<u>Codename Cottonmouth</u>

Daniel Stuart

Codename: Cottonmouth

Published by Angel Publications

Trade Paperback

This novel is a fictional work. Any resemblance to name or character of actual persons alive or dead is purely coincidental. Incidences in the story are from the author's imagination.

Published May, 2008

Reprinted October, 2013

ISBN: 978-0-9881628-0-8

Codename: Cottonmouth

Daniel Stuart

Table of contents

CODENAME COTTONMOUTH
PROLOGUE

The image of the blue Pacific Ocean washing up onto the white sands was always the same as his mind replayed the episode he truly wished would never again surface. The Hart's Puerto Vallarta vacation had begun as a refreshing, relaxing interlude as they lay under the large umbrella and breathed in the warm salt air. It was just his wife and himself on their fifty square feet of beach. The sun, sand, and surf turned Dave's thoughts to his wife Bev lounging next to him. He reclined his chair only enough so that he could keep her alluring bronzed body in sight.

His eyes feasted on her auburn hair waving down over her perfectly tanned shoulders while also framing her high cheek bones and large eyes. Although Bev was only five foot four, she was full figured with long legs that gracefully stretched down to petite feet. She had her chair down on the sand with only the back propped up and as Dave took in the outer natural attractiveness of her glistening bronze torso, he knew it didn't compare with her inner beauty. Bev took a sip of her frosty drink.

"Can you believe we're finally here?" she said "With all that official stuff you had to do; I didn't think we'd ever make it."

Life is grand, Dave thought as he took another sip of his Colada.

"Yeah, it took more time than I thought to get my files caught up but here we are hon' and we've got lots of fun ahead." He studied her curvaceous body again, raising and lowering his eyebrows several times trying to give the impression of a pervert.

Bev groaned and then laughed. "Oh give me a break."

"Seriously," he said as he leaned over and gave her a peck on the cheek. "I'm already enjoying it."

She laughed and held up her frosty drink, "Here's to---"

At that moment, four men coming from different directions converged on the happy couple grabbing Bev from behind. While one man held an automatic pistol to her head, another pressed the hard barrel of his against Dave's ear. Quickly the men bound the vacationer's wrists with neoprene cuffs and threw cloth bags over the couple's heads. The man behind Dave spoke softly towards his ear using the weapon to punctuate his point.

"We have been instructed to escort you to a meeting. If you resist *Signore* Hart, we have orders to shoot your wife first and, if necessary, you. Please *Signore*, you and your wife will come with us. Now!"

As they wrestled the Harts off the beach Dave tried to make it as difficult for them as possible without flat out resisting in the hope it may help gain attention. Dave felt the cement under his feet shortly before he heard the creaking of a vehicle door open. The next thing he knew he was pushed in the door onto rough plywood and Bev landed on top of him. Bev was sobbing and Dave tried to comfort her for which he suddenly felt a boot in his gut causing the air to be pushed out of his lungs. He doubled up in pain as the vehicle careened around corners seemingly at breakneck speed. The drive took less than twenty minutes and then they were pulled out of the vehicle and again wrestled across what seemed to be a parking lot. Dave was hammered into the doorpost as they pushed him through a door and down three flights of stairs. As he descended into a basement, the coolness, humidity, and smell made it obvious it must be some kind of dungeon. Dave was steered over to a heavy wooden chair where his hands were secured to its arms, and then the sack was removed from his head. Instantly he searched for and found Bev who was directly across the small room facing him. Their eyes locked and Dave could see the panic in Bev's. The face of a young man with cold dark dead eyes suddenly blocked Dave's view of Bev. He stared directly at Dave.

"Mr. Hart, how nice of you to join us for this little, shall we say -- demonstration. I hope the men here were courteous in bringing you here?" He snickered and waited for Dave to reply.

Dave did so with only a nod which instantly brought the searing pain of an object crashing across his head.

"My name is Mahir Abdul Al Aziz. It means skilled servant of the Almighty. To you it would be Aziz or Sir but not to worry you won't be talking too much." He motioned to the men. "Ensure those straps are secure and gag them!"

As soon as the men finished, Aziz moved closer to Dave so as to make it appear this was only for his ears.

"I would like to remind you of that little skirmish we had up in Canada last summer. Can you recall when you and your cowboys slaughtered our entire group? How could you have known that included my younger brother Amhid? Of course why would you care?

My employer, who will remain anonymous, felt you might have forgotten so we organized this little presentation so your people will forever remember it and understand the eastern concept of an eye for an eye. How will I do that you ask?" He backed away and waved his hand toward Bev. "I direct your attention to your beautiful wife."

As Dave watched in horror, one of the men walk over to Bev and with a razor sharp knife drew a red line of blood from her chin to below her stomach. Dave could see the pain and terror in her eyes as the blood oozed and spurted out of the incision. Dave's eyes filled with rage and tears as his six foot four inch frame vibrated pulling and tearing at the bindings. He tried to pull free, but as the pain and the wet slipperiness of his own blood covered his hand he realized it was useless. Dave couldn't stand to see Bev like this and tried to look away but one of the men grabbed him by the hair turning him back towards the mutilation. Now as Dave watched, the men went into a maniacal frenzy and slashed Bev with the knives until they and she were covered with her blood. As her life's blood pooled on the floor her head slumped forward for the last time in unconsciousness and then death. Dave became limp. He searched his mind trying to will this was just a nightmare and he would wake but Bev continued to hang in her bindings. Again Dave went into a rage now to try and break the bindings and kill every last one of them.

As Dave twisted and groaned trying to lose himself, Aziz calmly walked over to the door, took an Uzi from one of his men and sprayed the room. All four of his men, unluckily, were at the right height and caught two or three slugs each in the chest, killing them instantly. Dave on the other hand caught a line of five bullets from the right shoulder to the left hip. Somehow the projectiles managed to avoid any vital organs. Each slug slammed his body like being kicked by a mule, followed by the sensation of searing hot pokers from the burning lead. Dave's chair fell over and then the colors of the room dissolved into total white. A strange buzzing filled his ears. He fought to regain his conscious mind. The sound was the phone and he had dreamed *that* dream again.

Chapter 1

Dave squinted through sleepy eyes at the clock on the dresser as he anticipated ignoring the phone. It was zero five hundred hours. He was still gasping for breath with his heart pounding like a one cylinder outboard and he was soaked from sweat spawned by that all too frequent dream. The psychiatrist's diagnosis that Dave's mind was replaying traumatic events, which was normal, led to a prognosis that given an indeterminate period of time the mental wounds would heal and the dreams diminish.

Dave struggled with top sheet of his bed which was wrapped around him like the bonds in his dream. He found it difficult to move without ripping it and the phone rang off the hook on the night table. Forcing his right hand out from the taut cloth he fumbled the receiver to his ear.

"You've got the wrong number," he mumbled into the handset and clumsily smashed it back on the cradle. He'd just collapsed into the pillow and rolled away when the incessant ringing started again. He picked it up but this time the person on the other end spoke first.

"Don't you dare hang up on me again or I'll send the MPs," said a shrill female voice.

"Okay Joanne, what's up?"He said in a defeated tone.

"And that's another thing; didn't they teach you anything in your

military training? I'm a Colonel and you're a,—a,"

"What was that? I couldn't make it out."

"All right, so you got a promo, but I'm still the CO so I'd like some respect."

"I respect you, Joanne. So what's up?"

"I hope you were standing at attention when you said that mister. Be at CSIS headquarters in Burnaby at ten!"

Dave smiled as he hung up the phone and slowly unraveled the sheet around him. In his mind he thought of the many crossroads that had brought him to this point in his life. He was now a Lieutenant Colonel and second ranking officer of Global Tech Security.

He remembered the firefight he had been in as a civilian under Joanne's husband, then Colonel John Benton. His thoughts returned to the mountains west of Jasper where he had become entangled with a terrorist group. He and his wife with their friends had stumbled on a terrorist camp and as a civilian he and his friend and their wives had overwhelmed a very well armed and trained group. When he was finally able to call for reinforcements Colonel Benton had led a squadron of helicopter gunships to assault and wipe out the terrorist camps. It was during mop-up operation that a brigade of the terrorists from yet a second camp had set up an ambush that had it succeeded, would have neutralized most if not all the choppers. He remembered how he had sensed more than seen the enemy and suggested what he perceived to be the ambush. Colonel Benton had acted on Dave's perception and it gave them the initiative that saved the mission and allowed the gunships to carry the day. Dave was offered a place in a special operative unit of the CSIS which at the time he wasn't sure he wanted. The Puerto Vallarta incident with Bev being murdered, no, much more than just murdered; she had been sadistically mutilated; had changed his mind. The awful memories of Bev's murder brought his mussing to a temporary halt.

It wasn't until he was on the freeway heading to Burnaby that he resumed his reminiscence. He had searched out Colonel Benton following his own recovery from multiple bullet wounds and applied to enter JTF-2. He passed a rigid entrance exam and physical and was allowed to join the unit.

John recognized Dave's natural abilities which made it easy to apprentice him in the arena of covert operations. Colonel Benton had developed a small security company called Global Tech as a front for the more clandestine activities and he inserted Dave into that slot. Dave worked hard at training and eventually was given a squad of men who became known as the Kodiak Team.

Kodiak Team was already well established when news came that John had been promoted to General, inheriting an inexhaustible amount of pressing National Defense issues. It didn't require a great deal of insight to realize that General Benton couldn't give Global Tech the kind of attention it required. Dave mused about his favourable agreement when informed that Benton's wife, Joanne, also an Officer in the Canadian Military had been asked to transfer to Global as its CO. Dave knew Joanne through her husband and knew she would be the perfect replacement.

His Kodiak Team evolved into a unique specialized unit that discharged certain tasks, which were too hot, dirty or inappropriate for any other branch. The Government refused to admit they even existed but when the need arose for a small discrete strategic force with serious firepower and training, Global Tech's Kodiak Unit would be called to deliver terrorists or other subversives to the infernal regions.

*   *   *

Dave drove slowly down the line of late model cars looking for a space to park. Joanne had just arrived in her shiny new BMW and there was an empty space next to her so Dave pulled his '65' Chevy Biscayne in beside her. As they both exited their cars Dave noticed Colonel Benton in a very expensive business suit fixing her attention on him. He felt a little too casual in his ever-fashionable blue jeans, sports shirt and cowboy boots, but it was comfortable.

As he moved toward her he noticed again his Commanding Officer was a very slim trim fifty year old and as good looking as she was at thirty. He was very much aware of her daily two hour workout schedule and knew she expected no less from everyone under her command. Although she was the CO for Global Tech and could be as rigidly aggressive as Patton, Dave knew she also had a soft side and cared deeply for each individual under her authority.

Dave as second in command was expected to be every bit as aggressive and physically fit as his CO. Like Joanne he also had a soft spot for his team members.   When it came to apparel and vehicles however, there were definite gaps in expectations and results. Dave wasn't of the same breed when it came to his clothing or other chattels. His attitude, when out of uniform, was if it works don't fix it and if it's not comfortable you probably didn't want to go there anyway. Out of uniform he enjoyed a very casual lifestyle.

"When are you ever going to dress for these meetings?" She gazed at his clothing and sniffed her nose at his beat up old Chevy. "And when are you going to get a new car?"

Dave glanced down at the lower half of his six foot four frame as if he were checking to make sure he had remembered to put pants on.

"I am dressed. Next thing you know you'll have us suiting up in uniform for these get-togethers.   And I'm thinking of getting a new car next year, but there's really nothing wrong with this one."

"You're impossible. You've said the same thing since you first joined Global Tech over three years ago and there it is, the same old rusted out dented bucket of bolts."

Dave smiled. "So what's the meeting about?"

"You and your team will be heading to Edmonton. Seems the computer snoops have found

something interesting happening there, but hey--"
She glanced at her watch. "--we'd better get in there."

Dave entered the conference room and scrutinized the upbeat young people standing around the long large oval mahogany boardroom table. An onyx triangular prism nameplate with his or her name and position was located in front of each individual's placement. Dave noted that most of them had the appearance of being so young they might run for class president at a high school rather than investigators for an intelligence agency. He was sure all of them had no less than a degree in physics or some other high-end IQ pursuit. On the downside he speculated, due to their body language, none of them had done an hour's worth of real fieldwork.

As everyone began taking his or her place, Joanne motioned for him to sit next to her. A distinguished looking man topping forty-five sat at the head of the table, behind the nameplate of Richard Sage – Assistant Director-Intelligence. He called the meeting to order.

" Colonel Benton, Lt. Colonel Hart, I think you're acquainted with the people around the table so we will dispense with introductions."

"Lt. Colonel, we have reason to believe a group of international terrorists are working out of this house." Sage directed everyone's attention to the large plasma screen on the wall where a picture of the house was now illuminated.

"It is these men--," he said as individual pictures of the men living in the house came up on the screen. "--who are planning an attack somewhere in the Edmonton area. Each of them has been identified with known terrorist organizations. We have obtained several intercepted computer and phone transmissions which although not indicating any specific targets, they do point to a military style operation. We are sure from these intercepts that their target will be some kind of large petrochemical structures such as one or all of the refineries in the area. We would like you to take Kodiak Team to Edmonton and quietly close down this terrorist cell and their safe house. We want any information you can gather and as little collateral damage as possible. Arrest all cell members and turn them over to the Federal Authorities. Now my colleagues here will bring you up to speed with the information they have and of course this is all top secret. Questions?"

Dave was studying the papers being handed to him and only glanced up to respond.

"None Sir."

The young people in turn finished passing Dave one or two sheets of paper and then verbally presented the information they had researched from their expertise area. Scanning the papers, Dave followed each respective speaker after which he placed the notes in his brief case for later reference.

Almost as quickly as the meeting had started, it was over. Mr. Sage stood without another word, turned, and exited by way of a separate side door. Everyone else left through the door at the opposite end of the large room.

Colonel Benton stopped Dave just outside the building.

"I want you to be very careful Dave. I know we have our little digs but I don't want you or your team getting hurt or killed."

"Why Colonel Benton, I didn't know you cared."

"I don't but do you realize how much it costs to train you people?" A smile let Dave know she did in fact care a lot. "Stop by my office before you leave, I'll have a last word for you."

Dave called Captain Julio Rodriguez his second in command on the Team as well as a very close friend. The two conversed in generalities for a few moments and then Dave jumped into the purpose of the call.

"I got some work for us."

"Okay, when and where?"

"Edmonton. Muster at the barracks, twenty one thirty hours. We leave at twenty two hundred hours, today. Fatigues, no patches and each man will need night tactical dress."

"Sure, just body weapons or the whole enchilada?"

"Basic tactical as well as eighteen C's and of course the shooters will need their MSG's with night scopes."

Julio whistled.

"Tactical, Glock automatics, MSG-Nineties? Sounds like an evening of fun."

"Only for our side, but if all goes according to plan we should be back here within twenty-four hours."

Dave left his car in Surrey, and took the Sky-Train to Vancouver city center. From the depot he walked the few blocks to 1001 West Pender, where the Global Tech Offices were located. Entering the third floor reception area, he immediately noticed a curvaceous, blue-eyed blond receptionist and thought she definitely improved the office aesthetics. As he went to enter the CO's office, the cute receptionist jumped up.

"Hey, you can't go in there!"

"And why the hell not?" Of course there had to be a catch, he thought, she just couldn't sit there and look pretty.

"Do you have an appointment?"

"No," he said with his hand still on the door handle.

"Then you can't go in there."

"And I suppose you're going to stop me?"

"If I have to."

At that, Joanne opened the door and stepped into the outer office.

"Ah, I see you've met my new assistant," she said to Dave. "Lt. Gail Levine, this is Lt. Colonel David Hart. Lt. Colonel Hart does some special consulting for us. And as unlikely as it may seem he is second in command here." She turned to Dave. "Lt. Levine comes to us with special forces background so I'd watch out if I were you." Joanne smiled glancing back and forth between the two.

Dave looked at Gail with an altered point of view. She's beautiful and can take care of herself, he thought. Next thing they'll tell me is she's smart too.

Joanne smiled and raised her eyebrows as though she read his thoughts.

"And she's got a Doctorate in Social Sciences as well as Bachelor's in Education." Dave shook his head.

"Sounds like you've got all your bases well covered."

It may have been the sun reflecting off the peach coloured walls or the red oak furniture but

Dave noticed the faint hue of red on Miss Levine's face.

"Thank you Sir, I mean sorry Sir" she said as she awkwardly tried at a late salute.

"At ease Lt., we generally try to keep things on a friendly first name basis here in the office." Joanne said with a smile.

Joanne motioned for Dave to enter her office and after the door closed, she raised an eyebrow. "Well what do you think about my new admin assistant, she's pretty, smart, unattached and---" Dave smiled and waved her off.

"And so now you're Colonel –Cupid--Benton?"

"I just thought you two might hit it off."

"Well don't. I'm not interested and I'm not ready to get anyone else killed."

Joanne looked at him with sadness in her eyes for a long moment.

"Look Dave, you can't blame yourself for Bev's death and it's been over three years. Don't you think it's about time to move on?"

"Hey, hey, I'll decide when it's time to move on, as you put it. Just leave it alone." Dave was not overly upset but wanted to make sure Joanne knew she had pushed too far and as he glanced at her he seen his point had been taken.

"Sorry, I just thought Gail might be someone who could help heal some wounds."

"I doubt it. Was there anything in particular you wanted me here for or was it just the cupid thing?"

"One very important item as a matter of fact, your rules of engagement. You will offer them the opportunity to comply and if they will not you will use lethal force and then clean up after yourself. None of them walk. And of course if you screw up, this conversation or your orders for the mission never happened."

"That bad, eh?" Joanne nodded.

"Okay, well we won't 'screw up', but you know we'll get it done."

"And Dave, be careful."

Chapter 2

The Challenger CC-144 cleared for takeoff from Abbotsford regional at twenty two hundred hours, and quickly screamed into the clouds on its way to Edmonton. The flight over the Rockies would take a little over an hour so Dave had already reclined his seat and dozed off. He had hoped he might snooze without his mind replaying his nightmare but that incident always seemed to be waiting to invade his thoughts. He had just finished the last part of the dream when he was aroused.

"Hey man, you asleep?" Julio asked, forty minutes into the flight. Dave lifted one eyelid and glanced over at him. "The guys were wondering if you wanted to join in on a few quick hands of poker. Hundred dollar pot, twenty dollar bet, max."

"No thanks," he said with finality. "Last time you sharks got me into a game, well suffice to say I just started to afford groceries again yesterday, but thanks for waking me up." He yawned. "I need to go over the information on this safe house." At this the poker game crashed to a grinding halt as all of the men's attention was diverted to their leader and what he would say next.

"You think there'll be much trouble?" Julio asked.

"Hey, if it was a cake walk they wouldn't call on us," Dave said casually. "But nothing we can't handle."

George Seagram and Marty Mussleman leaned over the seat.

"Don't worry LC; if they get aggressive I'll pick them off," George said.

"I might be the spotter but I couldn't miss with a pea shooter from that distance," Marty chimed in. Dave glanced at Marty and then George. He had followed their practice scores and they were equally matched as sharp shooters, but because Marty had come to the team later he was given the spotter designation.

By now, the five others had abandoned their card game and gathered closer to the discussion. The men were keyed up with adrenalin flowing and although professional enough to keep it in check they wanted to know any details that might be divulged. The team members were all highly trained combat soldiers, but each man also specialized in at least two other disciplines.

Troy Williams was a construction engineer and demolition expert. He could build structures with seemingly little materials or make a bomb out of almost anything and blow the enemy's hardware to hell.

Harvey Shaw excelled in hand to hand combat and although the other members were at the peak of physical fitness, none had ever been able to pin Harvey. He served as communications officer and electronics specialist. Harvey was a Blackfoot Indian and he told everyone if things got really bad there were always smoke signals although security took a beating using them. It was sort of like using the old telephone party lines.

Kelly Jones was designated the team pilot with multi engine license. He was also the team's weapons specialist on the ground with a degree in metallurgy. He could make a weapon out of almost anything and carried a large Kukri he had made in Kosovo from a leaf spring of an army jeep to prove it. The spring came from an enemy vehicle.

Jack Lewis' claim to fame covered electronics and languages and Tron Kowomotto was a Medic and mobile equipment operator. If you were injured, Tron was a good guy to have around and if you had any kind of mobile equipment he could operate it or fix it.

Dave opened his laptop.

"Seeing you're all here anyway, I guess this is as good a time as any to have a briefing." Dave took them systematically through the operation, showing them a map of the area and a reasonable blueprint of the house describing where each person would deploy. He gave them the word that if any of the combatants surrendered they would be processed and then turned over to the RCMP, but none would be allowed to escape. Dave managed to wrap up his mini presentation as the jet made its final approach to Canadian Forces Base Edmonton.

Once on the ground the team moved swiftly to transfer their equipment into a full size van with blacked out passenger windows. Dave drove them to the south side of the city. He toured the streets near the University of Alberta which was adjacent to the target area, Old Strathcona, to help get the team geometrically accustomed to the area. He proceeded down Whyte Avenue and on into the business district where the chic, the rockers, the visitors, and a few out and out weirdoes all mixed into a swelling ebbing tide of people. Dave wondered if one more person could be squeezed onto the busy sidewalks. They rounded the block at the old train station, which had been transformed into an outdoor pub, to retrace their path back to the residential area and do a closer reconnaissance of the target area. Dave cruised through the neighborhood a few times as each man marked distances and angles, fine-tuning his personal attack plan with regards to how it coordinated with the others. They slowly drove down the streets where many of the houses were large old wooden framed two story dwellings designed long before people concerned themselves about energy efficiency. Although they were centered on large lots because of the size of the buildings and the mature aspens, evergreen, and plenty of shrubbery they seemed crowded.

It was just after zero one thirty hours when Dave asked if they wanted a bite to eat; the team was too keyed up for food but several opted for coffee. It took some searching but they found an all night drive through. As the men drank their coffee in the van they quietly discussed the coming assault and then headed back to the Old Strathcona area to do one more recon of the objective.

Dave crisscrossed the area noting as many angles to the target building as possible. Then as he took a wide swing near the University he glanced at his watch. It was zero two fifty and time to go to work.

Dave slowly idled down the rain swept street towards the objective, an old rundown two story wood frame building with heavy overgrown foliage. The headlights illuminated the pavement more than normal because of the large aspens that grew all along the road nearly blocking out the streetlights. The seedy neighborhood was almost all pre Second World War houses and a few, like this one, went back even further to Strathcona's hay day in the first part of the nineteen hundreds. Most of the houses on this street were let to junkies or juiceheads but now most partygoers had either passed out or gone home and things were quiet.

He pulled the van up to the curb, shut off the lights, and killed the engine. He stared at his watch and at exactly zero three hundred gave the order to deploy. Eight men in black tactical apparel silently slipped out to their designated locations. Two of the team, George and Marty found their way to a Mack's convenience store roof across the street west of the old two-story target house. Three others moved stealthily around to the back door of the house. The remaining three positioned in the shadows at the front ready to move through the doors on command. The darkness plus foliage made the men of Kodiak almost invisible. Dave spoke into his Com-Tac.

"Team one, if you two old ladies are just about in position we'd really like to let the rest of the troops get on with the mission"

"Sorry sir," George said. "It's just that Marty's afraid of heights and I had a hell of a time dragging him up here."

"Don't you believe it sir," Marty interrupted.

Dave chuckled but knew he had to bring it back to business. Dave hesitated until he was sure the others were in position

"Team one, do you see any movement?"

"No movement, sir."

"Team two, three, move in." Then he repeated it very slowly and clearly.

The two groups quickly and quietly disabled the locks of the front and back doors and moved in. Instantly there was the silenced clicking of eighteen C's from inside the house.

"Team two, they're not complying Sir," Harvey said with a hint of alarm. "We got four hostiles down."

Dave listened as the men's transmissions told him Team three was clear and proceeding to level zero one, the basement. Team two was moving upstairs. Then Marty reported that there was movement, at least three people, in the upstairs west bedroom. Team two heard the transmission and acknowledged it. Seconds later, Dave heard two thuds from the high powered rifles across the street with window glass breaking from the bullets. Cracks of gunfire were almost instantaneous and then the silenced staccato of the automatics again.

"Thanks one, you saved our bacon. There were five of them and they almost got the drop on us." Kelly and Harvey quickly checked the upper floor and Kelly informed Dave the house was cleared.

Dave left his command post in the van.

"Okay guys, heads up. Team leader is coming in."

"Team three to LC? You've got to see this. It's Semtex and C-4 and there's gotta be a hundred pound of each here. These guys were prepared to do some serious damage." There was a brief silence. "We got two hostiles down here as well, Sir."

Dave checked the basement and was amazed to find ten crates each of the two explosives. He didn't like the idea of transporting unknown explosives but he knew he certainly couldn't leave it here. He checked it over very carefully, and although he would use some of the C-4 to cleanse the scene, felt certain it was safe to move to CFB Edmonton.

The team searched the entire house, one room at a time to insure all hostiles were accounted for. In one of the storage rooms Kelly reported a dozen P90-TR submachine guns with laser guides and an equal number of M-4A-1 assault rifles. Dave checked the cache and then ordered two of the men to move the weapons out to the van. He then told the rest to gather all IDs, credit cards, computer CD disks and get DNA samples from each individual. Dave pressed the point for them to be very careful to mark and identify every item. As Dave and Julio wandered through the house looking for anything that would add to information about the terrorists, Dave stopped and stood in the living room taking one last look around. He did a double take at a picture on the wall and then pointed at it.

"What's wrong with this picture?" Dave asked.

Julio glanced around the room which was nicotine stained with areas of the wall cracked and peeling. "It definitely needs cleaning and paint."

"No, no I mean the pictures on the walls. Two on the adjacent walls are classic cars and then this one--" he said pointing to the wall in front of him. "-- is a very good copy of a tall ship in a tempest and notice the frame is clean, where the rest have nicotine and dust from hanging for years."

Dave ran his hand over the frame, and after carefully checking for booby traps, he removed the picture from its place. There in the wall was a rectangular opening twelve inches across by six inches high. Dave carefully glanced in first and then reached in and pulled out a brown canvas bag as well as a handful of papers and a journal. He opened the bag and found it was full of bundled hundred dollar bills.

Julio whistled. "We are gonna have some Christmas party."

Dave ignored the comment and opened a large briefcase containing all the other evidence they had accumulated. He carefully inserted the brown canvas bag with the money and the papers he'd just found and relocked it.

One of the men called Julio over and pointed out a computer. The two were trying to get into the information files but they didn't know the password. Dave stepped through the entrance to the room, saw what they were doing and ordered Julio to physically remove the hard drives. He called the team together.

"Let's clean the scene gentlemen. Shaw and Lewis, get those explosives into the van." He spoke into his Com-Tac. "Squad one, cover us while we sanitize the place."

Dave stepped into the kitchen, hit the speed dial on his Sat Cell and Colonel Benton answered on the second ring.

"Mission accomplished. Lots of Intel and even cash by the way, but no-one wanted to stay for the second show."

"Okay, our employer will handle the media. Are you out of there?

"Just starting sanitation. We'll be airborne within a couple of hours."

"Good, I want you in my office the minute you get in."

"Roger that." Dave slid his cell closed and switched on his Com-Tac. "Remove any lead from the bodies and eradicate those entry incisions with the sulfuric acid. Rig the place with the C-4 for a steady burn and then bug out. Let's do it."

The men went about the grisly task of eliminating the evidence. Tron and Julio carefully made an incision at the bullet entry sites of the cadavers and with forceps, dug for, found and removed the lead slugs. They poured sulfuric acid over the incision area and proceeded to the next body. The acid would eradicate the surgery site just in case the fire didn't accomplish its intended task.

The men combed the entire house collecting all shell casings and removing any stray bullets from the woodwork. They sprayed areas where there were bloodstains with special chemicals and when they felt the area was sanitized for forensics, they placed the C-4 throughout the house and around each body, setting ignition timers for fifteen minutes. It would light the plastics and the burn would be total. The team, their job completed, headed toward Canadian Forces Base Edmonton to deliver the rest of the plastic explosives and then fly back home to Vancouver.

   *   *   *

   Dave was in Colonel Benton's office when she arrived back from lunch.

   "I see you found your way in."

   "Yeah, you really should get better security. I just don't think the lieutenant there is up to the job."

   "You out rank her Dave and besides you're the one who designed the security here, remember?"

   Dave smiled and put his finger to his lips as he turned up the radio.

   "In news a little further away, City of Edmonton Fire Department was busy in the early morning hours trying to bring multiple house fires under control in the Old Strathcona area on the south side of the city."

   The news anchorman announced that three houses were totally destroyed and several others badly gutted. An unconfirmed report said that authorities believed there may have been as many as eleven partial corpses in one of the destroyed houses. The news man went on to say an unidentified source connected with the investigation is following leads that the cause of the original blaze was unknown but it is believed to be drug or gang related. The reporter quoted the Edmonton Fire Department Chief James Woolcock as calling for an inquiry into the possibility of changes to the building codes to prevent fires from spreading so easily. Just before Dave turned off the radio the newsman listed the damage estimates to be in the five million dollar range.

The Colonel stared at Dave.

"Seems to me I remember someone saying, *keep collateral damage to a minimum.*"

"Yeah and that same someone said, arrest them and turn them over to the Federal Authorities."

"Touché."

Dave smiled and pointed to a large briefcase. "The Intel's in there. These jokers were playing big time. Looks like they were going to try to shut down the Imperial Oil Refinery there and with the plastics they had they could have easily done it. That refinery processes more than a hundred-ninety-five thousand barrels a day. Can you imagine the impact?"

Joanne raised her eyebrows just thinking of the chaos.

"All the intel we collected as well as a couple of hard drives is in the briefcase. We'll need a computer specialist to see what's on drives?" He nodded toward it beside her desk. "I skimmed through most of the paperwork and came up with an interesting character, too, a General Beauregard Smith. Ever heard of him?"

"No, can't say I have. Does it indicate what his connection is?"

"He seems to be the top man or very near the top, but even more important to me, and get this, the data indicates a possible connection somehow with my wife's murder."

"If that's true, maybe this thing is getting to close to home for you. I'll leave it up to you, but if it comes to the point that it might impair your ability to make clear decisions, I want you to take yourself out of command."

"And just who in hell would lead the team?"

"My first choice would be Julio, he knows your moves and the team knows him."

"I can handle it." Dave grew tense.

"All right, we'll analyze this and then turn it over to the CSIS. Meanwhile, Lt. Colonel, get some rest, I promise I won't call you for sixteen hours."

Dave stood, nodded at Joanne and left her office.

As Dave closed the door, he almost ran into Gail who was carrying coffee for her boss.

"You shouldn't have." He said with a put on surprised look.

"I didn't. This is for Colonel Benton."

Dave made a dejected face, which he figured looked worse because of his beard's two day growth and was happy to see it made the desired results.

"Well, if you really want some?"

Dave chuckled. "That's all right. I was just giving you a hard time."

"Speaking of time, excuse me, Sir." She hurried through the door to deliver the coffee.

Dave smiled as he left the office giving a last thought to his teasing. On the sidewalk he decided to grab a late snack at the little bistro half a block down Hornby Street. It was a quaint little spot that Global employees used a lot. He purchased an apple Danish and coffee, found the only vacant small table and sat down. The Province Newspaper was folded on the table so Dave decided to browse through it. He was half way through the Danish and coffee when he caught a glimpse of Gail entering the café. His interest in the paper now gone he watched to see what she would do. She ordered a bowl of soup, a sandwich, and coffee and then looked around to find a table. Dave couldn't help but smile when she noticed there were no empty tables and then noticed him

He indicated she was welcome to share his table which she accepted.

"Kind of late for lunch isn't it?" Dave asked.

"Oh, I'm updating the filing system and didn't realize the time until Joanne, I mean Colonel Benton shoed me out of the office for my lunch." They bantered back and forth for nearly an hour with Gail asking him about what he did and Dave responding with only what she could know. Suddenly Gail noticed the time on Dave's wrist watch.

"Oh my god, its fourteen thirty. I only get half an hour for lunch." She quickly grabbed her dishes, deposited them on a conveyer, said her goodbyes, and headed back to the office. Dave meanwhile, although not smitten by the love bug had some indication he had been at least nipped. He sat finishing another cup of coffee musing about this Lt. Gail Levine. *Was it her looks? She was a looker. Was it her spirit? She was definitely feisty. Maybe it was her strength or presence? That too!*

Riding the sky train back to North Surrey and his car he mused about Joanne's introduction of Gail and he pictured the curvaceous Lt. in his mind's eye. As the RTS smoothly cruised along the rails over the choked city streets below, he fantasized dancing with the girl and was amazed at the absence of guilt. As they slowly glided across a dance floor Dave held her close giving him an all but forgotten, but nice feeling as it raised his spirits. As the music played in his mind he suddenly realized it was Bev and his song and suddenly the idea of holding any other woman than Bev became repulsive. He could think no more of romantic interludes and he shut the vision of Gail out of his mind.

The thought of Bev brought the new information he had stumbled onto about General Smith to mind and he felt perspiration on his forehead. As he looked out over the city of Burnaby, the abduction of him and his wife in Vallarta once again took over his mind. Dave had begun unknowingly grinding the fist of one hand into the palm of other and cursing under his breath. *If this animal was responsible for Bev's murder, he would find him and Smith would pay in spades.* He made himself a promise that as soon as the agency had the results of the latest Intel, if it showed complicity, he would begin a pursuit that would end in the death of General Beauregard Smith.

"So help me God," he whispered.

As Dave gazed out the sky train window, now the mighty Fraser River was below him and he focused on the two islands upriver past the Pattullo Bridge. As he did a small voice from deep inside admonished him.

"You swore to serve and protect, not to exact vengeance. Vengeance is mine saith the Lord."

The words almost chocked him. Was he after vengeance or was he doing his job to protect Canadian citizens from subversives? He thought about this until the train stopped at the end of the line bringing his contemplation to an end.

Chapter 3

Dave's sweat saturated grey flannel-jogging suit clung to his body as he increased speed near the end of his five-kilometer run. The morning exercise always invigorated him and he imagined it helped push away the memories of Mexico. This was his secondary hallucination, because no matter how far or fast he ran, the flashbacks and nightmares always caught up. He did, however find solace in the narrow mountain road to and from Vedder Crossing. It permitted him a chance to get closer to nature and view the flora, which at some places grew up to the edge of the blacktop giving the perception of a hallowed place.

He ended the run at his beach house drinking in the spectacular sunrise as the golden ball inched its way over the mountain peaks. He stood awhile and watched as the sun inched higher and thought how Bev would've said *that alone made the trek worthwhile.*

After an extended shower, he headed for the small Lakeside Café and slipped into a booth. Kathy, a hefty woman in her fifties who had owned the Cedar Inn and was also the cook and waitress, motioned toward the coffee pot. Dave gestured to his cup and blew her a kiss to which she rolled her eyes. She came over to the table and filled the cup.

"Just coffee - or are you eatin' today?" she said, trying to look stern.

"I'll have the steak and eggs with hash browns, pancakes and toast with some strawberry jam on the side."

"You're joking right? Or maybe you're entertaining a lumberjack convention?"

"Cheez, okay, leave out the pancakes."

Dave looked around the café and noticed the only other customers were a couple who were smiling as they stole quick glances at him. As he finished reading the newspaper, he thought Katie might have ducked out to do some grocery shopping, but then she proudly appeared carrying his steaming hot breakfast and placed it in front him. He sampled his first piece of steak.

"Mmmm, done to perfection as always." He was in mid-savor when his cell buzzed. It was Lt. Levine informing him that Colonel Benton wanted him in her office at eleven hundred hours. Dave thanked her and went back to his breakfast.

*   *   *

Dave entered the reception area of Colonel Benton's office and Gail greeted him with a smile.

"Is the boss in?" he asked, nodding toward Colonel Benton's office.

"Yes sir, she's waiting for you. Go right in."

Quite a change from yesterday Dave thought as he opened the heavy mahogany door and entered the Colonel's office. Colonel Benton was mulling the papers on a small table in the corner and as Dave strode in she glanced up waving over the pile of papers.

"Well here it is. Grab a chair and I'll review some of the highlights with you." Opening a heavily filled manila folder Colonel Benton moved over behind her desk and sat in her large executive chair.

"First, this General Smith you mentioned is a very big fish. He, in fact, seems to be at the center of most terrorist activities we're focused on." As she turned the pages, she summarized the data. "He apparently plans with precision, stealth, and ruthlessness and because of this has acquired the nickname Cottonmouth, as in snake. One unique item I've realized from these notes is that he's not into terrorism for anything so noble as religion or national pride but rather power and money. I checked with the CIA and they say he's not one of theirs. Either it's true or he's gone rogue because they offered any assistance they could give to apprehend him. Second, it looks like it was one of his brigades you helped eradicate up north with John a few years ago."

Dave grew agitated. "And so Bev's hit was revenge?"

"That would be my guess, as well as a warning that to mess in his part of the jungle is deadly and from the reports I've read as well as what you've told me, you really danced with this guy."

Dave smiled.

"Yeah we didn't just win a battle with his group we eradicated them, but then they weren't exactly there for a Sunday picnic." Dave reflected in the past for a moment longer and then went on. "So what else do we know about this scum bag?"

Joanne glanced toward him with an all knowing smile as she pulled out another manila folder with the CIA logo, stamped top secret and opened it.

"I had to pull in some markers for his military record but there are still a lot of blank spaces. Apparently Smith was always somewhat of a renegade officer but he went over the line on a mission in South America, handling over five hundred innocents with extreme prejudice. The military, or CIA, or whoever hushed it up and transferred him to a special desk in Florida. It sounds like Black Operations from there on." She pointed toward a page. "It says here his main objective while there was to prepare the American people for the war on terror, the Afghan and Iraqi invasions, and the subsequent removal of the Taliban and Hussein regimes. Apparently the 'good' General played two sides against the middle because after nine-eleven he disappears and there's some inference he was working with Saddam in Iraq's chemical nuclear department."

"Very smooth. All Saddam has to do is put the watch dogs off until Smith has the weapons moved and poof, no weapons of mass destruction to be found."

"Here's another footnote. You're going to love this one because it lends a little credence to your conspiracy theory. Their records show General Smith had serious involvement in high tech remotes for commercial jet liner's, and mini nuclear devices. Leaves a lot open for speculation but there are just too many spaces for any definitive scenario."

"What? Too many spaces? Do I have to spell it out for you? The low-life scum bag used replacement planes loaded with extra fuel, and flew them into the towers by remote control. Once the planes hit the towers and everyone's attention is on the *black* smoke, he eliminates the witnesses by putting them on a 737 that we know as UA ninety-three and then blowing the airliner out of the sky. At the same time, he sends a missile into the Pentagon. While this is causing untold confusion, his people bring the Towers down with pre-placed C-4 and 'mini' nuclear devises. That's why there was seismic activity just before they came down as well as the melted steel underneath the rubble. My God, doesn't anybody listen to the witnesses anymore? Professional firemen and ambulance personnel telling how they heard the boom, boom, boom of the plastics going off." Dave was visibly shaking with anger now. "That murdering son of a bitch, he's a mad-man and he's got to be stopped."

Joanne looked at him somewhat sardonically.

"So you're trying to tell me that there are thousands of Americans who conspired to carry out an attack on their own people and not one has leaked the truth?"

"Didn't take thousand, didn't even take hundreds. A few highly placed people and forty or fifty on the ground, and if anyone becomes a liability, that person is *removed*. You know how it works. For

Bev and those people murdered on nine-eleven I'm going to get him, no matter what it takes."

Joanne stood up. "Lt. Colonel Hart," she shouted, "You will do this professionally, or you'll not do it at all! The last thing the world needs right now is a loose cannon."

"So what do you expect me to do? Just sit on my thumbs and let this dirt bag continue his killing spree?"

"I expect you to conduct yourself in a professional military manner. What we need to do now is fill in the blanks in this report with proof. If we can do that, then we will nail his ass to a windmill, but I'll have no Lone Ranger antics. Is that clear?"

"Crystal. Meanwhile this guy gets away."

"Come on, Dave. Where is he going to go, another planet? We'll use the system and that's an order."

It will be between him and me, Dave thought.

"Yes Ma'am," he said, betraying his true thoughts.

There was a long silence before Dave stood to his feet, faced Colonel Benton at attention and stared straight ahead. "If that will be all Colonel, Lt. Colonel Hart requests permission to leave."

"Request denied. Now sit down Dave and quit acting like a jerk. Let's get this meeting done so you can buy all of us lunch."

"All of us?"

"Oh, ah, I invited Lt. Levine," she said with a surprised *you didn't know* look. "Thought it might be nice to have her along," she said slyly.

Dave sat down and stared at Joanne and then out the window for a long while trying to organize his thoughts. He knew Joanne was right about procedure and he also knew his emotions were overriding sound judgment. "I'm sorry," he said after a few minutes. "I guess I let personal feelings override common sense."

"Good, now let's get this meeting finished. The Intel you brought back from Edmonton indicates one of the General's close associates, a Sal A Din, is the leader of a group of insurgents in Iraq. Here's a picture of him and here's his last known location. I want you to take your team, grab him if you can find him, and acquire as much information on the General as possible."

Dave looked at the picture and the colour drained from his face. Colonel Benton glanced at him and then took a second take.

"Dave is there a problem?"

Dave hesitated. "This Sal A Din is Al Aziz, the one who led the mob that murdered Bev."

"Dave, are you sure?"

"In spades Colonel. I'll never forget those eyes as long as I live."

Joanne moved papers around on her desk while searching for the proper response.

"Are you certain you're going to be able to lead this mission?"

Dave's colour had somewhat returned. "Joanne, just between you me and the walls, I wouldn't miss it for the world. So are you saying kidnap him?"

"Detain him for questioning without council."

"Sounds simple enough, just go into, where is it? Oh yeah Kirkuk, and ask around. Everyone there co-operates and tells us where their Muslim brother is, so we can just go and arrest him, probably in front of two or three hundred blood thirsty insurgents. This is not going to be easy."

"That's why we use only the best, Lt. Colonel," she said with a smirk.

She focused on her desk calendar. "Today is June twenty-first. I'll expect a briefing by eleven hundred hours June twenty-third."

"Yes Ma'am."

"Now let's get to lunch."

Dave suggested The Morgue for seafood, which caught Gail unawares. Joanne explained that The Morgue was just a nickname because it was born out of the old Vancouver City Morgue building. The proper name was the Burrard Seafood Factory and has some of the best seafood in Vancouver.

The maitre d' escorted them up the carpeted stairs to their table and they bantered back and forth finally ordering some wine. Gail appeared uncomfortable, being very quiet, as she eyed the deeply varnished tables with expensive crystal and silver which was exquisitely set. The nineteenth century lighting was augmented tastefully by modern fixtures and she noticed the satin drapes in royal colors matched the carpets.

"Is there something wrong Gail?" Joanne asked.

"I wondered if you ate at fancy eateries like this all the time."

"No this is special." Joanne said. "It's kind of a welcome on board for you and celebration for a successful mission for our brave warrior here." She nodded towards Dave. "Besides Dave here can afford it can't you?" She smirked at him and he just grinned.

They discussed the menu and decided. Dave pulled the cord and the waiter appeared almost instantly.

"We think we'd like to order the Castaway Special. Could you give us a brief description of it?" Dave asked.

The waiter informed them it was the restaurant's signature repast. He described how the chef began with a bed of white rice on a large platter imitating the sand on a desert island and then added asparagus shoots here and there indicating fallen palm trees. He told how a small pineapple top is inserted in the center to enrich the jungle scene. Mussels, shrimp, oysters, crab meat, and pineapple squares were spread around the *island* to enhance the image. He finished by adding that the shells from the morsels are also spread over the rice for effect so that the platter becomes a terrain model of a south sea's desert island.

"It is not only artistic but delectable. Add to this our Hawaiian sunset drink and your meal will be the best Vancouver has to offer," he said with evident pride. He asked a few more questions about add-ons and then left while the three casually talked and laughed. The meal was served and was all the waiter had described. They ate, talked, and laughed as the time passed and by the end of the meal Gail declared it the best seafood she had ever tasted. As they waited for the cheque they teased back and forth about who would pick up the tab. Joanne actually won out and Dave and Gail thanked her for the wonderful dinner. They left the restaurant and while Gail and Joanne walked back to Global Tech's offices, Dave went in the opposite direction to catch the Sky Train for the trip back to Surrey. As he was walking, he called Julio. This time Dave teased Julio about having such a high voice that he'd mistaken him for Julio's wife. Next he invited Julio over to his house to discuss an upcoming *hunting trip.*

The next morning Dave had no sooner finished his run and showered than the doorbell rang. He looked at his watch and opened the door. "Right on time. Go on into the study and I'll be right with you."

"The study?" Julio said laughingly as he looked around at the kitchen, living room, bedroom, and bathroom; the only four rooms in the house.

"The study," Dave said nodding and waving his arm toward the living room.

"Had me worried there. I thought you'd have us chatting about this thing in the John."

"You want a cup of Java?" Dave yelled from the kitchen.

"Now that's clairvoyance. I take it black."

Dave poured two cups and joined him in the living room.

"Well old buddy, we got a dicey one this time. The boss wants us to go to Kirkuk and detain this guy." Dave threw him the picture. "Do you know who that is?"

"No, should I," Julio said looking at it and then up at Dave.

"He goes by the name of Sal A Din, or Maher Abdul Al Aziz. He was the leader of the group who killed Bev. The bastard had her killed, and then shot his own men and me."

Julio sat looking at the picture as Dave continued.

"We need to find him, capture him and then wring all the information we can out of him." Dave envisaged wringing something else entirely. "And then give him to our southern neighbours. So we need to develop a plan how we're going to do it."

Julio whistled. "I suppose a third Desert Storm is out of the question?"

"Totally, unless you can figure out how to do it with nine men. Oh, by the way, this is a volunteer mission." Dave paused to see Julio's reaction and when the captain nodded he continued. "Okay, let's get into it. We land at Kirkuk Airport, and then I'll have my asset contact us there. We find out where this slime ball is, snatch him in the night, and then move him to a safe house. Feed him some anesthetics, dig for info for several days and turn him over to the local CIA. Bing, bang, boom. A few days maybe more and we're out of there. What do you think?"

"Think? Have you lost your mind? In case you've forgotten, there are a lot of people over there that hate our guts and they show their feelings by shaking our hands while they blow themselves to hell? How many of us did you say are actually going to go?"

"Nine, but only the two of us will go after the guy, the rest standby as a fire team at the airbase. If we need them, we call them." Dave snapped his fingers. "By the way you speak Farsi don't you?"

"Na baba."

"What the hell does that mean?"

"It means no, you must be joking."

"That's what I thought." Dave smiled and took a gulp of his coffee. "So I guess that puts you on point."

"Hey this just gets better and better. Is there anything else, like maybe we take Jay Leno to entertain the insurgents to keep them off our backs?"

The smile slowly disappeared from Dave's face. "Captain, if you don't want to participate in this mission I can have you replaced?"

Julio was caught by surprise. "Hey LC, chill out, I'm in, alright? I just want all the cards on the table."

Dave's smile slowly returned. "No Jay Leno."

"So is there anything else I need to do to prepare?"

"Take your wife out for a romantic candlelight dinner and dance under the stars. I'll call you as soon as the mission is a go."

After Julio left and Dave was alone with his thoughts, he reminisced about how Bev and he would pick a new and romantic restaurant for dinner and then take in a movie, a country western band, or even live theater. His memory flashed back to the time they just went to White Spot for burgers and then up the Grouse Mountain Sky ride. The phone ringing interrupted his reverie.

"Dave, this is Gail. Colonel Benton would like to see you in her office at fourteen hundred hours."

"Why is the Colonel making her appointments through you all of a sudden? She's always talked to me direct before." Dave knew why, but he wanted to see if Gail was privy to Joanne's matchmaking.

"I don't know sir. I suppose that's what I'm supposed to do as the Colonel's aid."

Dave thought on that for a moment.

"Yeah, I would suppose so." Dave was hesitant for a moment and then asked her if she would like to have dinner with him. He told her of a little place in White Rock that had good food, nice atmosphere, and a wonderful view of the ocean. She agreed and they set the date for the next night.

Dave was at Global at thirteen forty-five as much to speak to Gail as to be early for his meeting. As he entered the reception area, he saw a man in a very expensive looking suit sitting on the corner of Gail's desk. Gail was smiling from something the man had said.

"Excuse me Lt., is the Colonel in?"

"No sir. However, she said she would be back in time for your appointment. Lt. Colonel Hart, this is Captain George Day. He's from records at CSIS."

The man stood and the two shook hands. Dave noticed the excessive strength and roughness in the man's hand and wondered if he spent all his off hours at the gym or maybe tearing down mountains.

Colonel Benton came in at that moment and after the three went into her office she introduced Captain Day all over again. She told Dave the Captain was there to help in the planning of the Sal A Din mission. Dave thought the tall slim man with ample physique to be fit but somehow didn't belong in the roster for CSIS Records.

Dave never allowed anyone other than the members of Kodiak Team to *help* with any operational plans and he certainly didn't like the body language this guy put across. Still, given the

Captain was sent by their superiors, he decided to continue, but with caution.

"If you spell out your plan, I'll add whatever expertise I have to it," Captain Day said with a tinge of a Newfoundland or cockney accent.

"The more input the better." Dave lied. "The simple plan here is to have my team do a night jump about fifteen kilometers northeast of Kirkuk." He pointed to the place on the large world map on the wall. "We'll enter the town separately so as not to arouse suspicion and seek out our man. Once we find him we will," he gave a quick glance at Joanne, "detain him for questioning."

"A night jump? Northeast of Kirkuk? That's some very rugged terrain and especially for night jumps."

"My team has jumped into worse terrain than that, besides, we sure can't do it during the day can we?" Dave smiled at the thought that this captain was buying the story.

The Captain looked puzzled. "I don't see how I can help with the insertion but we do have assets in Kirkuk that you might use." He gave Dave a description, name and location of a man to contact whom Dave had already decided to shelve.

"When did you expect to proceed Lt. Colonel?" The Captain enquired.

"We leave exactly six days from today, on the twenty ninth at zero two thirty Zulu, of course dependant on the weather in that area. Giving us twenty-four hours to drop zone, it should get us there about the right time."

Colonel Benton had been watching this exchange with a gentle smile.

"Then that about wraps it up." She said as she shot a glance at Captain Day. "Do you have anything else to add?" He didn't so she dismissed him.

"Lt. Colonel," she said without looking in his direction. "Stand fast. I have a few things to go over with you."

The door closed behind Captain Day before she turned to Dave. "Now what the hell was all that nonsense about? Night drop north east of Kirkuk," she said with a disgusted tone.

"I don't trust him, I don't discuss my plans with outsiders, and I only use my own assets. Your husband taught me that and it's part of the reason I'm still alive."

"Were you planning on letting the CO in on *your* mission?"

"Day after tomorrow we leave at zero five-thirty on one of our transport jets for Windsor, Gander, Paris, Rome, and then onto Kirkuk Airport. We contact *my* asset and find good ol' Sal. Detain and interrogate him without counsel for a few days, turn him over to the CIA, and return home. Minor collateral damage. All I need is your approval."

"Of course you've got it. What about the Captain?"

"What about the Captain?"

"He's been flirting with Gail. I'd hate to see him sweep her off her feet and leave you high and dry."

Dave broke into an incredulous laugh.

"I don't believe this. I'm risking my life on covert missions to get information and stop some deranged psychopath from plunder and destruction and you're worried about who will sweet talk your assistant." Dave sniffed over his shoulder.

"If you're really concerned about Captain Day try doing a thorough background check. I don't think they gave you all the dope on him." Dave gave her an all-knowing glance and smiled "And just for your information, because enquiring minds need to know, I've already asked the lady out tomorrow night to dinner and she accepted. Now mother, can you leave it alone?"

Joanne beamed. "Do you want to borrow my car? You should make a good impression on your first date you know."

"No!" Dave yelled. However, it didn't diminish Joanne's smile and as Dave left the office, he was smiling too. Once he was out of the building, Dave called Julio and informed him the mission was on and he should have the team at the hanger June twenty fifth at zero three hundred.

Dave spent the next day on edge and preparing for the dinner date with Gail. He was as nervous as a mouse with a cat staring at it and at six fifty-five Dave drove up to the front door of the Princess Margaret apartments. He was just about to ring the entrance buzzer to the apartment building when Gail exited the elevator.

Dave had to double check to ensure this wasn't some apparition and was actually the woman he had asked out to dinner. No longer was she in her drab office pantsuit, but had altered her appearance by wearing a blue dress that highlighted her already perfect figure. She also had used just enough make-up to accentuate her natural beauty while her golden blonde hair, like gentle silk, flowed to her shoulders and seemed much nicer than the French braid she kept it in at work. He escorted her to his car, fought with the passenger door until it opened and helped her in. As he got in behind the wheel, he felt a tinge of embarrassment.

"Sorry about the car. I've been planning on getting a new one but just can't seem to say good bye to the old girl."

Gail looked around at the interior. "Nothing wrong with this one, '65' Biscuit isn't it? 6 or V-8?"

"It's the 327." Dave was beginning to like this woman for more than her looks and intelligence. She seemed so down to earth in a heavenly kind of way.

"My older brother was into cars and I tried to keep up with him by getting a classic, a VW Bug, but the motor went and parts for those little things were super priced so I sold it cheap. I've been using transits and taxi's ever since."

As they traveled south towards White Rock, Dave eased the conversation to Captain George Day. "So what about this Captain Day? Is he someone you've known long?"

Gail gave an impish smile "George? Just met him yesterday and he's already asked me out, but I haven't accepted yet."

"Yet?"

"I think he's a bit too aggressive, even pushy," she said with a sarcastic smile, "but he is quite handsome," being coy.

"Are you trying to make me jealous?"

"Could I?"

"Touché."

The journey to the Pearl of the Ocean restaurant flashed by as they enjoyed a running conversation.

At The Pearl, the waiter led the couple to a far corner terrace, which allowed a spectacular view of the bay. A sparkling white linen tablecloth with an ornamental candle in the center adorned each table. Dave held the chair for Gail to be seated and then sat down across from her. A light breeze rippled the water in the bay giving a glorious kaleidoscope of slashing silver and gold colours as the sun silently slipped towards the horizon, but to Dave this golden haired angel sitting across from him upstaged it all. As he stared at her, it seemed he was seeing her for the very first time.

She's gorgeous, he thought, as he noticed her shining golden hair, her eyes, almost as blue as her evening gown, and that evening gown, how she filled it...suddenly he caught himself, realizing he was gawking and his face flushed.

"I'm sorry," he said, "It's just that you look really gorgeous tonight. I mean you look good every night, I mean all the time. Ah jeez, you know what I mean."

Gail smiled and without missing a beat, put on her best Mae West impersonation.

"You're not so bad yourself cowboy." They both laughed.

She was referring to the sports coat, light blue shirt with tie, blue jeans and alligator cowboy boots Dave was wearing.

"Yeah, sorry about the duds, but I just don't spend much time off work looking for clothes. Other than fatigues, uniform or work clothes, this about answers the call if I want to go out, but seeing you, I wish I had of taken time to buy a suit."

"Hey, don't be silly. I like you exactly the way you are. Kind of dressed up but ready to protect and to serve. It's you Dave."

He signaled a waiter to the table.

Could I impose for a bottle of champagne on ice and then we'd like to order."

The waiter gave a nod.

"Certainly sir, right away."

Dave smiled at Gail.

"I haven't enjoyed an evening like this for a very long time. I'm glad you agreed to be my dinner date this evening.

The waiter began serving the meal and they enjoyed the food, the atmosphere of the restaurant, and each other's company. After the leisurely meal and conversation they sat admiring the reflections of the bay. Now after sunset, the reflections of the lights from Blaine and some assorted boats at anchor glittered in the water

"Would you like to walk along the beach?" Dave asked.

Gail nodded. They left the restaurant and walked along the moon walk enjoying the fresh salt air, the sea, and each other. After walking and talking, Dave took her back to her apartment building and stopped at the front entrance. He turned the ignition off and Gail turned to him.

"Thank you for a great evening," she said

"You're welcome," he said as they gazed into each other's eyes.

Slowly they came together, embraced and kissed long and deep until she pulled back taking a quick deep breath. "Thank you again," she said and gave him a quick peck on the cheek before getting out of the car. Dave walked her up to the door and after another short embrace said good-night.

As he drove home to the lake, he realized he had spent the entire evening without flashbacks or thoughts of the Mexican fiasco. He also was well aware his sleep tonight would still be permeated with the nightmarish dream of an incident he had lived through a thousand times.

Chapter 4

The morning sun had burned away the coolness of the night as General Beauregard Smith strolled through his Columbian villa. Glancing through one of the arched openings that embellished the verandas on both floors he drank in the view to the west, observing how the deep blue sky accentuated the emerald green jungle flora beyond the courtyard. This normally might have helped lift the General's spirits, but not today.

Continuing his morning promenade, he descended the wide sweeping circular staircase scrutinizing with immense satisfaction the galactic ballroom. It was by far the grandest room in the building with a row of ten giant chandeliers running along the center of the high arched ceiling as well as other ornate decorations. The General envisaged a Gala Ball of some type being held here as he glanced around the overall area. He considered with pride the master craftsmanship of construction using cement, rock, and wood incorporated into each of its three levels, each stretching over nine thousand square feet.

While the dining room, ballroom, and study took up much of the main floor level, the upper level was spaciously allotted to bedrooms as well as his own exclusive private living area. He had left the basement for the kitchen, staff offices, living quarters for the domestics, and whatever trades people would be needed for maintenance.

Reaching his destination, the study, he gazed around the cavernous room. The entire décor of mahogany and brown leather blended with, as well as complimented, the nineteenth century American furnishings and artifacts. Even the computer and monitor on the highly polished reddish colored desk were wrapped in a wooden covering and harmonized with the room. Behind the large desk sat a dark brown leather manager's chair, custom designed to fit the General's six foot four, two hundred and fifty seven pound frame.

Moving around behind the desk and sitting down he contorted his face into a scowl. He was in a miserable mood since he'd received the news that his task force in Edmonton, Canada had been neutralized before they could carry out their mission. Jonathan and Andres, his two top advisors, both dressed in expensive looking British buttoned down fashion, rushed in responding to the General's buzzer. The General glared at them; his face red with anger.

"What the hell happened up there? That refinery was to be put out of commission for at least a year. It probably wouldn't have driven the price up much, but more importantly it would have added more pressure to the already overburdened dependence on other refineries in which I happen to be heavily invested; my stocks would have soared in the billions. Now the timetable is set back at least six months. Don't I pay enough money to ensure these jobs get done?" He squinted straight at the two nervous men in front of him. "Let me tell you two boneheads this; if I don't get all the information on this screw-up within the next few hours some people here and in Canada will be less their heads---starting with you two! Now get the hell out of here and get me some answers! Pronto!"

The two hurried out of the room almost tripping over each other.

"And Tom," yelling at one of his guards. "Send them two girlies in here!"

Smith poured himself a large brandy and lit a reefer as the two prostitutes sashayed in. He glanced around at his two bodyguards and nodded toward the door.

"I can take care of this myself; close the door on your way out." He turned his attention on the two girls.

A few hours later, he stumbled out of the study in a delirious state with blood covering his clothing. He had already passed the anteroom where his two bodyguards were playing poker when he realized it and turned around. He cursed the two guards up and down and then ordered them to get rid of the two prostitutes. The guards gave each other a defeated look.

"Right away, sir."

He spun around, almost capsizing and headed for his bedroom and the shower. The guards proceeded into the study reluctantly and found the one woman naked, bruised, and cowering in the corner of the blood spattered room.

"Asshole! Why can't he just screw them and leave it at that. Where is the other one anyway?"

The other guard was searching the room and when he opened a closet door, the body of the second girl unraveled out onto the expensive Indian carpet which began to turn a darker crimson with the woman's blood. As he stared in shock at the body he saw that the head was twisted at a macabre angle towards the back and attached to the main torso by only a narrow cord of tissue.

"Oh my god, he almost cut her head clean off. That scum faced son of a bitch. Ah shit, I think I'm gonna be sick."

He rushed to the lavatory at the back of the study, stuck his head into the toilet bowl and threw up. After several violent heaves, he came back out wiping his face with a cool damp washcloth.

"You know for fifty bucks I wouldn't have to be asked twice to blow his brains out!"

"Yeah and I'd make a contribution too," Tom said, "but you'd better keep your voice down or we'll be the one's getting our brains blown out. Now come on and let's get these two out to the van. I'll call housekeeping to get this mess cleaned up."

*   *   *

The next morning Smith sat in his sanitized study with his two bodyguards when Andres and Jonathan buzzed and then entered. They looked haggard as if they hadn't slept all night which they hadn't.

"General, we managed to get the information you ordered and much more," Andres said with a smug victorious grin.

"Well, don't just stand there with your dicks in your hands, tell me!"

"Yes sir, we found out a Lt. Colonel David Hart led a team in a night assault against our safe house. His team killed all our men there."

This immediately started the General to fly into a rage.

"What Lt. Colonel Dave Hart? Who the hell is he?"

At the General's question, Jonathan stepped forward.

"Lt. Colonel Hart was the one credited with the Valmont thing and the one in Vallarta." Now Smith's face was red and the veins stood out on his neck.

"That interfering son of a bitch. He's done it to me again. I, I thought I had him wiped out in Vallarta. Sal said he blew him away; put two or three slugs into him. God damn that lying son of a bitch, Sal. I'll make him wish he was never born!" The General gave a mean stare at the advisors. "Is that all?"

"Well n-no sir." Both advisors were visibly shaking now.

"You'd better hurry up, I'm really losing my patience here," he said with a growl in his voice as he pulled a nickel-plated H&K forty-five out of the desk drawer and slammed it down on the marble desktop.

"W-well it seems somehow this Lt. Colonel found out about Sal and has a mission in the works to find and squeeze him for information."

At this Smith went ballistic, now turning white with rage, choking in anger. But almost like a little light came on in his brain, as quickly as the anger had irrupted, it dissipated, and a gentle transformation of a smile came across his lips.

"Did your little birdie happen to tell you when this was going to take place?"

Jonathan now checked his notes. "Y-y-yes sir, twenty-nine June between twenty-four hundred and zero six hundred hours. Apparently they're jumping in darkness northeast of Kirkuk."

Smith was jovial now. "Well, well, well. I think we should arrange a welcoming committee for our little group of Canucks."

*   *   *

The pilot of the aircraft flicked on the seatbelt warning and intercom and almost immediately the jet with the Kodiak team dipped into an excessively rapid descent from forty thousand feet.

"Gentlemen, we are now making our approach to the Kirkuk airport. We need to make a fast steep slide in there to avoid everything from rifle shot to SAM's. Fasten your seatbelts and hang on kids. I'll have you on the ground in ten minutes, hopefully alive."

As the bird swooped quickly to the ground, then thumped, and lurched, braking hard, Dave gave the team a final pep talk.

"Alright guys, we've got our own rooms and we chow down with the rich kids and you all know your tasks." Dave searched the men's faces. "Julio and I will be hunting and if we get into trouble," He knew if they got into trouble, there was a minimal chance his team would be able to rescue them but he went on, "--do your best."

The Challenger taxied to a stop and the co-pilot opened the door. The ground crew had wheeled a mobile boarding stairs to the plane and the team grabbed their carry-ons. As they left the plane, the hot dry breeze seemingly slapped their faces and they joked about not needing a sauna in their rooms. Dave and Julio were met by the US liaison officer with whom they shook hands.

"Lt. Fowler sirs. If you'll follow me I'll escort you to the Base Commander." Fowler turned to a marine private and ordered him to escort the rest of the team to their quarters. Fowler then turned back to Dave and Julio.

"This way sirs, I have a ride waiting. Oh, and you had better wear these helmets," he said as he passed them each a helmet. The officers donned the 'pots' and jumped into the well-used Humvee for the one mile ride to the command post.

"Lt. Fowler," Dave asked, "is it true you fellows never got a grader over here and the hospital treats more kidney damage from rough roads than from enemy fire?"

"Almost Sir, I see you've noticed the roads aren't exactly--" They hit an especially deep pothole and both Julio and Dave hit the roof and then came down into the hard metal seats. "--smooth." They all laughed.

They arrived at the Command center and Lt. Fowler escorted them into Colonel Jackson's office.

"Come in gentlemen. That will be all Lt. Fowler." The Lt. left closing the door behind him. The two Canadians stood at attention in front of the Colonel's desk.

Colonel Jackson sat behind his desk and looked to be in his late thirties. Although his physique was well built he looked more like a weight lifter than a body builder.

"Oh, at ease officers and grab a chair. Well, Lt. Colonel Hart and Captain Rodriguez, I've been advised of your arrival and your mission. Welcome to Camp Renegade. Now I'm gonna get real up front with you people; I don't like this one damn bit. You spooks come over here, push the people around, stir up a hornets' nest, get your damn information, and then leave. We're supposed to clean up after you." He glared at the men, threw the papers he was holding down on his desk and nodded again for them to have a chair. "Ah hell, it's already been decided anyway and higher powers demand I be hospitable." Again he glared at them with his beady eyes. "So how can I be of service?"

Dave cleared his throat. "Thank you Sir. I guess my first concern is has my contact arrived on base yet?"

"Yes, he's working over in the old terminal as an electrician. We'll have him escorted over to your room as soon as you're settled."

"Thank you Sir, and after I've met him I'd like to have him quarantined until the end of the mission as a precaution. He'll require Marines to guard his room?"

"What the hell for? Never mind I suppose I don't want to know. Okay, done." The Colonel was becoming exasperated.

"Second, we'll need a quiet place with absolutely no personnel access when we bring our captive back in about a week or so. Your intelligence people will want to question him."

"I see, and when did you plan on executing this maneuver?"

"The Captain and I will leave at sundown and hopefully be back in about seven to ten days. My people will act as an extraction team if we run into trouble, but we don't anticipate any. They will need a chopper if any problem arises."

"I'll have a chopper stand by while you're out and when you return I'll have the MPs escort you to an empty Yugo at the end of the airstrip and post a guard. No one gets in or out."

"Ah, one more thing Colonel, would you happen to have an inconspicuous ride? Like something a little smaller than a Humvee or a bus?"

The Colonel, his patience wearing thin, shuffled through some papers until he came to a list of vehicles on base. He followed the list down.

"You may be in luck. We captured some insurgents who were using a little Chevy S-10 pickup. Had a damn fifty caliber mounted in the back. We had the gun removed and the truck's over at the motor pool. It's yours, but be aware of the mines and other explosives on the roads around here. The enemy seems to have a relish for blowing the hell out of everything and everybody in sight right now."

"Yes Sir, so we've heard," Dave said with a grin.

"Right, well if that's all, I suppose you'd like to get some food and rest before sunset. I'll have

Fowler escort you to your barracks and then have the electrician brought to you. Your ride will be outside your barracks at nineteen hundred hours and you'll be issued a gate pass."

"Thank you Sir." They stood and saluted, which the Colonel returned lazily, and they left the office. Lt. Fowler was waiting down the hall to take them to the barracks.

Dave and Julio had just got settled when a knock came at the door. Julio opened it and there stood a well tanned, middle-aged, man.

"I'm Oscar. I was told to report here to fix up a special electrical outlet."

"Great, come on in and close the door," Dave said.

Once the door was closed, the man sat down at the small table and pulled out a map of the city.

"I've got you a basement suite for your center of operations right here."   He pointed to a circled spot on the east side of the city. "It's only two blocks from your objective, here, where Sal A Din is staying. We're sure he'll be there at least for tonight." He took another paper out of his pocket and opened it up.

"This is a rough blueprint of the building he's in."

"What's our best access and egress?" Dave asked staring at the rough diagram.

"The same, a door in the alley on the west side of the building."

"Are they posting sentries?" Julio asked.

"Hey, this isn't Canada. Of course they post a lookout, but he's on the roof and they're watching for military sweeps, not nuts like you," Oscar said with a chuckle.

"Is there any way to access the roof without alerting the sentry?" Julio asked.

"None, he's got a three sixty sweep and the entrance to the roof is through the living area."

"Well thanks much for the Intel as well as your evaluation of us. You realize you'll be held on base for about a week in solitary?" Dave smiled as he asked.

"And just how the hell do I explain that?"

Dave winked at Julio. "Can you see the yellow in his eyes?"

"Oh for sure, skin's kind of greenish too. He definitely has Jaundice, who knows what disease he's carrying. I'd say quarantined for at least a week."

The man fish eyed them. "You wouldn't dare."

"We're really sorry but we have to. I'll make sure your account is properly credited," Dave said as he opened the door and waved for an MP. "I want this man escorted to the hospital and placed under strict quarantine for jaundice and I want a guard on his room until further orders. It's already been approved by the CO."

Julio grabbed a coffee as soon as the door closed.

"Do you know that guy? I got the impression you two had met before."

"Yeah, he's Mossad. That's one reason I had him quarantined. Don't get me wrong, they do good work but you just never know what angles those guys are playing."

"You mean like our southern spooks?"

Dave just gave a nod.

"I guess we're going to have to bring a shooter with us too, to take out that sentry. You give George the heads up."

Julio finished the last slug of coffee and headed for Marty and George's room.

At nineteen-thirty hours, Dave, Julio and George crowded into the little pickup dressed in sports clothes and drove off the base. They made a left and headed for the east side of the city twisting and swerving through traffic. Dave left the truck first about six blocks before their destination and George got out three blocks later. Julio continued past their quarters for about three blocks and parked the truck in an inconspicuous spot. They each did a walk past to ensure the place was free of hostiles.

The entry to the basement accommodations was at the bottom of a long narrow stairs in the alley. It was a windowless stone and mortar flat with a solitary light bulb hanging from its wire in the center of a large room. An old wooden table and three chairs stood directly under the light. Across the room was a small bathroom with a makeshift shower which doubled as the toilet. Along two walls were three cots with spartan bedding. Although the upper two floors appeared to be functional, they were supposed to be vacant.

Dave used his leather attaché case to motion to the far side of the room and a second set of stairs that led to the upper floors.

"You two check the floors and George, see if you can find that sentry."

George grabbed his scope from his duffle and with his eighteen C holstered he followed Julio up the stairs.

Dave checked out the entire lower floor and found Oscar had outdone himself in stocking the cupboards with western type easy food from Kraft Dinner to Minute Rice.

"Almost a fast food deli," Dave said as he searched the cupboards, found the coffee and began to brew a pot. He was just pouring himself a cup as Julio and George came back down the stairs.

"So, could you spot him? Dave asked.

"It's not him, it's them. They've got four sentries. The only plus is they aren't moving around. Each one has a position at a corner watching ninety degrees. I can take two maybe three but the fourth sucker is going to vanish before I can do him. I wish we had brought Marty. We could easily take two each but four on one is lousy odds."

"Suppose I should have brought the whole damn team," Dave said sarcastically.

"Why don't I just take the S-10 back to the base and pick him up? I could be back here in forty minutes," George suggested.

"Because there's a possibility it's been spotted. If it was from around here, someone might have recognized it and put two and two together." He pulled out his Satellite phone. "I didn't want to risk it, but I'll get the team to escort him out here. We have until oh three hundred which is," he glanced at his watch, "seven hours away." Dave punched the number. "Kodiak, this is Badger. I need you to deliver shooter two."

"You got trouble out there, Badger?"

"Negative. Everything is quiet. I just need an extra shooter. Put on some area clothes and escort him on foot to within about six blocks of our position. Spread out so you blend. You'll wait at that rendezvous point for his return to base. I'll expect him within four hours."

"Roger that Badger." Dave slid the phone closed.

Marty arrived just after midnight.

"Did you guys make it without shaking up the whole town?" Dave asked.

"Not a squeak Sir. The team divided into two squads and moved a block apart. They're about five blocks west and closely dispersed."

Marty turned to George. "Couldn't work without me, aye?"

"We needed your weapon. You're just a necessary nuisance" George said.

"LC, are you going to allow an inferior shooter to talk to me like that?" Marty asked with a grin.

Dave shook his head with a chuckle. "Just make sure you take out all four with no noise. And don't screw up."

To help the time go by faster the shooters cleaned and checked their weapons while Julio honed his khukri. Dave took the time to fill several syringes with a mixture of valium, phencyclidine and alphaprodine. The given mixture would render a person unconscious almost immediately and keep them in that condition for up to four hours unless an antidote was administered.

At zero two thirty Dave gave the shooters the order to move to the roof and pick their targets. Dave was very precise with his words.

"When I give you green, you take them out. Do it fast and quiet. Captain, once they have neutralized the sentries, you and I will make a silent entrance into Sal's domain. Khukris only, silenced Glocks if necessary."

George and Marty took their rifles and headed for the roof while Dave and Julio slinked through the allies toward the insurgent's hide out. In a crouch they quickly and quietly crossed one street and then down another alley. Dave gave Julio a heads up when they had reached the end of the alley which was across the street from Sal's building. Dave checked his watch. It was zero three hundred.

"Shooters have you marked your target?" Dave whispered into his Com-Tac.

"Yes sir," they replied in unison.

"You have a green, that's green."

Instantly four clicks sounded in rapid succession, and then silence.

"Four down Sir, no noise, no feathers."

"Roger that. Stay on post and keep the area."

"Yes Sir."

Dave and Julio moved stealthily across the street and into the alley. They stopped at the door. Each man slipped his night vision eyepiece down over the right eye and then silently slipped in the entrance to the building.

Almost instantly, Dave motioned to Julio, pointing out a lone guard who was in a semi-conscious sleep on a chair. In total stealth Julio slipped up behind the man, pushed the Kukri blade quickly between the second and third cervical vertebrae. Julio held the man who was trying to scream but could not because he was paralyzed from the neck down. The guard wanted to lift his arms or legs but nothing worked. After his heartbeat raced and his eyes darted to every area they could get to for a couple of minutes of sheer panic, the lack of oxygen to the brain rendered him first unconscious and then dead. Julio secured him to the chair and then released him.

Dave meanwhile scanned the room as he cautiously moved past four other sleeping men and then to Sal off in the corner. He quickly inserted a needle into Sal's carotid artery and pushed the plunger on the syringe. Sal almost awoke and let out a small jagged yell before the drug rendered him unconscious.

The shallow yelp from Sal woke up the four other guards in the room and as they rolled out of their cots they charged at Dave. Instantly as the first one was leveling an automatic toward Dave at point blank range Dave stuck the empty syringe into his face and grabbed his weapon hand. He twisted it back, removed the weapon, and then flipped the guy into the second attacker. He high kicked the third and the snapping neck was quite audible as the man landed on top of the first two. The fourth one almost managed to hit him but Dave went down, kicked his feet out from under him and dispatched him with a heavy kick to the temple. Dave quickly flipped back onto his feet and seeing the first and second men again charging, he chopped across the neck of first unfortunate one, crushing his larynx and then grabbed the second by the throat and severed the carotid. As the spurting blood gradually diminished, Dave held the jerking man until he went limp and then let him drop the few inches to the floor. Dave was breathing hard from the sixty second workout.

"You could've let me help you know," Julio said.

"Next time, maybe," he said, grabbing for breath.

They searched for any intel that might be of use and then while Julio struggled to lift Sal over his shoulder, Dave cracked open the door and checked to ensure the alley was secure. The two slipped silently out of the building and smuggled their silent captive back through the alleys the way they had come.

Once in their basement flat, Julio deposited Sal on a cot, carefully cuffed his hands and feet and then checked him for any hidden papers, weapons, or pills.

"Shooters, are we clear?" Dave asked.

"No movement sir, it's clear."

He ordered the shooters to find the fire team and return to base.

The sun had risen by the time Sal gradually regained consciousness. As he woke he gazed around the room until he came to Dave. The Lt. Colonel watched as Sal's eyes grew large. Dave was amused at Sal's recognition of him and he thought maybe this is going to be enjoyable after all.

He gave the high ranking insurgent his first injection of the analgesics Dave liked to refer to as love potion number nine. For the next forty-eight hours, they would continue to inject the analgesics every four hours while slightly increasing the dose, but always letting Sal see it came from the blue syringe. After the first few days, Sal would do anything to get his 'fix' and that would signal step one was successfully completed.

"Why have you not given me my injection?" Sal said in slightly broken English on the morning of the third day. After some dialogue about information for continued injections Dave realized Sal was ready for interrogation.

Dave moved over to the cot and made sure Sal focused on him. "Captain, give him the needle."

"But he's got to pay for it. You know the rules."

"Yeah that's right. We do have to go by the rules." He got closer and whispered, "Now if you were to give me your name, that might be information enough for this time." Then he spoke louder as if tricking Julio, "So what is your name?"

"Salah Al Din," he said quietly like someone who had just given up some pride.

"Did you hear that Captain? He paid, so he gets the needle."

Sal received it eagerly and slipped back into his dream world.

Dave knew this was the first step so to speak and the next crucial step would be to scare him with a bad trip making sure he was aware the syringe was a red one. This was a dangerous step because if he got too far out on the bad 'trip' he might never find his way back. They actually gave him two bad trips before his spirit completely broke and fear took over, which made it very difficult to refuse to answer their questions.

Julio was about to give him his third red injection when he noticed Sal began to shake violently.

"Please, I'll tell you anything you want to know, just give me a blue one not the red. Please?" He was crying like a baby.

Dave moved closer now.

"Will you answer our questions now?"

"Yes, but please give me the blue needle," he sobbed.

"What is your alias? What other names do you go by?"

"When I'm on a mission I call myself Mahir Abdul Al Aziz."

"Good boy," Dave said.

Julio gave him the injection from the blue syringe and Sal was floating in a few minutes. Dave started the satellite phone recorder and motioned for Julio to begin the questioning.

"Sal, do you know where you are?" Julio asked in Farsi

"No."

"You're in General Smith's house."

"Ah-h-h, which one?"

"How many does he have?"

"Several. There's the villa in Columbia, another off the coast of Myanmar, the place in Syria and the Hacienda in Argentina. There are others but he hardly ever uses them."

"Which one do you think this is?"

"This must be Columbia. That is where he said I was to meet him at the end of the month. It isn't the end of the month yet is it?"

"No you've got plenty of time. Okay Sal, maybe you need some rest now and we can talk again later."

"Yes, I need to rest and think," and he submerged into a semi consciousness.

Dave shut off the recorder and took a sip of coffee.

"So did you get anything?"

"Yeah, not bad for a start. He said Smith has several houses. He mentioned one in Argentina, Syria, Columbia and Myanmar. Poor Sal figures he's at the Columbia Villa."

"We're doing good but next time let's try and get some operational Intel."

"You don't think we're moving too fast?"

"No. Hell no, we've been at this for five days. I think a few more sessions should do it and that might be about all old Sal will able to handle."

The next session started as Sal began to come down and Julio held out the syringe but wouldn't give it to him.

"How soon you forget. Information first, then the goodies."

"What do you want to know?" he said.

"I'd like to hear more about Mr. Smith." Julio said as Dave started the recorder.

"You mean the General?"

"That's right. What can you tell us about our friend the General?"

"Hah, that's a laugh. The General isn't anybody's friend." Julio pulled out the red needle and Sal cringed.

"Okay, alright." Sal said and proceeded to answer as Julio spoke to him in Farsi, his native language. When Julio noticed Sal becoming very agitated he motioned to Dave who administered another injection. Sal dropped into his own physiological sandbox, soon to be out of touch with reality. He drifted off to sleep.

Julio joined Dave at the table where Dave had already poured him a coffee. Dave smiled.

"Sounded like he gave you a lot of material."

"He did and some of it is good intel. Let's see now." Julio turned to the beginning of his notes. "I asked him where the General's home base is. He replied he mostly stays at the Columbia Villa at the apex of a triangle about one hundred and fifty kilometers southeast of Buenaventura and roughly the same distance from Bogotá. He even explained that at one time, a Medellin drug lord had used it as his home and headquarters but a combined covert mission from several U.S. law enforcement agencies neutralized him and the estate was mothballed which allowed the jungle to reclaim the grounds. It sat empty for several years until the General happened to see it from the air and acquired it. He had military engineers design defenses on the entire property and then landscaped it better than the original. When they were finished, the flora completely canopied the entire estate except for the Villa, guard barracks and heli-pad in the back courtyard."

"I then asked him specifically about the estates security. He says the General had some of the most sophisticated detection and anti-personnel equipment available installed. He says all of the detection equipment is operated by a large computer, which uses heat, light, and motion sensors to aim and fire the weapons. There are three gates on the one kilometer driveway that automatically close without the proper RF signal and without that signal the sensors through the computer will aim and fire the machine guns in a cross fire. If in fact the intruders were in a small armored vehicle or small tank, the computer would deploy anti tank missiles. These the General assured him would destroy anything less than an Abrams." Julio turned the page in his notebook.

"He continued that the entire perimeter has a ten meter cleared kill zone. This cleared area has anti personnel mines, and fifty-caliber machine guns. The computer uses sensors to operate these as well. Finally, if an attacking force was able to make it to the villa, a platoon of elite heavily armed guards would be ready to defend the grounds and the General with their lives if necessary." Julio glanced at Dave who had raised his eyebrows.

"I then asked what he knew of the General's business. He said Smith had been working on a thing they called the Manhattan Two Project when he first met him. He was having some kind of mini bombs built with next generation nuclear fission, something they called Purple Lightning. He was also in charge of getting America ready for a new kind of war. The war would first neutralize the Taliban in Afghanistan who were holding up pipeline construction from the east." Dave had come alert.

"Was he telling you Smith was working with Al Qaida and Osama against the CIA?"

"That was my next question and he asked if that was an infidel's joke. He said Osama is CIA, always has been and the General was his Commander. He said when Iraq was invaded, the General was there and working with Saddam and they were calling it the Bekka Valley Project. That's where most of the Weapons of Mass Destruction went from Iraq. Actually, only the best, mostly nuclear, biological equipment and lab supplies were transferred but it made quite a few of truckloads. After that, the General aligned himself with Syria and Iran and used Hezbollah to guard his cache hidden in the Bekka Valley. He said it's been whispered they've almost perfected a weapon they've labeled the Scorpion. He overheard something about purple lightning technology again as well. He said this Scorpion is supposed to be the size and weight a man can carry but with the power close to a one megaton nuclear bomb. " Again Dave's eyebrows went up in surprise.

"I asked if he knew what the General was planning to use these weapons for. He looked at me incredulously and said he's going to wipe out Israel of course and in the process he will destabilize an already volatile Middle East. He said the long end of the plan is when the American's jump in to protect their interests in Israel, then Russia will back their alliance with Iran and Syria. After the Americans and the Russians get done throwing their military hardware at each other, the General will step in with his latest ally, North Korea and a new Middle East will rise out of the ashes with the General as the wealthiest and most powerful President in the world. Sal says somehow the General believes if he controls the Middle East he will control the world."

By the next day, after a few more sessions, Sal was singing the Jewish Victory song and Dave decided they had pretty well got every secret Sal ever knew which meant this part of the mission was complete. Dave pulled out his sat phone and punched a special sequence of numbers and was soon connected to the Vancouver CSIS headquarters. He talked to a special communications technician and transmitted the tape of the interrogation. When it was completed he requested a transcript on CD be sent to his office.

Dave smiled as he slid his phone closed and turned to Julio.

"Captain, let's get our friend here back to the base. You get the truck, but be careful."

"That's one order I wouldn't fool with."

When Julio returned with the S-10, he parked it in front of the alley by their headquarters. Dave wrapped Sal in blankets as camouflage, threw him over his shoulder, and carried him out to the truck. He laid Sal in the box and began to walk around to the front passenger door when a volley of automatic weapon fire raked across the truck. A heavy caliber machine gun punched a line of holes from the back passenger side to the driver's front corner.

Before Dave ducked down behind the truck, he saw at least three of the large slugs rip across Sal's body with chunky splotches of Sal's bloody body tissue ripping out where each bullet hit. Julio had gone to the basement to retrieve the weapons duffle or he also would have been greased in the driver's seat. At the sound of the machine gun, Julio traversed the stairs three at a time and as he reached ground level in the alley he saw Dave crumpled on the ground beside the truck. Julio stopped breathing as he surveyed the scene. Dave lay with his back to him, his left side already soaked red and a pool of his blood formed on the sidewalk.

Chapter 5

"Dave, Dave, answer me. Dave, can you hear me?" Julio yelled down the alley. Julio was under cover in a step well in the alley and was just about to rush out to pull his friend out of harm's way.

"He's west down the street in a second story window," Dave said loud enough to be heard but without moving a muscle. "Check it out, you'll see the muzzle."

"Shit, you had me scared," Julio answered as he darted a glimpse around the corner of the building. "Yeah, yeah I see him."

"Flank him to the left, get to the second floor and nail that son of a bitch. I'll bother him from this side as much as I can. Go!"

Julio ripped his assault rifle from the weapons duffle and took off down the narrow alley to circle around the block and enter the back of the building where the bushwhackers fired from.

Dave waited until he figured Julio would be in position in need of some cover fire and then squeezed off short blasts with his Glock. It wasn't much, but his rifle was still in the duffle on the other side of a perfect kill zone.

Firing at them with his side arm resulted in a concentrated and heavy pattern from the big automatic weapon but Dave reasoned it might keep them occupied long enough for Julio to get into position. It seemed an eternity passed before Dave heard the report from Julio's weapon. Dave used the diversion to charge into the alley and retrieve his rifle, but as he did the heavy caliber opened up again spraying cement at his heels.

A shell must have hit the truck again because just as Dave passed the corner of the building the truck exploded, flipped into the air, and come down on its roof in a flurry of flames. In almost a single motion he grabbed his H&K, checked the clip, grabbed two spares, and spun to retrace his steps back out past the blazing truck. He burst down the street sprinting as fast as he could as the shells ricocheted off the sidewalk and stone buildings just behind him. As he zigzagged flat out, he laid a pattern at the window where the heavy caliber was coming from. He emptied the clip, dropped it out of the weapon, slammed in a full one and sprayed some more. At last, all went silent and Dave, pumped with adrenalin, rushed over to the back door of the building to check on Julio. He hammered a fresh clip home as he charged up to the entrance. With his back to the cement wall he quickly glanced in the doorway and then with his weapon at the ready rushed through the door. Julio sauntered coolly across the room.

"There were five of them. I got three on the lower floor and one upstairs and you took out the gunner at the window."

"Well let's not hang around and wait for their friends. Let's get back to the base."

"What about Sal?"

"His friends there shot him and then incinerated him. They must have hit the gas tank on the truck. Come to think about it, my guess would be someone must have rigged the truck with explosives. I've never seen a gas tank blow with that much intensity except in the movies. Lucky it didn't blow when you were driving it."

"How about you? Are you okay?" Julio asked, eyeing the wound on Dave's upper arm.

Dave put the first two fingers of his right hand over the left side of his jaw to mimic a check for a carotid pulse. He frowned for a minute and then broke into a smile as if finding something.

"Hey I still got a pulse. Guess that means I'm still alive." He noticed Julio staring at the blood trickling down his left arm. "And from what I could see of that nick on my upper arm it's just a flesh wound."

The blood was oozing out of a half inch deep by three inch long ragged wound and had already saturated his ripped shirt. Julio pulled a field dressing from his pants pocket and wrapped it tightly over the wound which helped the bleeding to subside.

Julio glanced at Dave with the 'what the hell do we do now' question written all over his face.

"LC do you think we should call for an extraction? We do have the team and a chopper standing by."

"No, we'll head over to Main Street and try to blend with the locals. We got pretty good tans but I'll have to keep my head covered, the sandy blond hair would be a dead give-a-way."

Julio raised his eyebrows.

"I think the key word there is dead."

"Captain Rodriguez, you worry too much."

*   *   *   *

Dave and Julio arrived at the gate to camp Renegade and were immediately arrested with an MP escorting them to the CO's office.

The Colonel was seated behind his desk and Dave could see by the CO's red face he was wroth.

"What the hell did you think you were doing? The Iraqi police say you killed nearly fifty civilians. In case you're not aware, we already did Operation Iraqi Freedom, and without your help. You can't just come over here and kill people you know."

"They were insurgents," Julio began.

"You shut your mouth Mister. I didn't give you permission to speak! One more word and I'll have the whole bunch of you thrown in the stockade and you can wait for your government to negotiate your release." He turned his attention again toward Dave. "Well Mister, what have you got to say for yourself?"

Although Dave stood at attention, in due respect of rank, the Colonel was not causing any undue alarm, except possibly the fact he thought the threat of the stockade might be real.

"We were on a sanctioned secret mission sir, and that prevents me from disclosing the reason for, or the information gathered; but I can say the Iraqi police are, for whatever reason, inflating the numbers. We killed ten men in self-defense or in conveyance of carrying out our mission. They were insurgents and they actually shot one of their own, but that still only brings the number to eleven."

"And what about the prisoner you were supposed to bring back?"

"That's the one they shot sir."

The Colonel gave a defeated sigh and moved some papers on his desk. "Ah hell, what's the difference? Stand at ease gentlemen. Seems some of these Iraqi police have closer ties to the insurgents than they do to us. I've already talked to Middle East Command and they say you're to be given every available courtesy, take any necessary heat and spirit you out of here as quickly and quietly as possible when you're done."

Dave was respectful.

"I understand sir. We would like nothing better than to be airborne a.s.a.p. It's just a matter of making the necessary arrangements Sir."

"Lieutenant Colonel, nothing would make me happier than to see the ass end of your plane disappearing over the western horizon. So anything you require to get the hell out of here will be made to happen. Do I make myself clear?"

"Perfectly sir."

"Then get over to the infirmary, get that arm taken care of, and then disappear."

"Yes sir!"

The Comanding Officer glanced up and when he saw they were still standing there he pointed at the door.

"Dismissed."

After they had left he punched his intercom and told his aid to have every possible courtesy made available to aid in the departure of the Canadians.

Dave and Julio headed for the infirmary as Dave called Joanne to update her on the status of the mission.

"Lt. Colonel Hart, how nice of you to call. Seems like ages since I got a report from you. Is this a business call or did you just want to chitchat? I've been hearing all sorts of nasty things about you."

"Nice to hear your voice too."

"I see you got some good Intel from the man though. Do you think the CIA will be able to get anything further from him?"

"I'm sure they won't."

"So when are you finished there? I've heard the Base Commander there is not exactly a giant fan of yours. Nor is he ecstatic about your continued presence." Dave had to smile at how fast Joanne got news.

"Roger that. We narrowly escaped the stockade. Anyway we're out of here within the next couple of hours."

"Good, I've got tons of paperwork here for you and once I finish debriefing you we'll talk about how we might secure a sanctioned mission to rope the Cottonmouth in."

"Roger that, sounds like things might be moving in the right direction."

Five hours later, Kodiak Team's jet just reached altitude after a routine refueling stop at Rome's Aviano Air Base. Dave gazed around at the team members. Harvey was playing solitaire, Tron was reading a Popular Mechanics magazine and Marty and George were quietly arguing about some shooting technology. Everyone else was asleep.

*   *

*

After a sixteen hour layover in Paris, giving the men a chance to see the sights, the plane was airborne by zero five thirty and would make two more brief fuel stops before crossing the four western provinces of Canada to Abbottsford, British Columbia.

It was early afternoon when Dave entered the reception area to Colonel Benton's office. Gail's face lit up when he walked in. Then she saw his arm in a sling. She jumped out of her chair ran around her desk.

"What happened to your arm? No-one said anything about you getting wounded?" She pushed the intercom button and told Colonel Benton that Dave had arrived and that he was injured. Joanne flew out of her office and both women questioned him about how bad the injury was. After some minutes, Dave was able to be heard.

"Now listen up. This is nothing but a simple flesh wound caused by some flying cement so let's not over dramatize it, okay? The doctor used a few stitches and told me it'll be as good as new in a few weeks. So although I thank you for your concern, this is really nothing."

Gail reluctantly returned to her chair behind her desk and Joanne ushered Dave into her office. She motioned for him to sit in a chair and proceeded into a quick debriefing.

"Now tell me the truth, did you kill any civilians?" Joanne asked.

"None."

"And what about Sal A Din, was it the way you reported it?"

Dave saw Joanne was watching him, trying to assure herself he was telling the truth.

"It happened exactly as I reported it. The insurgent's M-60 opened up the first time and hit Sal at least three times and that's when I got this." He nodded to his arm.

"The second time they fired it might have hit the gas tank or maybe in hindsight the pickup had been rigged with explosives to get all of us, but at any rate it exploded with Sal, who was already quite dead, in the back. The truck went up in the air, flipped and landed upside down totally engulfed in flames with Sal under it."

Joanne continued to question him, trying to dredge any facts omitted from his report and when she finished there was complete silence except for the tapping of the keys while she completed her report.

"Did you do that background investigation on our Captain Day?" Dave asked.

"As a matter of fact I did."

"And?"

"There were no flaws in his record at all, but something, I can't quite put my finger on it, just didn't seem right." Joanne passed him a manila folder with personal and confidential marked on the front and Dave read it. After looking the entire report over Dave passed the folder back to Joanne.

"Nothing, right?" Joanne asked.

"I think that may be exactly the point. Did you happen to notice, this guy doesn't have one reprimand, one problem, one citation, one nothing. I don't know of anybody with such a sterile record."

"You wouldn't be a little envious would you? Just because you've been hauled up enough times to warrant a courts marshal doesn't mean a soldier can't have a career without problems. It's what we like to call a good officer." Joanne smiled at the thought.

"Or a cover story, and look at where this guy lives, The Wall, on Nelson. Those places cost at least a million and a half per. Does the CSIS really pay some of its people that well?

"He was a multi millionaire before he entered the service. I guess having all that money was just too boring." Joanne was smiling again.

"I'm sorry but I'm just not buying it. I'd like to put some men on good old bored George and see if we can find anything more. I'm betting we'll find something that'll smudge up that crispy clean record a bit. I've just got a gut feeling about this guy. Will you authorize it?"

Joanne stared at Dave for a long moment and then nodded. "Okay Lt. Colonel Hart. I authorize you to use your team to gather real time intelligence on one Captain George Day using whatever technology or equipment necessary to complete your mission."

"Yes Ma'am," Dave said with a grin.

As Dave was leaving he stopped at Gail's desk. Gail gazed at his arm in a sling.

"Does it hurt much?" she asked.

"You can't even begin to know," he said with a smirk on his face.

Gail feigned a swat at the injured area. Side stepping her swing, Dave chuckled.

"The pain wouldn't bother me half as much though if you would have dinner with me tonight," he said.

"Okay," she answered but then recanted. "But oh, I can't."

"Why not?"

"Uh, George is taking me to an adaptation of 'Les Miserable's' at the Playhouse tonight."

"Oh, I'll bet he'd like to *play house* alright," Dave said in an almost inaudible voice.

"What was that?" Gail asked.

"Oh, that's damn good of him." Dave lied.

"That's not what you said. George is a very nice man after a person gets by his surface pushiness. He's just self conscious."

Dave could feel the anger building.

"Let's stop beating around the bush shall we. He's a jerk!" Dave blurted.

Gail glowered at him.

"David Hart, for two cents I'd say no to any dinner date for you saying that."

Dave took a quarter out of his pocket, threw it on her desk.

"Keep the change!" He stomped out of the reception area and down to his office. It took Dave until the end of his paperwork plus another hour before he cooled down and realized the ramifications of what he'd done. He knew he wasn't really jealous but it frustrated him to think that Gail was being hoodwinked by this character. After contemplating it for awhile he realized if he had Day pegged right, the good Captain was doing the same to the top information bureau in the country? How could he expect Gail to see through him?

Now what was he going to do? He couldn't tell her that he suspected the Captain. Of what? It was still just a gut feeling but he didn't want to see Gail getting mixed up with a – what could he be, a spy? However, if he didn't apologize there would be no way he would keep her away from him. There was only one thing to do. He picked up the phone. It rang several times and then the automatic answering came on. Dave wondered why no one answered the phone so he went to the reception area. Gail was there. He continued to her desk.

"How come you're not answering the phone?"

"I seen your name and number on the display and I supposed you just wanted to yell at me some more."

"Actually I wanted to apologize for that immature outburst. Can you forgive me?" Dave knew if she didn't, she would have to admit she was being immature.

"Okay, but George really is a sensitive guy."

"So could we maybe do dinner tomorrow night? I promise I'll make it fun."

"Well, I don't know." She said playing hard to get. "But I guess I'd be miserable if I said no."

Dave glowed as his step took on a spring that hadn't been there on the way to the reception area. Once back in his office he whistled and smiled as he closed the door and called Julio.

"Hi kid. I have an interim assignment for the team. I want our team to set up surveillance on what's supposed to be one of our own. His name is Captain George Day. He resides at 938 Nelson Street, apartment 3, level 48. I want video-audio bugs and phone taps in his apartment; tracking devices in his clothing and vehicle. I want the closest pay phones tapped and a special internet and cell phone listening station set up. Any mention of General Smith or calls to or from Columbia will trigger an instant alert to me, no one else. I want our team on this guy like wallpaper twenty-four seven and I don't want him having any idea we're there. The team has to really blend on this one. Any questions?"

Julio whistled. "Level 3 surveillance. This guy selling Canada to the North Korean's or something?"

"Could be a lot worse. Make it happen, Captain and let me know when they're set up."

"Yes Sir! It will probably take a couple of days."

"No way, I want you set up by tomorrow morning. I want a priority one on this."

"Yes Sir!"

Dave hung up the phone and began thinking about Gail and his dinner date. On his way out he stopped by Gail's desk.

"Give me a hint. What kind of entertainment do you like, other than live theater that is?"

Gail twisted her face to indicate she was really searching the far recesses of her mind.

"Just about anything you would like. The fun is really who you do it with more than what you do."

Dave knew he was being punished and somewhat felt he deserved it.

"Okay but if I book an African tribal dance you can't leave. I'll see you later." Hoping that would give her something to wonder about, he cranked around and with a spring in his step left the building. His large smile would definitely make most Vancouverites suspicious.

*   *   *

As usual Dave was restless. He had slept for a short time but the dream had used more energy than if he had just stayed awake. He glanced at the illuminated numerals on the night table clock. It was after midnight. It was evident he wasn't going to get back to sleep any time soon so he rolled out of bed, dressed in his sweats, and walked down to the lake.

The moon was full and shone silver across the small lake. The small mountains all around the lake were dark and it was barely possible to pick out the trees and only a few cliffs were slightly illuminated. Dave traversed the dock and sat down on the end, dangled his bare feet in the cool water, and gazed out across the lake. He tried to dwell on the beauty of the moon reflecting off the ripples, but visions of Bev still overrode his thoughts as he wished she was sitting here with him.

Strange as it seemed to him once he relaxed with that notion another thought came into his mind. It was the recollection of Gail telling him about her date with George Day and the two thoughts kept cycling back and forth to the forefront of his thoughts seemingly souring any future relationship. Finally, with his mind in more turmoil than it was before, and not being able to partition the different thoughts properly, he stood and began to swagger back up the dock. He was so engrossed in this mix-mash of musings, he didn't notice the dark shadow that had stalked him and stopped under cover of a small boathouse. He stepped off the wooden dock and onto the sand and heard what sounded like a very short low whistle from behind the boathouse. Instantly his mind tried to list what would make a noise like that. It almost sounded like a knife sliding out of a sheath. At that instant, an alley cat darted away from the boathouse. Dave allowed the cat probably made the noise... *Dave*, he thought to himself, *you're really getting paranoid*. Even so as he passed the corner of the building, ingrained training made him give a quick glance toward the shadows. What he saw was a man in black tactical apparel springing towards him out of the darkness.

The shiny chrome reflection of a sleek switchblade knife led the charge. Dave instantly slapped the arm of the hand grasping the knife as it speared towards him. He only had time to rotate his body, deflecting the attacker. With the initial attack thwarted, the element of surprise was lost. The attacker having a knife while Dave was unarmed could never have made up for the lack of proper combat techniques. Dave had already decided it wouldn't even be necessary to seriously rough up this novice, but rather incapacitate him and find out who sent him.

As the man plunged the knife towards him a second time, Dave, in a lightning fast move side stepped the stab while he grabbed the wrist of the knife hand with both hands. With the momentum from the attacker's forward movement, Dave wrapped the attacker's arm around behind his back and removed the knife from his hand. To Dave it was more like a training exercise with a lazy recruit than defending himself. Once the attacker was subdued, Dave escorted him to the house. He shoved the young guy into the kitchen and crashed him down in a chair. He grabbed a neoprene handcuff and secured the attacker's hands behind his back. Dave moved around in front of the man.

"Okay, so who sent you?"

The attacker just stared back at him.

Dave grabbed one arm and lifted him out of the chair.

"I said who the hell sent you?" as he back handed him so hard the man went sprawling on the floor, blood seeping out the side of his mouth.

Dave lifted him up off the floor and pretended he was straightening the black garment, but before the attacker could get comfortable, Dave laid a heavy right to the midriff emptying all the air from the man's lungs. Just to emphasize his point he gave him a smashing blow to the face. Dave grabbed him again and sat him back in the chair.

"Now look my friend, I'm not going to kill you, but if you don't tell me what I want to know, by morning you're going to wish I had." Dave smiled and grabbed a chef's knife. "On second thought, maybe I could use a different tack."

The young man's face grew ashen.

"Wh- what do you mean a different tack?" he asked hesitantly.

"Well, I have only performed the surgery on a dog I once owned. Damn thing would never stay home and all the neighbours were complaining. Old Shep didn't make it, but I think I know what I did wrong. Of course if it works you'll never be able to procreate again, if you get my meaning."

Dave could see he had found the key that would open a multitude of doors and present a wealth of information. He moved forward as if he was ready to begin performing the operation.

"Alright! Alright! Hold it! I'll tell ya. Just put the knife down okay?" The fear in his eyes told Dave he was going to get the whole truth and nothing but the truth. "A group from Vancouver who are connected, hired me. They said, do you,,, and I'd get free drugs for a year and they'd erase my gambling debt. They didn't say anything about going up against a Steven Seagal type."

"Give me some names."

"I've never seen or talked to them face to face. They always contacted me by anonymous email. I figured they've got to be with the mob since they knew about my debt."

Dave went to the phone and called Joanne. He told her about the young would be assassin and his suspicion the fellow was unknowingly tied to Smith. He requested she move the team to safe housing and send a couple of MP's out to pick up the man.

While waiting for the MP's Dave used the time to ensure his prisoner wasn't holding any information back. Once the MPs took custody of the young man, Dave managed to get a couple of hours sleep.

Chapter 6

The office building was quiet except for the clicking of Dave's keyboard and a janitor moving his wheeled wash bucket down the hall. Dave had managed to reduce a sizable amount of his backlogged paperwork before the offices began to populate, but now he heard the sound of Joanne's familiar clip clop footsteps echoing down the hall. He had left his door cracked open a hair for the express purpose of knowing when she arrived and now he followed her into her office. Joanne glanced toward him as he entered and motioned him to a chair.

"So we had a little training exercise did we?"

"Yeah, the kid got all the training and I managed a little exercise."

Joanne studied him and then moved on.

"I'm going to try and get a mission on Smith's Columbia residence sanctioned. If we can arrest him we might be able to close a good many files."

"Joanne, are you still working under the assumption the General can be taken alive? I thought after Sal's interrogation, you would have realized

Smith won't allow us that option. I'd suggest just sending in a few F-18's and blow his little fortress to hell, but he keeps a lot of innocent people in his employ as insurance against that option. I also know if he had any idea we were going to take him out he'd situate himself in the middle of the largest crowd he could find and probably kill off half of them himself just to muddy the waters."

Colonel Benton opened the file on Sal's interrogation on her computer and began reading the information.

"Perhaps you're right, but I know how the Assistant Director is going to react if I ask for a sanctioned mission with lethal force into Columbia. *'Why Colonel we're not at war with Columbia,'* he'd say,*' we can't just go barging into a sovereign nation, shooting from the hip as the mood moves us.'* No, I'm afraid it's arrest him or leave him alone. It's the only way we'll get this mission approved so we can get the job done."

Dave stared at her with an unbelieving solemn glare.

"Then we just won't get the job done." Dave said flatly.

"Sir, I think you had better explain yourself. You're edging on insubordination."

"Anyone who can indiscriminately have three thousand of his own countrymen killed just to get a war going is not the kind of person who opens the door to honor an arrest warrant."

"Oh boy! Here we go with your conspiracy theories again. Well maybe you should give me the whole thing and get it off your chest," she waved with both hands up in the air before speaking again. "Go ahead Dave. Explain to me how everyone has it all backwards except you."

Dave took a deep breath and wondered where to begin.

"First off it's not just me. There's thousands who can smell a rat. Okay, primarily our man Smith was never regular army except on paper. He was CIA just like it says in the file there. He starts his career as a Major with the CIA in Argentina working with DINE and SHINE, the names for the Chilean and Argentina secret service. He helped put together their death squads and when he used some of his own men to murder some innocent people and the heat got too high the CIA pulled him out of there and gave him various other morbid jobs.

Next he's moved to Florida to head a black operation to bring in some of Osama's people. They used only men portrayed as Muslim extremists. They were the fifth column who at the right time would draw the American and Canadian people to their attention. In the end everything to do with 9/11will be blamed on them.

Have you ever wondered why, with all the satellites and high tech equipment the big O hasn't been caught or killed? He's CIA, that's why. Always was and still is. Hell, send our boys after him with the equipment they've got and we would have him in irons within a month. Meanwhile back in the good old US of A, Smith works on airline remote guidance systems and next generation mini thermo nuclear explosives. He has literally billions to spend if need be from Bin Laden's poppy fields and with companies like Boeing and Honeywell, to name only a couple, he can get his job done. Now don't get me wrong, the worker's on the floor of these large companies knew nothing about the finished product. They just unknowingly built the pieces to be put together later on.

Anyway over the years planes are built with safety equipment which when required is used in a not so safe fashion. I'm talking about the anti-hijack system that was in all the so called hijacked planes on nine-eleven. Doesn't it make you wonder just a tad why if all these planes had an override built into them to thwart hijacks how come not one was thwarted. The answer is simple. They weren't hijacked; they were already being controlled by the very remote that was installed to protect them. Smith had the whole system set for the presentation and the passengers from all the planes were on the supposed flight ninety three which never crashed but was blown out of the sky by explosives and possibly an A-6. Ever see the crater that giant plane was supposed to have made? Hell one of its engines could have almost made that, but it was more than likely a 737.

Meanwhile this was all to keep people's minds busy so that when the mini nuclear bombs go off in the footprints of the twin towers as well as the other well placed demolition explosives, it will be just too difficult for people to grasp. Doesn't it seem strange that approximately twelve young Middle East men board aircraft with nothing suspect and within such a short time after the fact they are all identified with even a passport being found on a Brooklyn street, supposedly blown out of an aircraft that flew into the side of a skyscraper at its top speed and turned into a flaming inferno. It really has overtones of the magic Bullet theory of Healy Plaza with the Kennedy assassination. And why wouldn't it. It worked for them then and they seem to be pulling it off now as well.

As for the Pentagon attack, there were so many common sense holes in that one, excuse the pun, that it's hardly worth discussing. Here comes a guy who couldn't probably land the plane on a landing strip designed to put down the space shuttle. He maneuvers this big 767 whisking in just above the ground, a technique that would make a twenty year veteran commercial pilot quake in his boots and wham!,- he manages to put it right where the least number of people will be hurt. Throw in a couple of homegrown witnesses and discount anyone who doesn't tell the official story and send it to the media.

Anyway, Smith is not going to just fold for us. He's a big player and he has muscle, so unless we outsmart him, catch him where he doesn't think we'll be; and be ready to use as much force as is necessary, we might as well take our bat and ball and go home." Colonel Benton punched the exit button on her computer and left the file.

"Sorry, I still don't buy in. You make some points I can't figure either, but if I was to find a conspiracy every time I couldn't fill in all the details,- I mean, even if your right where does that leave us? It's just too horrid to think about."

"I think that's the exact same thing I heard witnesses say about the Kennedy assassination and I agree, but if we don't face it; if we just 'sit this one out', where will it go from here?" The Colonel sat back in her chair.

"Okay, okay, we won't get anywhere with this, so now unless you had anything else I'll ask you to leave. I've got to word this request exactly right."

Dave was back in his office thinking about the sleep he hadn't got and trying to work out how this mission to Columbia could be carried out without lethal force. The phone rang.

"LC? We're up and running on the surveillance with everything in place. We were able to get a lot of the taps in last night. He was out until after midnight. And what about this middle of the night move? What the hell's going on?"

Dave thought for a moment and chose his words carefully.

"I had an aggressive visitor at my place last night. He tried to take me out, so given the circumstances with this General Smith thing the Colonel thought it would be prudent to have us tucked away safe until the situation is cleared up. I'll get back to you as soon as I have any new information." He disconnected and dialed Joanne's number. He thought getting out of the office might clear his mind and allow him to think.

"Uh, I just wanted to let you know I'll be out of the office for the rest of the afternoon. I thought I might buy some duds and maybe even check out a car lot or two." There was an extended silence on the line. "Hello?"

"Yes, I'm glad I was sitting down. Is this Dave Hart?"

"Go ahead; get it out of your system, make fun."

"So when is the wedding? I don't think anything less than that would cause this kind of turn around."

Dave was beginning to get flustered again.

"Look I just decided I needed a few duds and maybe the old Chevy *is* ready to pack it in so I called to let you know I'd be out of the office, Okay?"

Colonel Benton wasn't fazed by his defensive stance.

"Why don't I assign my assistant to help you? You told me she knew about cars and unless I'm racking it up all wrong, she's the one this is all about. Yes, Lt. Colonel, that's an order. You use my assistant as a consultant for your purchases."

Dave wasn't altogether against the idea so he chuckled and shook his head.

"Yes Ma'am!"

Dave and Gail shopped the men's stores and Gail helped Dave pick top quality suits for bargain prices and when they had bought him a couple of dashing suits with all the accessories they headed for

Richmond to explore some of the car lots there. They were in the showroom of a GM dealership and Dave was looking at a cherry red Corvette convertible.

"What do you think about this one?" Dave asked.

Gail peered in the passenger door window.

"They're nice, but very expensive, and definitely not you."

"Why not me?"

"I've always thought these 'toys' are for guys with inferiority complexes. You don't need a flashy car to prove who you are. I mean, I fell for you in your old Chevy. This macho mechanical muscle car would only take away from you, not add."

Dave didn't hear much else after 'I fell for you'. Now for some reason he couldn't care less if he bought a bicycle.

"Well, what would you pick? Or maybe I should ask what would you be comfortable in?"

"My brother always used to check out the back of the lot," she said enthusiastically. "That's generally where the cheap ones are and sometime you can get a real bargain."

Dave trekked to the back of the lot with her and found a few older vehicles, mostly beaters. He thought if he were going to get something like these, he might just as well keep the one he had. He told

Gail he didn't like any of them but as they wandered around the acres of cars, he spied a grey Cadillac DTS. It was a couple of years old but very clean and well taken care of. When he pointed it out to Gail, he could see she liked it too. Dave motioned for the salesperson who had been watching them like a hawk and who hurried over, getting there almost instantly. Dave bargained for nearly an hour with the salesman running back and forth to try to seal the transaction.

Dave's smile was ear to ear as they drove off the lot with his new wheels. Gail raised one eyebrow and gave him a sidelong look. "What did you say to him anyway? You got five thousand dollars knocked off."

"I started off by telling him you'd scalp me if I tried to spend a penny more than twenty-seven five. I really didn't expect him to buy that linc but I also knew they had the price jacked up. He finally agreed to the right price. I got a two year warranty, and old 'Biscuit' paid the sales taxes."

Gail smiled and settled back into the seat, pressing it down with her fingers. "It's comfy too."

Dave put the new car through its paces on Freeway 91 and drove Gail home promising to pick her up later for their dinner date at six o'clock.

*   *   *   *

The restaurant was on the outskirts of Langley and was more of a country nightclub. Many Country and Western stars had performed there and tonight Jimmy Frazer was headlining. Dave had managed to buy the last two advance tickets but he wasn't at all sure whether Gail would enjoy this type of show. After all it wasn't exactly Les Miserable's. As they were taking their seat Gail, in a very feminine dress and pumps put the first finger of both hands over her lips and let out a whistle just as the opening act finished their first song. Everyone was clapping and the lead singer thanked the crowd and they began a new song.

"This one is for GL," she said as she smiled straight at Gail. Dave looked at her incredulous.

"You know her?"

"Yeah, I helped her with some security and body guard placement. I even guarded her for a while."

Dave realized there were many things he didn't know about this lady and just as many he wasn't too sure he wanted to find out.

Dave had never seen Gail look so relaxed and happy and he could feel his heart slipping into an area beyond just friendship. No other woman had ever made him feel like that except of course Bev. The opening band finished their set and the lead singer told a couple of corny jokes. When all was ready he finished the jokes and raised his voice.

"Okay ladies and gentlemen let's put our hands together and give a warm Canadian welcome to The Navaho Chief, The King of the Tennessee flat top box and the number one Country Gentleman , Jimmy Frazer!"

Just as the fans roared, clapped, and whistled, Dave's Sat phone began buzzing. Dave searched his suit pocket and came up with it.

"Yeah!"

"LC this is Julio. I think you might want to head down here."

"What's that?"

The crowd uproar died down. Dave could now hear that Julio was telling him to hurry to downtown Vancouver where they were staked out at Captain Day's high-rise. Julio told him Day was about to bolt for Columbia and they had just listened in on a call from a person named Andres ordering him there. Julio finished by telling Dave, Day was now filling his suitcases.

Dave's adrenalin was splashing over the top.

"Stay on him and keep out of sight. I'll – ah -- we'll – ah—I'll be there as soon as possible."

Dave leaned over as if he were going to kiss her ear.

"I'm sorry sweets, but duty calls. I'll have to take you home and get into Van, fast."

As they left the parking lot, Dave tried to tell Gail that he had had a team watching George Day. Gail was visually upset.

"So what did your boys catch him with, double parking in front of the drycleaners?"

"I wish," Dave said. "Your man is working with General Smith, who in turn has a bad habit of killing people. In case you're not aware of it, he hired a young punk to kill me the other night."

Gail wasn't buying it.

"Come on Dave you're just after him because you're jealous of him taking me out."

Dave careened the car over to the side of the road and brought it to a screeching halt. He glared daggers at Gail while having a hard time sorting out the proper words.

"That - man - you are so enamored with, and have totally the wrong idea about, works for one of the most degenerate, twisted psychopaths I've ever run into. Smith doesn't just kill people he slaughters them. Believe me I've seen his handiwork from a front row seat. He even ordered me killed and I've got five scars where the bullets entered. My wife wasn't nearly as fortunate. I had to watch his men slice her until her life's blood drained onto the floor and she died. And he doesn't do it for some misplaced twisted ideology, although that may also be part of it, but rather greed, lust, and I probably wouldn't be too far off if I threw in sport. Your man there works for him, so I suspect he has to be just as perverted and twisted as his boss. When we try to arrest him tonight he, or myself and some of my men, or both, may be killed."

Dave sat back in his bucket seat behind the wheel and stared straight ahead.

"So don't talk to me about double parking." He cranked the car back onto the pavement. Gail sat quiet for a few minutes contemplating her past and future moves. Finally, with tears welling up in her eyes she turned toward Dave.

"I'm sorry for being a brat but I really didn't know. I thought he was just a kind considerate man. Are you going to take me with you?"

"Not a chance. There will probably be violence and I don't want to be responsible for getting you hurt or killed."

Gail grabbed her small purse, "I don't know if you're aware of it but I always carry a sidearm and I am an expert shooter. You know what that means." She opened her purse. Dave glanced over and spied the full size Beretta ninety-two FS. He then reached under his arm and pulled an automatic from a small holster. He motioned he carried one under the other arm as well.

"That thing will probably give you just the edge you need to get yourself killed. We're not dealing with local hoods that robbed the local liquor store here. We're not dealing with a regimented military on the battlefield or even Guerrillas in the jungle. The military doesn't train you for these guys. They carry full automatics and when you knock it up a notch they come out with RPG's, explosives, dirty bombs or high tech stuff the army hasn't even tested yet and just when you think you've stopped them, they blow innocent people to pieces and make you feel like hell. They work in cells, individually or in mobs." He holstered his weapon. "Still want to be there?"

Gail glanced at him with a smirk from one side of her lips.

"Somebody's got to watch your six." The smirk transformed into a coy smile. "Look what happened the last time you were out there without me." She pointed to his arm.

Dave gave her a double glance with a chuckle. "I give up. But you stay with the car and away from the action. He headed for Highway One and downtown Vancouver.

Dave picked out Julio on the corner as he turned onto Nelson across from the Wall. He pulled up to the curb and hit the down button for the passenger window. Julio came up to the car, leaning down to see in.

"Lt. Levine, I didn't expect to see you here."

Dave leaned a bit so he could see Julio. "So, what have we got?"

"I think he's about ready to bolt. He's been in his condo packing suitcases and making calls."

Dave thought for a moment. "I think I need to pay him a little visit."

"You don't think he may be waiting for you?" Julio asked.

"Well, if he is, I guess his waiting is just about over."

Gail went to get out of the car.

"Hey, where do you think you're going?" Dave asked.

"Someone has to watch your six."

"No way! No way at all. You'll wait here." Before she could argue Dave motioned to Julio. "Get a couple of the team to make sure she stays put. Cuff her if need be; in fact have them do it anyway and make sure the exits are covered. No matter what happens up there, Captain Day does not leave the building. If lethal force is necessary, use it, and make sure she stays out of the action."

Dave headed up to the forty-eighth level and Julio took Gail around the corner where he put Tron and Marty on guard duty to detain her.

As Dave stepped cautiously out of the elevator, he heard the click of a door closing. As his eyes followed the sound, he seen it was indeed the entrance to Captain Day's flat and began to realize that this possibly was a trap. Part of him said fall back and wait for reinforcements while a second part yelled carry on and get it done. He chose getting it done as usual. He slipped over to the door listening for any movement, his right hand on his automatic in the left holster but not drawn. He pressed the door buzzer and heard a voice on the intercom. "Come in Lt. Colonel Hart. The door's open."

Dave slowly opened the door and carefully stepped in. George was in another room and came to the entrance after Dave was in.

"Well Lt. Colonel, to what do I owe this unannounced visit? Or were you just in the neighborhood and decided to drop in for a social call?"

Dave walked over toward the large panorama window. "I think you're well aware of why I'm here. The gig's up George or whatever your name is. We had the pay phone tapped and we know you work for Smith. Are you going to come peaceably?"

George's eyes darted from one area of the room to another.

"No, I think you're going to have to *try* and take me by force."

Dave drew his side arm from the left side and held it pointed at George.

"Your choice."

Meanwhile Gail had tried to pull rank on Tron and Marty and when they refused to listen, she had quietly unlocked her cuffs, taken them by complete surprise and cuffed them to an iron hand railing. She grabbed her Beretta from her purse and in minutes, she was on the forty-eighth floor. As she moved with total stealth to the partially cracked door, she could hear Dave.

"One thing I've got to know, did you have any real feelings for Gail?"

"That little twit? The only thing she was good for was to get bits of information about you and what you were up to. I've never seen such a frigid bitch. If we were down in Columbia I'd hand her over to the General. He's known to have his sport and then murder the bitches." George changed the subject. "You know, you really got me in trouble with Smith by telling me that story about night jumps at Kirkuk. I'll be lucky if he doesn't have me shot."

"Smith will have to wait his turn; you'll be charged in a military court for espionage and we take a particularly dim view of a turn coat."

"Turn-coat? Hell I've never been a Canadian. Smith's people worked out my cover. Even the name was retrieved from a tombstone in Toronto." He shrugged his shoulders.

"Well, I guess it's time to dance." George had a remote concealed in his hand and hit the lights button. Instantly the lights went out catching Dave off guard. George knocked Dave's weapon to the floor while removing his second weapon from its holster. He pulled his own sidearm from his belt and then switched the lights back on.

"I'm sorry I can't give you the same choices you offered but your death will redeem me in Smith's eyes. So long Lt. Colonel" Dave heard a shot from behind him and then the Heckler & Koch followed by two more shot from behind him and then the H&K fired again into the carpet as George nosedived into the velvet plush carpet. Dave glanced over at the living room picture window and saw the bullet intended for him had put a hole and spider webbed crack in the glass. He rolled George over and checked for a pulse. There was none and the cream colored carpet had acted like a blotter with a huge round crimson stain. He turned and noticed Gail standing there with the Beretta hanging in her hand by her side and a blank expression on her face. Dave slowly and carefully moved towards Gail.

"Is this the first person you ever killed?" he asked.

"K-Killed? Is he dead?"

"I would think so. Three rounds in the heart will usually get the job done. He was dead before he hit the carpet." She was just standing there starring at the large area of blood on the carpet. Dave slowly reached over and took her Berretta and then pulled her into his arms giving her a hug as he carefully moved so her line of vision was away from the corpse.

"You did good, but maybe we should go down to the lobby and get the MPs to take care of this."

Dave called Joanne and filled her in. She said she'd get the R.C.M.P. on it. Dave then called down to Julio and ordered him to have the team cordon off and secure the scene. He led Gail to a small coffee shop in the lobby where they ordered a coffee, talked, and waited for the police to arrive. Gail was visibly shaken but the coffee helped.

"I thought you were supposed to stay down on the street?"

"Hey, that's no way to talk to the backup who just saved your life."

"I guess I can't argue with that. Oh man what am I going to do with you?"

*   *   *

The next afternoon Dave sat in Colonel Benton's office with the typed report listing the phone taps, the taped conversations and all the other evidence the team had gathered in their short surveillance. George and Dave's entire discourse was recorded, leaving no doubt it was a justified shooting.

Joanne passed Dave a folder.

"Sorry Dave, but the Board just doesn't see Beauregard Smith as the total threat that you do and I sure as hell wasn't going to try that conspiracy spiel you did on me. You will carry on preparations for the mission and the Wainwright maneuvers are still a go. If things change and they can quickly, I want you and your team ready to go."

Dave checked the folder that indicated the assault on the Columbia Villa was being considered and would require further investigation. He gave a sign of defeated resignation and slipped the folder back onto the Colonel's desk.

"I'll get the team to Wainwright and we'll spend a couple of weeks honing our skills doing maneuvers and jumps. I'll get all the geographical data and sat photos of the Villa area while I'm there and study them for the best insertion."

"Alright, there is one more thing. I want to recommend you for a promo to full Colonel and I'm pretty sure it'll go through, but it will mean you'll be confined to more office work and regular nine to five days."

Dave was aghast, but tried to cover.

"Uh, that's good, I suppose. But let's not rush it, at least not until I've finished with this Smith. I'm really not all that sure I'd fit very well into a regimented office routine." Suddenly he began to feel uncomfortable.

"I happen to know you'd do just fine as a Colonel and maybe even commanding officer." Joanne smiled as she walked him to the door.

Dave liked the thought of a promotion to full Colonel, but wasn't sure about the office or the commanding officer part.

Chapter 7

Dave and the team were en route to Wainwright when the message light flashed on his satellite laptop. He flipped it open.

Lt. Colonel Hart, Kodiak team will divert and proceed to Comox, transfer to a waiting CC-130 Hercules and Proceed to point Cactus Plain where you will deploy with a High Altitude High Open (HAHO) jump. Detailed orders at CFB Comox. All necessary arrangement complete. Addition one extra team member. Signed Colonel Joanne Benton.

Dave informed the Captain of the new destination and then told the team.

"So where the hell is point Cactus Plain?" asked Marty.

"I suppose it's the old military need to know. I'll get the particulars at Comox. Sounds like we'll be jumping out the back with oxygen," Dave said as the plane banked hard to set a new course.

Julio read the orders.

"Who is this new member?" he asked.

Dave put his hands out palm forward and gestured that he also was in the dark.

At CFB Comox the Hercules was already spooling up when the Challenger touched down. The utility jet pulled up near the 'Herc' and the men quickly transferred their gear running up the rear ramp of the giant plane. Dave was given the complete new orders and was fuming when he saw who the newest member was to be. They were to proceed to an area south-east of Spence's Bridge near the Fraser Canyon and carry out a ten *man* HAHO jump at or above forty thousand feet, after which they would drift some twenty miles southeast. They would trek southeastward staying invisible, overtake a virtual fortress, traverse Nicola Lake, and stay at a resort hotel before being picked up and returned to home base in Abbotsford. The entire practice would take eight days. Dave skulked up the rear ramp toward the belly of the large plane as the hydraulics started pulling the huge ramp closed and the big bird taxied toward the runway. He searched the entire plane and finally found Gail near the pilot's deck.

"You're not going on this maneuver."

Gail was in field fatigues, smiling, and visibly excited as she pulled out her orders.

"With all due respect sir, yes I am. Our CO says so."

As the plane struggled to gain altitude in a short distance, Dave was upset with the situation Colonel Benton had pushed him into. He had lost Bev and was concerned with putting Gail, whom he was beginning to realize he cared about, in harm's way. Why couldn't she see that?

"Why are you doing this? Why can't you just work in the office like you're supposed to?"

"Sir, I'm a soldier and a damn good one and this is what soldiers do. I may not be as strong as you brutes but I guarantee you Lt. Colonel I'll max out with most if not all of your men in the field."

"Lt., have you passed the JTF-2 entrance and have you ever participated in a HAHO?"

Gail stood at attention. "As Colonel Benton told you sir I came from special forces, JTF-2 top of the class. As for the HAHO, twenty-seven times Sir."

Dave raised his eyebrows as he stared at her. That was more than he had done.

He could see she was determined and she had orders in her favour but he didn't think the team was ready for a female and he had his own problem with her deployment as well.

"Alright Lt., if you can pass a little indoctrination, you'll jump with us. If not I'll reverse your orders and you'll go back to Global and tell Joanne I refused to allow you to go. Agreed?"

She nodded her head cautiously and Dave set up a small makeshift table, blindfolded her, handed her a HK-G36, and told her to field strip and reassemble it within one minute, thirty seconds. He handed her the weapon and to his surprise, she checked it over, identified it, field stripped, reassembled it and presented it ready to fire in one minute twenty-five seconds. The men all cheered and whistled and Lt. Levine was well on her way to becoming a member in good standing of Kodiak team.

Most of the men congratulated her on being able to field strip the weapon on the vibrating aircraft but Dave wasn't one of them. He had managed to get her accepted but was still gravely concerned about her safety. He was also having a difficult time trying to see Gail as little miss warrior. Of course, until the maneuvers ended she was Lt. Levine. He had stewed over this dilemma for some time and was brought back to the task at hand when the alarm sounded with the flashing orange light. It was ten minutes to jump.

Everyone had already donned their jump gear and were breathing near straight oxyGeneral With the warning light flashing they readied for the final phase; to disconnect from the onboard oxygen and use the body unit. The team worked toward the rear of the plane just as the giant back door slowly opened. The sun was just disappearing over the horizon but they were at forty thousand feet so geography below was in darkness and there was little they could see. The jump alarm sounded and at arm's length they jumped off the back of the plane in groups of four with Dave and Gail bringing up the rear. The plan was to freefall six thousand feet, open their chute below the Jet stream, steer twenty miles south east using global positioning system and then land in the middle of a two square kilometer clear cut. Dave always enjoyed these jumps, not so much for the thrill but for being able to use the high tech equipment and trusting his men and himself. As he glanced over at Gail she waved. Dave moved into position, checked his altimeter, and pulled the ripcord. The chute opened more like a large overhead billowing wing than a parachute. He checked the GPS and adjusted his direction and to some degree his decent. Dave could still make out Gail to his left. She was in exact formation.

As they drifted toward the ground Dave mused *maybe the Colonel knows what she's doing after all.*

The team would land along the clearing and rendezvous at the center of the upper northern tree line. Dave touched down and adjusted his eyes to the dark. As he got out of his harness he glanced over to see Gail land with poise and exactly in sync. Dave and Gail moved to the rendezvous point and were greeted by all the rest of the team except George Seagram. Dave noticed his absence immediately.

"Captain where is Lt. Seagram?"

"I don't know LC. I thought I'd give him ten and then send out a couple of patrols to search."

"Good, three patrols of two men each." Dave glanced over at Gail. "Lt. you'll team up with Lt. Mussleman there." He pointed to the man and turned to the entire group. "Okay, listen up. Julio, Tron, Harvey, and I will stay here and if George should show up we'll call you in on the hand held. Now go find him."

The couples left to search and were only gone five minutes when a feeble voice sounded on the hand held. "Team member to Badger, do you read me?"

Dave grabbed his handheld. "Team member this is Badger. Is that you George?"

"Yeah, seems I landed right on an old momma mountain lion. She didn't bother to warn me until she was on top of me. I managed to kill the devil with my knife but not before she ripped some pretty bad chunks out of me." His voice was raspy even though he was trying to put up a good front. Dave could tell from his voice he was in bad shape.

"Where are you George? George, where, are, you?"

Marty cut in. "I've found him LC. He's about five hundred yards at seven o'clock. Check out my light." He flicked his flashlight several times.

Dave and Julio headed in the direction of the light but were not prepared for the scene that awaited them. George's blood and the blood of the full size mountain lion were mingled together and covered both of them. The big cat lay dead close by. George's jump suit was in tatters with some of the parachute and its cords still wrapped around the animal. Dave could see George had put up a valiant fight, but the lion had ripped his chest open and torn his face and scalp. An especially gruesome gash across his eyes left one hanging out of the socket and the other had the flesh slashed away exposing the bone. Dave called Tron, the medic, on the handheld telling him to get to the flashlight beacon on the double and to bring his pack. George was unconscious now and slipping fast.

Dave pulled out his sat phone and ordered an evacuation helicopter from Abbotsford telling them he had a man in code blue condition from a cougar attack. He read them the exact co-ordinates and they immediately dispatched the chopper, but then tried to confirm what exactly Dave meant by a cougar attack as if it were some kind of code.

Dave finally convinced them it was indeed an honest to god cougar attack. In awe they confirmed the ETA for the chopper was forty-five minutes. Dave slid his phone closed as he turned to the team.

"Okay guys we've got about forty minutes. I want a set of beacon lights around a fifty meter perimeter. That's going to be the LZ for the Chopper. Use flares and light them when I give the order." Dave clapped his hands as he yelled like a football coach. "Now, go, go, go!"

The medic dressed the wounds as best he could, he valved a sucking chest wound and elevated the foot end of the gurney. George was still unconscious but his vital signs held their own and he seemed to have regained some colour. Dave checked the landing site and asked about George's condition every five minutes. He went over to George and knelt down beside the gurney.

"Son, I don't know if you can hear me or not, but I want you to hang in there. A chopper will be here soon and we're gonna take care of you. Just in case you got any bad ideas, you **are** going to make it and I want my best shooter back. So you hang in there."

Dave got up and walked out of eyeshot of the team. He felt so bad for the young boy that tears welled up in his eyes. He was sure George would never be in a recon team again.

The CH-149 Cormorant arrived ten minutes ahead of the ETA and medics aboard hooked up an IV on George giving him badly needed blood volume. They hooked up oxygen and put on a set of trauma pants before loading him aboard. The chopper lifted off quickly and headed for the Royal Columbian Hospital in New Westminster. Dave ordered the lights extinguished and the team returned to the rendezvous point. Julio was the first to speak.

"You think he'll make it LC?"

"Of course he'll make it." Dave said it without hesitation but in his mind he wasn't as sure as he let on and even less assured about the man's eyes. The gash across both eyes could very well blind him in one or both. It was almost a sure thing his shooting days were over and Dave wasn't at all sure George wouldn't consider that worse than death. Dave was just about to call in a replacement when an idea struck him unexpectedly.

"Lt. Levine, front and center." She quick stepped to his area.

"Yes Sir?"

"You say you came from Special Forces and that you were an expert Shooter."

"That's correct Sir!"

"Then for the rest of this mission you will become Lt. Marty Musselman's Spotter and the backup Shooter. You grab Lt. Seagram's equipment and his M-107. The rest of us will divide up packing your gear."

Gail had a grin on her face. "Yes Sir!"

"And Lieutenant.?"

"Yes sir?

"Wipe that grin off your face or I'll give you such a load you'll never smile again." Immediately her smile vanished and a stone hardness took its place. Even Dave gave a double take at the change in her countenance.

"Dismissed"

The team had time for coffee and rest before huddling around Dave for orders.

"Now listen up. We've had a terrible start, but from this minute on we will be the definition of stealth as if there were every enemy we ever dreamed about in our worst nightmares across the next or last clearing. Our shooters," he pointed towards Marty and Gail, "will move about a thousand meters up and down the slopes and guard our flanks." He gestured toward Marty for the upper picket and Gail for the lower. "Everyone will be invisible so if any of the locals happen around, make damn sure they do not see us. We'll move by night. Four days from now we storm a mock compound here." He pointed on the map. "And then move onto Nicola Lake which we will cross and land at this Hotel Guest Ranch. Any questions?" The men, all solemn, shuffled, some taking a step back awaiting orders. "You two get going," he said addressing the Shooters. "The rest of us will move out in fifteen minutes. Dismissed."

Dave eyed his team as they made stealthy progress over streams, through gullies, up mountain passes and down the other sides. He continually scanned a thousand meters down slope with his scope and by the beginning of the second night, when he still had not so much as caught a moving branch, was content Lt. Levine was doing her job. Either that or she was lost on some other mountain, but he knew Marty would watch her, although he thought hopefully not too closely. By zero five hundred of the fifth night, they had crossed the Coquhailla Highway, slipping under a few of the many bridges. Dave waited until they were out of sight of the highway and then called in the shooters. He wanted to update their orders but he also wanted to be sure he didn't have to mount a search and rescue.

Dave was bewildered when Gail strolled into camp as if she had just taken a jaunt through a park. Marty hadn't seen her since they left the clearing and trudged in like he was dragging the world behind him. When he saw Lt. Levine however with a spring in her step however, he straightened up as if to say if she can do it I can do it. Dave had to smile, but he was glad to see both had done their jobs admirably.

As the team sat among the rocks of a washed out gorge, their camouflaged apparel blended with the boulders so well that if they didn't move, it was impossible to pick them out from more than a hundred meters. Dave called the team closer together to give them the attack plan. He told them that the supposed villa was being guarded by a larger team and it was his team's job to infiltrate the center and get a cell phone. The winning team would get two weeks R&R, the loser one week. He reminded them in the real battle losers usually didn't live. Dave laid out a paper with a diagram of the villa.

"The shooters, Alpha team, will work their way as close to the villa as they can, finding as valuable a piece of real estate as possible. Once in position, four men will move in from the left side. We'll call them Baker team, and four from the right, which will be Charlie team. This whole exercise has to be with total stealth. When everyone has taken out as many of the enemy as they can with silent weapons, knives, garrote, or hand to hand, then silencers will be used. We will hold our shooters in reserve for emergencies and a safe withdrawal. Now, some things that will be different here from Columbia are the foliage, the moisture and of course, we don't have fences or walls. These guys we're coming up against know we're coming but they don't know when. Be careful people, there will be more of them than us. Watch for everything from shooters on the extended perimeters to booby traps and warning devices new and old. Any questions?"

"What do we do with the cell phone when we get it?" Bill asked.

Dave smiled. At least someone was still awake.

"When you pick it up it will ring, which ends that part of the maneuver. Answer it 'Kodiak has prevailed' and that instantly gives our team the two weeks. The objective is about four hours from here and we leave at dusk so finish your coffee, hunker down out of site and get some sleep."

        *   *   *

Dave looked at his watch as they crept through the sparse brush. It was one thirty hours. Gail's voice came on the Cam.

"LC I have a bogey fifteen hundred meters at two o'clock. I'm moving around to neutralize."

"Negative on that Alpha two," Dave replied, "Let Charlie team cover that."

"Team leader I have another at nine o'clock," Marty said. "He's about a thousand meters out."

"Roger that Alpha one. Baker team did you copy?"

"Roger LC, we're on it."

"This is team leader, listen up. When those two are taken out we move in. Alpha team will stay in position as we're neutralizing the villa."

Everyone confirmed and as soon as the opposite two member guards had been neutralized the Baker and Charlie teams began to work their way in. Julio spotted, by pure accident, a laser trip line which became visible in a small amount of dust. He notified the rest of the team and they avoided it. The team had just entered the rectangle of the supposed Villa when Lt. Levine and Musselman confirmed they were in their perimeter position. Knowing they had neutralized far too few of the opposition Dave thought to himself, *this is definitely moving forward too easy*, and he searched the area with a night scope and trained eyes to pickup what he knew they must be missing. Suddenly he noticed several areas that were whisked clean of foot prints in a twenty meter perimeter from the phone and then with little difficulty picked out several more. There were eight altogether circumventing the phone. It was an ambush and Lt. Bill Mixing was getting very close to the phone. Dave took one more sweep knowing what they had stepped into. Alpha and Baker teams with their weapons at the ready were slowly and cautiously moving inward but they were still ten meters from the phone. Lt. Mixing eyed the phone. Dave spoke softly into his Com-Tac,

"Everyone, slowly turn and do a Buffalo Guard around the phone. They're in Spider holes in a perimeter about ten meters outside of your position."

The Team slowly turned without a sound and readied their rifles. Dave gave the Lt. the order to go slowly for the cell phone. As he made a slight movement toward it, eight men, each of which was ten meters outside the circumference of Dave's team and armed with H&K G thirty-six's pushed up from spider holes. Dave's team had already leveled their weapons at the enemy team who immediately stood down. They had gone into the spider holes the day before and two guards had spread a fine but total covering of the surrounding dirt over the lids to the holes. The men had lain in wait throughout the night. The camouflage was almost perfect but to the learned eye became too pat and it gave them away.

Lt. Mixing picked up the phone which instantly buzzed.

"Kodiak has prevailed," he said and the exercise was over.

The opposing Captain who was neutralized earlier stepped over and shook Dave's hand which began a chain reaction of all members of the opposing groups following the example.

With the exercise ended in a positive light, Dave led his troop off in the two day trek to Nicola Lake. They spent the day hunkered down, reveling in their victory. Dave was happy to see the team in high spirits and increased self-confidence.

"Okay people, it would be very difficult to cover a well set ambush like that. That's why we get the big bucks. But let it ever be known when the real thing comes up, to miss is a failed mission, plus some will probably die. We won this by sheer luck, and that's not good enough."

With that Dave could hear several groans.

Julio smiled through his grease camouflage.

"What about the two weeks LC. Does the team still rate it?"

"You bet." He raised his voice a couple of decibels. "Two weeks R&R for everyone, starting as soon as we get back to Abbotsford."

Dave could see it brought up the confidence higher than where he wanted it but these were pros and they were well aware of their capabilities. He also knew now that the plans for taking the Villa would have to be re-organized. He would have to get something that would give his team the edge.

The evening brought a four hour march to the lake and with three rafts (I.P.R.'s), the team crossed over to the south side of the lake. Once their gear was stowed in the bus parked in the lot Dave dismissed the team and they made their way to the coffee shop. Dave went to the office and checked them in for the night.

By zero six hundred, the grey camouflaged bus was on the highway for the two-hour run down to Abbotsford. At the barracks, Dave gave the team a two-week leave and then offered Lt. Levine a ride home.

Gail accepted gladly and teased Dave about the fraternizing policy. The freeway was reasonably clear of traffic and Dave and Gail laughed and talked about the maneuvers until Dave took the exit and headed for Gail's apartment building.

"Gail, how would you like to spend the next couple of weeks with me at that western resort hotel? Ah, before you say yes I think you should know I've already booked two rooms for two weeks there."

Gail gave Dave an impudent stare. "And what were you going to do if I said no?"

"Ask you again. Maybe whine a bit."

Gail was smiling now going along with the game. "And if I still said no?"

Dave let his face go sad. "I never thought that far ahead, but I guess I'd just go there, saddle up ol' Dollar and ride into the sunset."

Gail was laughing now. "Well in that case Mr. Hart, take me home so I can pack."

       *   *   *

*

Dave glanced over at Gail as he hung up the phone. He had called the nursing station to check on George who was still unconscious.

"He's still unconscious but the nurse says his vital signs are stable," he said as he lugged the last two suitcases out to the car in a light Vancouver drizzle. He wondered how a single girl could have five suitcases full of clothes and why she would need so many at a working cattle ranch. Gail walked out of the building with a small overnight bag.

"Is there any room left for this?" as she held it up.

"Sure it can go in the back seat, the trunk is full."

Dave smiled and closed the trunk lid. "Let's get going before you decide you need anything else."

"Just seems I'm forgetting something." She said with a smirk on her face. Dave just rolled his eyes.

The drizzle persisted until they reached a pass and started heading down into Merritt. From there on it was hot, sunny, and dry. Dave took the off ramp and headed for the guest ranch and hotel.

"What are we going to do here for the next two weeks Dave? Just walk, talk, swim, and relax?"

"Ah, did you ever see the movie City Slickers?"

"Billy Crystal's here?"

"No, what did they do in the movie?"

"Looked for Curley's Gold?"

"No-o-o,,, that was the sequel. No they went on a---," he smiled at her with his eyelids raised in expectation.

"A cattle drive? A real live cattle drive?" She pushed the down button on the window and yelled. "George, George Day, I take it back I'm sorry I shot you. It should have been him."

Dave was laughing so hard he could hardly drive the car and even at that the car was weaving a bit. Gail closed the window and smiled at Dave.

"I hope you realize I'm just teasing. I wouldn't even care if Billy Crystal wasn't there, I'd still think a cattle drive was cool but you're joking right?"

Dave was beginning to wonder if he'd done the right thing making reservations for the Trail Ride.

"Listen, about the Billy Crystal thing. He won't be there. About the Trail Ride, we can take it or we can leave it; your choice."

"I'd love to do a Trail Ride. Do we get to pick our own horses?

"You bet, its three days and nights under the stars. And after the ride I've rented a boat to cruise the lake, maybe water-ski, or swim. We shouldn't be sitting around too much."

"My goodness Mr. Hart, are you trying to impress me?"

"You bet."

They pulled into the parking lot of the hotel. In the western lobby Dave read one of the pamphlets. The hotel was built as a quality hostelry and opened in the early 1900's and although the accommodations had been modernized the structure and atmosphere were still turn of the century style. The ranch part of the resort was purely for tourists with a few docile cows and a couple of highly trained cattle dogs. The horses were also well trained.

After stowing Gail's wardrobe in her room, Dave took her down to the docks to check out their boat. He found it by asking the marina hand and following the directions. It was a white and sky blue Tahoe thirty foot run about with a three hundred and twenty horsepower inboard. Gail was all for taking it for a test ride but Dave informed her that even though the rental company had launched it here, the contract didn't start for three days. That would allow them to do the trail ride without paying for the boat at the same time.

The morning of the ride was clear and sunny and they left the stables at eight o'clock. The moist mountain air was drying with the morning sun and the world was fresh. There were four others with them on the ride aside from the guide. He led them up the small mountains, through a pass and by the time they had finished the first day, they had already seen some of the most scenic mountain country in North America. As dusk began to settle on their camp Dave spotted a glow in the north.

"What's that? He asked the guide.

"That's Kamloops, it doesn't look it but it's more than sixty kilometers from here and this is about the only point in the area you can see that glow because of our elevation. We won't see it again on this ride."

That night they slept under the stars. Although they had pup tents the forecast assured them of no precipitation and warm temperatures so everyone opted for the sky as the ceiling.

Midway through the next day they noticed the trail was beginning to circle around and by the end of the day they were headed back west in the direction of the hotel. In the mid afternoon of the last day, the group stopped on a ridge for coffee and pictures and Dave led Gail off to be alone with her. Dave found a boulder and the two sat down on it overlooking a picturesque valley. Dave took a deep breath and commented on the beauty and ruggedness of the area. He was so close he could feel the warmth of her body. He glanced at her for her opinion and saw she was staring at him. Their eyes met and seemingly drew them into an embrace.

*   *   *

The Columbian sun seemed to be heating the day even more than normal and with the moisture it was a day to sit on an air conditioner, if a person could afford one. General Beauregard Smith certainly could and the air-conditioned pool area, in which the General was now relaxing in, was a prime example of what money could buy. Andres was perspiring so much his suit jacket was soaked through. The General pulled up to the side of the pool for a rest as well as to hear what news his chief communications officer had.

"Okay, what's so important, you choose to interrupt my aquatic time?"

"I've just got word that our best agent in the CSIS has been killed."

Smith's temperament suddenly changed as his face went red and his eyes grew large.

"What do you mean killed?"

"He was shot, sir, three bullets, all in the heart. Seems two agents from Global Tech assailed him and killed him. One was that Dave Hart again and the other was a woman, apparently a Lt. and his accomplice."

"They killed George? He was my best and most expensive mole! I spend over five million to get him in there, five million---, dead?"

By now Smith was out of the pool and moving toward his lounging chair.

"T-That could make the rest of this information almost as bad. It seems the Canadian government has seized all of his holdings, bank accounts, stocks, bonds, companies and real estate."

"His holdings? His holdings!? That slime bucket never had any holdings. They were mine,

mine, and those stupid ignorant Canucks are stealing it from me and all because of that one nothing man."

Smith flew into a rage cursing and throwing anything and everything that came into his hands.

He picked up an automatic weapon and pointed it at Andres. Andres put his arm over his face as if to block the vision of the lead coming towards him.

"I want you to put together a file on this Lt. Colonel Dave Hart. Everything from when he filled his diapers till today. And I want it in the next forty eight hours. You hear me, or I might just have to shoot the messenger!" He pointed the gun at Andres.

"Y-Yes Sir, i-it might be a little difficult because like you said George was our best mole."

"Well use our man in Langley to get the dirt. My god, do I have to do all the thinking for you guys? And he let go with a short blast from the automatic pistol, narrowly missing Andres.

"For god's sake, get out of my sight," he looked at the trembling man with disgust. "And change your pants. I see you pissed them again."

Andres nodded his head and headed out the door.

"And send some-one in here to clean up this mess."

"Y-Yes Sir," Andres yelled back as he hurried to get away from the General before he decided to really shoot the messenger.

It took the General the rest of the afternoon to get over the news that some five million dollars worth of assets had been *stolen,* but he finally settled down and decided to make a trip to a neighboring province. If he could get any good information on this Dave Hart he wanted to be ready with the proper action team and his friend (as much as anybody could be his friend) lived in the neighboring province.

*　　　　*　　　　*　　　　*

"Mr. Smith, how good of you to drop in. Come sit in the study and elaborate that of which you told me on the phone."

Santana Escobar Gomez, the pinnacle of power in the Bogotá Cartel motioned to his left and a book lined room almost the size of General Smith's own study. Once in the study the host offered his guest a drink and Smith requested a brandy. Pouring the General a Brandy on the rocks, he carried it to the couch then with his own ginger ale, he sat in a matching chair.

"So how can I be of assistance to my, ah, neighbour?" He closed the double doors to the study nodding to his own security guards who would watch and listen to the conversation.

Smith decided he'd attract more bees with honey than with vinegar.

"I come in need of expertise and finely honed muscle which I do not have but you do. I need to eliminate a military agent in Canada."

"Whoa Senor Smith, we don't do such things for hire. We would even be careful to do it if it was to protect our business interests. You see we have all the heat we can handle with the Americans and Canadians on our door step, what with trading deals and pay-offs, we get by, but we don't want to upset those countries anymore than necessary. I may, however, be able to put you in touch with a very competent American assassin, but that's as far as I will go."

Santana scribbled a phone number on the back of a business card and passed it to Smith.

"Call that number and ask for Phillip. This one is as good as they get and if you say I sent you; you might be able to get a good price."

Smith glared at Santana for a long while and then took the card.

"Can I ask you a question Senor Gomez?"

"Why certainly Senor Smith but please let us use first names. It's much more cordial."

"Alright, Santana, actually I have two questions. The first is why, when you're head honcho in the drug cartel, don't you offer your guest any of the best stuff? The second is why won't you help me with some of your manpower?"

Santana was taken aback by the General's rudeness.

"First Beauregard, I don't allow the stuff, as you call it, in any form in my home and I certainly don't burn my brain with that shit. It's business and that's all. The answer to your second question is that as you're well aware, your alias is The Cottonmouth, and quite simply I don't trust you, period. At the same time I'm sure with proper payment Phillip will get your job done."

The conversation continued with the General becoming more obnoxious. Santana had had enough and ordered a few of his security men to show the General to his limo.

The General's ego was seriously injured and he cursed all the way to Buenaventura where he had the car stop and pick up a couple of prostitutes. Back at the Villa they partied all night and when it was over, two more prostitutes lay mutilated and dead.

*   *   *   *

The General was awakened by the incessant buzzing of the PA system and once he opened the door he was confronted by Andres who had taken the liberty to bring him the newly typed dossier on David Solomon Hart. Smith excused Andres, had a shower and got dressed. Later, he thought, he would try to discover how to slaughter these ladies of the evening without getting their blood all over him, but right now he wanted to read all about what seemed to be his very own nightmare.

As he read the dossier in his study he thought those CIA boys really have got their shit together sometimes. Almost at the tail end he spied what could be his best way to get to the Lt. Colonel Hart and his chance to get this guy once and for all.

The report finished with an inference that the officer had dated a female Special Forces Lt. by the name of Gail Levine. Miss Levine was the one who had helped Hart take out his man and Smith saw that she might be the bait this Phillip could use to get to Dave. The general retrieved the business card from his desk and dialed the number.

"I would like to speak to Phillip please."

There was a short pause and a woman came on the line. "Hello?"

"Yes, I said I wanted to speak to Phillip."

"So speak already. You're talkin' at me."

"I'm not sure that my friend wasn't playing a joke on me. He said Phillip could do a certain *'job'* for me but he didn't say anything about a woman."

"Listen friend, whatever your name is, you probably couldn't afford me anyway. I charge one big one per, plus expenses."

"Only a thousand dollars? I'm not after a rat exterminator."

"Yeah, well I don't do rats. Fact is I think they're kind of cute and you can add three more zeros."

"So if you did two---,"

"That's right pops, two million. Of course if you want special features, like a suicide with all the trimmin's, the price just went up. What's your game, pops?"

"I'd rather you called me, ah, General. And Escobar said to mention his name."

"O-h-h-h, scary stuff. Okay if that's your game go for it. You can email me with all the information at annieoakley@jobdone.com. Once I have the info I'll give you instructions on where and how much to deposit. Oh and by the way, *General,* the more info you give me the less the expense bill. Oh and another thing, do not, I repeat, do not ever come looking for me because I kill Generals right along with sergeants

and privates. Enough said; I'll see you on the web."
The line went silent.

Beauregard thought to himself, two million
plus expenses. No one was worth that, were they?
He finally sent the dossier to Phillip and awaited the
further instructions. He had told her to just get rid of
this guy and if it didn't cost extra, make it as bloody a
mess as possible. He'd also mentioned the girl and
that she was to be the bait but he wanted her
whacked as well.

The General was relaxing on the terrace when
Andres walked in.

"We just got an e-mail by some-one named
Phillip to the General."

"So what does it say?"

"She says it will cost you three million seeing
they're Military Intelligence and another million for
expenses."

The General again went into a tirade and
threatened Andres but finally told him to have the
money deposited in the proper bank account and
email this Phillip to proceed. The evening actually
turned into one of the General's best.

Chapter 8

The Computer growled as Dave continued to pour over all the information that had been fed into it. One thing he was sure of, Smith wouldn't be easy to get to. General Smith had surrounded himself with highly professional mercenaries and he paid them well. Smith outfitted them with the best weaponry available and the high technology security devices he employed enhanced their fire power.

Dave had also run across some very disturbing accusations. Several allegations had been made that the General had murdered many prostitutes he had hired and was rumored to be increasing this trait. Dave dwelt on this point and decided it would fit with the psyche of such an individual; after all he was a cold blooded killer very much like his counterpart the Cottonmouth snake. He would allow his victim to feel safe while slowly quietly moving into position for the kill. His nature was to plunder without any feelings of sadness or remorse and even displayed a sick satisfaction from some deranged mental aptitude. The murdering fed his craving for lust, wealth, power or in cases like the prostitutes simply entertainment or sport.

Dave looked at the report now on the screen. This psychopath had five hundred civilians slaughtered because they were afraid to witness against a South American Gorilla group. He had herded an entire village out into the jungle and had ordered his men to mutilate and kill them all, men, women, and children.

Dave opened another report, this time from Chechnya; two hundred and forty children were killed because a couple of rebels were hiding in the basement of the school building. The orders were given by General Beauregard Smith. He called in an airstrike knowing full well the kids were in there. Dave gazed up, not wanting to think about the grief caused by just these two incidences. Why in god's name hadn't he been arrested and tried for murder, and yet he is assigned to a command in Florida and begins a Black Op to ready Americans for the war on terror. He should have been the first terrorist the US took out and shot, but then of course he was working for them. Then something stung Dave to the very core.

In another report he read that many well known 'Christian' Evangelists frequently used Smith's '*Company*' airlines to fly them all over the world. Dave wondered if they had any idea who was supplying their transportation but digging deeper he found many of them received very sizable gifts from one or more of Smith's subsidiaries. It was so blatant it would be impossible for them not to know. He sat there pondering the depths that the tentacles of this monster had entangled itself into the day to day fabric of American life which as he was well aware included Canada and much of the world.

His sullen musing was interrupted by Colonel Benton as she strolled into his office. He glanced up to notice her as she passed him a very elegant magenta blue and white envelope with a Star of David inscribed on it. He gingerly took it and read the fancy gold inscription on the face. Lt. Colonel David Hart. He started to open it looking up at her.

"Do you have any idea what this is all about?" he asked.

She raised her shoulders and shook her head but a slight smile suggested she was telling a fib.

As he unfolded the expensive paper, he read and whistled.

"Seems the Israeli Government has invited me to a high level but secret meeting. It goes on to mention that I'll be an honoured guest." He glanced again at Joanne. "And it's dealing with Mr. Beauregard Smith. This isn't at all according to protocol is it? I mean isn't Sage supposed to do these things?" He looked over at her and then read it again.

"Joanne, you know I don't like these formal dues." Dave handed the invitation back to Joanne.

"Sage might get a twisted nose over this," she said with a smirk.

"Then I'll just decline."

Joanne glanced over at Dave with a knowing smile.

"I think you had better accept this one Lieutenant Colonel They invited you and so they want you. Who knows, they may have something that will help our case with Smith."

"I really doubt that, and besides Oscar might get me locked up for that spat of jaundice I diagnosed him with. I had him quarantined for a week for security reasons."

Joanne shook her head incredulously.

"That was a dirty trick to pull and especially to someone who had just given you so much assistance. Look Dave, if you want I can make it an order. I'm sure if it's important to them, it's probably going to be damned important to us."

"Okay, okay, I'll go to their meeting, but you sooth Mr. Sage. It's bad enough fighting the enemy without fighting friends too."

Joanne smiled and left the office. Dave on the other hand wondered just what such a meeting could be about. The rest of the day was taken with arranging air priorities and visas and generally preparing for the flight to the tiny country that could.

The next morning Dave was high above the clouds on an Air Canada flight to Toronto where he would connect to Tel Aviv. He relaxed and enjoyed the cross continent trip with no Julio to interrupt his snoozing. By suppertime he was aboard a Boeing 767 for the cross atlantic flight. It would fly through the night and arrive mid morning the next day in Tel Aviv.

Ben Gurion airport was crowded as Dave made his way over to the customs. All his papers were in order so he was surprised when the customs officer waved for two men wearing sports jackets and they approached him.

"Lt. Colonel David Solomon Hart?"

Dave nodded.

"We'd appreciate it if you would accompany us to a search room right over here."

Dave thought about not accepting their invitation just to see their mettle but then he noticed the Micro Galil each one had neatly shoulder holstered just inside their sports jacket. He decided it wouldn't be polite to reject their offer and by the flint expression on their faces he guessed it wouldn't be in the best interest of his health either. Inside the small room a third man joined them and their demeanor changed.

"Welcome to Israel, Mr. Hart. We will escort you to the meeting you have been invited to, but for security reasons we will need to blindfold you with a cloth bag."

They placed the bag over his head and lightly cinched it. Dave couldn't help but remember the last time this had happened and hoped the ending would be less lethal. They led him out a back door and then to an elevator which after it had stopped, presumably in the basement, they inserted him in the back seat of a very comfortable sedan. Dave estimated the trip took about twenty minutes but couldn't be sure. One thing he was sure of was wherever they were it was very close to the Mediterranean for he could feel the moisture and smell the salt water. On the other hand he mused everywhere in Israel is close to the Mediterranean. He considered this whole country was only three quarters the size of Vancouver Island and yet a great many people wanted its inhabitants annihilated. The men led him into a building, another elevator ride, down a hall and into a room where they removed the hood. Dave gazed around a large ultra modern board room and was amazed to see Oscar among five other men seated at a large oval shaped table. So all this was the Mossad and maybe he hadn't been entirely off the wall when he had suggested Oscar's revenge.

"Welcome to Israel." A tall lean man at the head of the table motioned for Dave to take a seat which had been left open for him. "I am Major General Joseph Zedvin. I called this most important meeting with the desire for some information exchange with the end result to rid the world of a very dangerous pest."

"Are you speaking of one General Beauregard Smith?" Dave asked.

"I am, and I was hoping together we might be able to put our information in a big pot, stir it around and come up with the elixir recipe to eliminate the scoundrel." The General eyed Dave and then the others at the table. "We know you have some information and we have quite a file as well so if you can help us fill in some of our blanks and we fill in some of yours then we might also be able to work in tandem to get him and his organization. What do you say Lt. Colonel?" The Major General waited for Dave's response and Dave decided he had better pick his words very carefully.

"Major General, I am all for working together and as long as I won't be required to divulge any operations we are, might be, or have already been involved in, I can see nothing to hinder us."

Dave searched the six man team to see their reactions. The General coughed and snickered and then spoke.

"We already know of the Ops you have been involved in from Major, ah, yes, Oscar here, who by the way has suggested some reprisal for his misdiagnosis and which I might quickly add, has been vetoed. He has turned in quite a file on your goings and comings. As for the things you're doing or going to do, of course we are an intelligence gathering organization, but right now we just want to bring an end to this Smith." The General let his words take effect and then went on. "So what I would like to do is fill in the blanks you may have by giving you the Intel we have and then with regards to your reservations you can tell us what you know about him. One final item I should mention before we start. This room is completely secure and everything said here is being recorded but the people here are as far as any of this Intel goes." He nodded his head to a man operating an electronic counsel in the corner and the stripped glass turned frosty with an almost inaudible hum filling the room. "John would you like to lead off?"

The fellow to his left pulled out a manuscript size stack of papers. Dave noticed the size of this one man's file was larger than the entire file Global had. The man cleared his throat.

"First of all General Smith was and possibly still is an operative for the CIA. If he is still connected he has covered his tracks very well but then they usually do. Although he is not a scientist or chemist, he seems to be able to find and bring together the world's finest minds to work his magic. He has recently, since operation Iraqi freedom, brought some of the top physicists together as well as other brilliant minds to put together what we have dubbed annihilation bombs. These are some type of small nuclear devices, something that's being referred to as Blue Lightning Thermal Nuclear, which can be carried by one person but have almost half the explosive power of the first US Atom bombs."

The first man continued to open a line primarily in the Physics area and left no doubt that Smith was dangerous to the entire world. He finished his presentation in forty minutes and had no one else added a thing, it would have been enough to yell an alert to every government on planet earth.

The General thanked him for his work and asked the next man to begin.

This fellow was more abrasive and spoke more to the point.

"Beauregard Smith should be in seclusion in the highest security prison available. He definitely shows signs of schizophrenia and also has severe symptoms of bipolar. What is meant by that is he seems to have the crest of the wave where he is euphoric but when he comes down to the trough he finds a need to kill which after committed, induces the euphoric state again. How much of this is drug induced and how much is he himself is very difficult to measure but make no mistake about it, as the waves continue they will get more pronounced and closer in rhythm. He has killed before and rest assured he will kill again, and again, and again, until he is ultimately stopped."

The second man finished his dissemination and then the third told of the general's allies which were mainly the Middle Eastern Muslim countries and North Korea. "These countries are a very loose coalition which are using the General every bit as much as he is using them. Our supposition is that if the General were to be removed quickly and quietly none of his allies would move into the fray."

The fourth officer, Oscar, had Intel on the fighting readiness of the General's terrorist cells.

"Dave, The General has built these cells over a number of years and they are battle hardened veterans. He also has set up several elite guards to protect him and his properties. Most of these guards stay put at the various villas and haciendas he has scattered around the globe, but he does take a few of the best of the best as body guards. He also ensures his properties are populated with many innocents which he hopes will reduce the possibility of large scale bombing attack.

The last speaker made known what they believed to be his financial capability and although it was only an estimate it was backed by eastern Muslim oil and maxed in the trillions.

Dave sat dumb founded. The meeting had lasted two hours already and although his people had put together a significant package, it in no way equaled theirs.

"What can I say? You have dwarfed my small package of intel. There are only a few small tidbits of Intel which I didn't hear that I can pass on to you. One is he is drawn to prostitutes and then kills them. Possibly he uses them as easy prey to give him his psychotic high and believes not as much protection will be afforded to ladies of the evening."

"At last count we have twenty-seven," one of the Israelis offered.

Dave was impressed.

"I supposed you knew he was in charge of black ops out of Florida and was in charge of getting America ready for the war on terror."

The Major General now sat up straighter.

"No, that's news to us. We've never had that come across our desk have we?"

He caught each of his men in turn and then turned back to Dave.

"What more can you tell us about his Florida days?"

"Just that he ran most of his operation from his office at Mac Dill Air Force Base and ran a network of small airports and Pilot Training companies on the east coast. This was a front to allow transport of large amounts of drugs which would finance his more exciting black ops. Fact is they were all Company run, ah CIA, and in some degree they were also used to confuse or blur the picture of 9/11. A prime example of this process is to take a glass window. Anyone can see through the glass to what is happening on the other side but when the other side of the glass is covered with a shiny material the glass becomes a mirror. The action continues to happen on the other side of the glass but all the person sees looking through it now is a reflection of themselves. Then all they have to do is set up the picture they want to reflect. They did this in 1962 and now in nine/eleven they've pulled it off again and not one of the perpetrators has yet to be caught. I intend to change that with our man, General Beauregard Smith. He ordered my wife killed and I took five slugs, so sorry if I get a little excited when I speak of this, but I also believe he was the lead operative in the September 11 raid and had his hand in many other plots. The latest Intel indicates he has an operation somewhere in the Bekka Valley and it has to do with the odds and ends he spirited out of Iraq. I suppose that is all the factual information I have."

The Major General was smiling.

"I'm impressed. Although we had suspicions we haven't heard anyone from the Intelligence community come right out and say it. Do you think he may be working on that Blue Lightning thing there?"

"I wouldn't at all be surprised. One thing I'd like you to know gentlemen. I don't believe those so called hijackers did anymore than Oswald did in sixty-two. I dare say they were probably as surprised as anyone else on those planes and a damn bit more upset. They were just the shiny covering on the back of the glass."

The Major General looked shocked.

"Who the hell piloted those planes then?"

"AWACS, gentlemen. The General's Black Ops pilots. Highly trained, highly paid, and high in the sky. Could have even been high on drugs for all we know. They were American CIA pilots with high tech remote control of the Boeing aircraft. Remote control from America's own AWACS all funneled through the CIA."

"What about Osama. He's put out tapes more or less confessing."

"He was and probably still is CIA. If they ever catch him, I doubt he'll be alive. Just between you and me, I don't think he's been alive for a number of years."

The head man gave a slight whistle.

"Sir, I could go on and on with this but it's just conjecture and the problem at hand is General Beauregard Smith. I suspect the General moved the bulk of the Iraqi WMD." He smiled at the Major General. "Or what there was left of them after Russia and a few others finished their recall, through Syria to Iran, and that only as another subterfuge. Now he can let them stir up a hornets' nest and cover his work here in the Bekka."

"Well Lt. Colonel you've given us some amazing insight, which I must tell you fit the puzzle. I hope you received some information you can make use of, as we have. Now my driver will escort you to your hotel and please enjoy your stay in The Land. Oh, you will be blind folded again for security reasons. There are many who would do anything to find out where we are located. Good-bye Lt. Colonel Hart."

Dave's escorts took the hood off as they pulled up at the doors of the Dan Tel Aviv Hotel. Dave stared at the grandeur of it and then to the north at the sea.

"Hey guys, I was booked at the City hotel. You think you could give me a lift over there. The two officers smiled a knowing smile at each other.

"The boss says you will stay here, all expenses paid. We'll pick you up on Monday in time for your flight back home."

Dave left the car and went into the lobby and straight to the desk where a young lady welcomed him in Hebrew. Dave said he was Canadian and gave his name. She followed the registry and then her eyes opened wide.

"Yes Sir Mr. Hart," she replied in English. "The Royal suite is ready for you now. It's the best in the house and I've been instructed to tell you, if there is anything, anything at all, you desire just call room service." She hit a small buzzer and a bellhop instantly came out of the office.

"Please take Mr. Hart to his room."

Dave was amazed. "Uh, I will need to have my luggage picked up at the airport."

"Your luggage was delivered earlier. It's in your room."

"Thank you," he said incredulously and followed the Hop to the elevator.

Dave entered his room and handed the Hop a twenty who gave him a quick nod and told him again if there was anything he needed to simply call room service at 7777. Dave walked through the large suite, which he mused was more than twice as large as his home. He checked the spacious three bedrooms with the king-size beds and then looked in the bathroom. The walk in shower was indeed large enough for an entire five person family to bath together.

After showering he decided to go souvenir hunting. He wanted to pick something especially nice for Gail and Joanne. Dave left the hotel and took a taxi to a street where there were many small shops and stores. He paid his fare, got out, and began the hunt for the perfect souvenir. He was looking for a solid gold Star of David either in a necklace, bracelet or pendant of some kind. The day was far spent when he found what he was looking for in a small jewelry store. He especially liked the inlaid diamonds. He had haggled for the price of the necklace which he had been told was part of the buying process. He paid the price the seller and he had come to agreement on and decided to try the Metro back to the hotel. He checked the schedules seeing number four would get him there and then searched out a bus stop just in time to catch it. He rushed over to the city bus and was just about to board when a man jostled his way around Dave and got on in front of him. At that instant several things happened. Dave remembered he wanted to get Joanne a memento as well and changed his mind, backing away from the bus. As he did he noticed the man who had just pushed ahead of him was now sitting in the bus and staring at him in a forlorn expression. Dave turned and as the bus pulled away, walked in the opposite direction. The fully loaded carrier hadn't got more than fifty meters when the sidewalk seemed to vibrate and as Dave turned to glance at the bus, he was shocked to see first the glass windows explode in a shattering blast and then fire chase the glass followed by body parts and metal. The concussion knocked Dave to the ground and stunned him. He stared from his vantage point on the cement sidewalk and could see many of the people who had been walking on the same sidewalk as he but had been much closer to the bus. They were now lying motionless on a blood spattered walk way. The instant carnage was surreal as Dave slowly surveyed the scene.

He was just beginning to get to his feet when two men in beach shirts grabbed him, one under each arm, turned and ran, half dragging him away from the scene. Dave was trying to resist but the men held fast and ferried him down an alley with hurried strides.

"Mr. Hart, we're IDF," one of the men said. "We were ordered to protect you and we must get you away from this scene in case you were the target. There may be more assassins in the area to finish the job."

Dave thought about it and decided the suggestion was plausible. As the three men crossed the next intersecting street Dave could hear the far off sirens of the ambulances and other emergency vehicles approaching. As Dave began to gain his stability the two IDF soldiers loosened their grip on him and they all slowed to a fast power stride. One of the soldiers used a cell phone and after traversing two more blocks a sedan pulled up. One soldier opened the back door for Dave and the other officer to enter and closed the door after them. He then quickly got in the front and the tires screeched as the car sped away. Everything had happened so swiftly that only now was Dave's brain replaying the order of events.

"I saw the man who blew himself up. He stared straight at me just as I changed my mind and decided not to take that bus. His eyes were like they had the words written in them that he had just made a critical mistake. My God, I was the target. Smith has teams on me. He just tried to kill me again." His speech was incredulous.

The car pulled up to the entrance of the hotel and his guards escorted him to his room. They told him their CO had assigned them to be his security until he left The Land.

Dave stayed in the hotel except for an hour on Gordon Beach and one brief sightseeing tour, where he bought an authentic menorah. Other than that he swam in the hotel pool and lived in the laps of luxury. Aside from his harrowing brush with death, he felt refreshed getting on the Air Canada jet for the trip back home. He had learned a great deal about General Smith. He had seen the horror the people of Israel lived with day in and day out, and he especially had seen the look in that man's eyes. Those eyes that wailed the loss of a victory but at the same time shrieked the twisted determination to terrorize his enemies at the cost of his own life. All of it made Dave more determined to stop Beauregard Smith.

*   *   *

Dave sat in Joanne's office, determined to persuade her to give him orders for an operation against Smith at his Columbian Villa.

"Joanne, give me a Cessna and I'll fly it myself but we got to stop this guy. You've got my report from the Israeli thing and it proves that this is one notorious outlaw."

"Oh come on Dave, what do you think I've been doing? I've gone over to The Hall every day, and called Sage two or three times in between, but they don't want to move."

Dave glanced across the desk at his CO and realized she would have done everything possible to get the Board to go forward but something was definitely holding them back. He speculated if he could only discover what that something was he might be able to convince them Smith had to be stopped and he and his men had the best chance of doing it. As he thought about the urgency of the situation his mind returned to the bus in Israel and that bomber's eyes.

"Joanne, do you have any idea why they're procrastinating on this? Surely they aren't so inept as to really believe this Smith would fold easily or that I would lead my men into a situation that's not tenable."

"Dave there's a lot of politics and legalities to be answered here. Don't go taking it personally but when and if the order comes, and I do expect it will come, you'll be expected to do your duty to the best of your ability. Just do the paperwork for now Dave."

He excused himself to return to his own office and stopped off at Gail's desk.

"Hi Sweets!"

"Hi yourself." She wrinkled her face as she glared at him. "Sweets."

"Hey what's wrong? Did I miss something here?"

"Oh yeah! Seems to me you didn't miss something is more like it."

Dave eyed her cautiously and wondered what had gotten into her.

"Okay, I give up. What didn't I miss? What's going on?

"While you were off gallivanting around the world did you even once think of *the someone* back here at home? And, to make matters worse you waltz right into the CO's office without so much as a wave." She put her hands to her mouth forming a blow horn. "Hello? Is there any intelligent life down there?"

Dave received the transmission loud and clear and was smiling now.

"As a matter of fact, while I was *gallivanting*, as you call it, through the commercial district of a certain city I *was* thinking of you, and I specifically bartered this." He pulled the little gift wrapped box from his pocket. "It's from a little Jewish jewelry store just for you." Dave passed it to her and her eyes filled with tears. She hesitantly began to reach for it and then pulled her hand back. She finally took the box and sat there staring at it.

"You really were thinking of me?" When she opened the little purple velvet box her eyes welled up again. For the first time since Dave had said hi, she was speechless. She stared at the gold Star of David with the small diamond at the apex of each point and then glanced at Dave and then back at the star again. At last she ran around her desk crying and threw her arms around his neck.

"I'm sorry for saying what I said and thinking what I thought, but I didn't mean you needed to get me anything. I just thought you hadn't even thought about me. Will you forgive me?"

Dave nodded.

"That's the nicest thing anyone has ever done for me," she said in between the sobs. "How can you ever forgive me for being such a brat?"

"Well, I don't know," he said as he feigned a complete cave.

They were quietly conversing when the intercom blasted with Joanne's voice.

"Lt. Levine could you please interrupt whatever you're doing and get General Benton on the line for me?"

Gail chuckled at the words *whatever your doing* and went back to her chair.

"Thank you." She mouthed as she picked up the phone and began punching the number for the General.

Dave smiled back as he returned a mimed "You're welcome." He headed down the corridor for his office feeling elated while he whistled a tune.

Chapter 9

That evening, Dave parked the car up the hill from the Royal Columbian hospital and walked down to the entrance. Once inside, he noticed Julio, Marty, Gail, and two other team members waiting by the hospital gift shop and moved toward them.

"How's he doing?" Dave asked. "I heard he was conscious."

Marty looked up. "Not so good." He hesitated as if having a hard time saying the rest. "I mean he'll live but I'm not too sure he wants to. Oh man, he's lost his right eye. They saved the left one, they think, but they're not sure whether it'll be that great either. LC, he's told me many times he'd rather die than not be able to shoot."

Dave grimaced at the thought of facing this man who had had such a close brush with death and now was maimed in body as well as in spirit. What could he say; what was there to say?

"Is he conscious?"

"Oh yeah, but he won't talk. He's really feeling bad."

Marty and the group walked with Dave to George's room. A heavyset red haired nurse on her way out stopped, looked at the muscular men, slim woman, and admonished them in an Irish accent.

"There'll be only two visitors allowed for fifteen minutes at a time. Hospital rules." She looked the four men up and down. "If you break the rules, I'll throw you out."

Dave nodded while admiring the lady's directness.

"Yes ma'am."

After she was out of sight the others snickered.

The others waited outside the door while Dave and Julio went in. The private room was a nice size with pastel colors and everything sparkling. George was already sitting up. He had been in and out of consciousness for the last week and had undergone three extensive operations but he now had started responding to treatment. Dave felt sadness wash over him as he gazed at George's bandaged head and body. He could see the oxygen tubes to his nose and the battery of IVs attached to his arm.

"Hey George, looks like that old mama cougar got the worst of the deal." Dave couldn't hold the smile. "Looks like you're doing pretty good though."

"Damn, looks like I'm not the only blind man here," George said with a growl.

"The doctor says you'll get to keep your left eye so you're not exactly going to be blind." Julio said

"Yeah, well it sure as hell finishes me with sharp shooting. If I had to lose one why the hell couldn't it be the left one and leave my shooting eye alone. It'll end my military career as well."

"Hold up there Lt., the three gold bands on my shoulder gives me some authority to make that decision. You may not be able to shoot in combat, but with your qualifications, you sure as hell can teach the new kids the craft and make a major contribution to your country. That's all any of us do."

George slightly shifted his head away from them, moving it as much as he was able, signaling the end of the conversation.

Dave raised his eyebrows in a sign of resignation and motioned to Julio it was time for them to leave. As Dave moved toward the door he stopped and turned back to George.

"George my father always used to tell me when things went wrong, *it's always darkest just before the dawn.*"

Without another word he turned and stepped through the door, into the hall and closed the door. Once in the hall, Dave informed Gail and the others that George didn't feel up to any more visitors.

*   *   *   *

The next day, Dave sat in his office and (among other problems) was trying to figure out the dilemma of how he would gain entrance to the General's compound without shooting someone or being shot by the General's mercenaries. He had tried several scenarios, but they all came to the same conclusion. The people Smith had guarding his domain wouldn't be interested in an arrest warrant except to exempt themselves and their employer from it. Kodiak team would have to go in with the ability to shoot first and ask questions later or be killed. Dave wadded up another diagram of the compound and chucked it into the garbage, which was already spilling over. Finally, he realized what needed to be done. He picked up the phone and dialed Colonel Benton's number.

"Colonel, I respectfully request a meeting with the board. I've been looking at this mission and as things stand---"

Joanne broke in. "It looks like a suicide mission and no-one comes back? I was wondering how long it would take for you to make this call. I'll request a special meeting, tentatively for tomorrow. Can you have a worthwhile presentation ready in that length of time?"

"If I have to work on it all night."

"Then get busy."

It was well after midnight and gallons of coffee later when Dave put the finishing touches on his presentation. He hoped it would impress the Board and the Commissioner enough to boost the level of the mission and change the rules of engagement to include the use of preemptive lethal force if necessary. Dave had also requested approval for the recruitment of at least three more members.

He checked his watch. It was too late to go all the way home to the Lake but the safe apartment in Burnaby was only a half an hour away so Dave decided to use that. He called Gail but didn't get an answer so he figured she had probably shut the phone off.

The taxi glided towards Burnaby and as Dave listened to the windshield wipers smack back and forth he noticed rainy nights like this one always seemed to make the pavement darker. As the driver piloted the vehicle through the light traffic Dave reminisced joining CSIS.

He had felt he would help make Canada and even the world a safer place. Not particularly by being a super hero or even a hero of any kind but just to let the bad guys know there were still those who would not let them brandish their threatening and murderous behaviour without consequence. He pondered how he had at first rejected an offer to be reinstated in the military with a commission and how the indecision had changed with the death of Bev.

His rational then was, 'how many other innocent people would these terrorist kill to change the way the people thought and lived. His mind went back to a speech he had heard in school social studies class by John F. Kennedy warning the American people of a clear and present danger to the nation. He had spelled out a warning that his predecessor Dwight D Eisenhower had also warned of, but had already become exponentially more dangerous.

In essence he was warning that the Intelligence Community High Archaists in tandem with leading military Industrialist were already a threat to national security of the United States. That was assuredly one of the major reasons why the establishment had to eliminate Kennedy with a Coup d'état. It was planned long before he ever left Washington for Dallas that fateful day and it was guaranteed he would not return alive.

Not one person ever answered to the American people for the assassination of their President. Dave's thoughts automatically superimposed 9/11. Again, not one person had been tried and answered for the crime of the century but now Dave was hot on the trail of a leader of the bandits and there would be a showdown.

Dave was jarred back to the present by the taxi careening through a red light with other car horns blaring and narrowly missing an intersection collision. The rude awakening was just in time to bring the lights of Salvatore's Pizza to Dave's view.

"Hey, pull over here and stop. I want to get some takeout pizza. Here's a twenty, wait for me."

*   *   *

Dave arrived early at the Office Tower, the building where the meeting would be held. As Dave stood outside the door enjoying the fresh air, he watched Joanne pull in and noticed her give him the once over.

"You know, I think I'm going to have to put Lt. Levine in for a promotion."

"I take it you agree with the choice of clothes?"

"And you're here at least ten minutes early," as she checked her watch.

"Being here early has nothing to do with Gail; Joanne this has to go through. I've struggled with it and there just isn't any other way to get to Smith. He won't listen to anything except brute force."

"You're right but I hope and trust you can convince the Board of that."

"Yeah, me too."

Joanne and Dave entered the boardroom and found the place where they were to sit. Dave noticed there was the Assistant Director of the Integrated Threat Assessment Centre or ITAC, D.L. Sage, three assistant directors, and each of them had an assistant from an appropriate department. Dave scanned the eight men he needed to win over. Mr. Sage looked relaxed and attentive but the other seven could have just as easily been a Court-Martial Tribunal. Searching their faces didn't at all leave him believing he would get a favorable response. Joanne read some self-doubt in Dave's demeanor and scribbled a couple of words on a paper.

Dave read the paper; *you'll do fine,* and nodded with a smile.

Assistant Director Sage called the meeting to order and requested Dave to begin. Dave stood and with a laser pointer in hand cleared his throat.

"We have a very complex problem on our hands ladies and gentlemen." He hit a key on his laptop and a picture of a huge man in a US Air force uniform with two stars flashed on the boardroom screen.

"This man, Major General Beauregard Smith, has become one of the most lethal and dangerous men Democracies around the world have ever known. From intelligence, which we have accumulated, we can tie this man to more than a dozen terrorist organizations worldwide as well as here in Canada. His Cohorts list like a Who's Who in the terrorist community.

From the Intel I personally have gathered and studied I believe he was deeply connected on the wrong side of nine eleven." After almost each sentence Dave flashed a different picture. "He's been involved with next generation fission bombs and reducing their size. Indications are he is close to reducing the size of these nuclear bombs to a size able to fit in a normal briefcase while retaining near total power; thus giving the term 'nuke in a briefcase' a whole new definition.

He's also been highly involved in remote flying of large jet aircraft. Consider it. Remote commercial planes with unthinkable weapons capability linked to a psychopath who kills without feeling and has no known religious affiliations that might inhibit his bloodlust. These are some of the places he has already hit with regular explosives and mercenary soldiers." Dave slowly flashed several pictures of destruction on the screen. "Ladies and gentlemen he has the knowledge, the connections, the equipment, and the will to make a pre-emptive strike anywhere in the world with no collateral for the defending country to counter strike." Dave showed several more pictures of destruction proven to be the results of Smith's organization.

"He, gentlemen is a military ghost who without conscience will kill one or one million people to reach his goals and with seemingly little or no retribution. He has picked up the sobriquet of Cottonmouth for good reason and so for our purposes I would prefer to call him just that from this time forward. Cottonmouth was working with Saddam before the last Iraqi invasion and managed to spirit away certain fission and biological weapon building equipment and supplies.

Because of his work while with the US military coupled with other Intel we have gathered, we have reason to believe this man is heading up an organization which is developing and perfecting nuclear weapons that can be concealed in briefcases and carried by suicide bombers dressed in suits and ties. These people could move almost anywhere without detection.

We believe his organization is bent on the destabilization of first the Middle East and then the entire world. He will probably strike first wherever oil is a major resource as this has the greatest impact on worldwide governments." Dave glanced at the people.

"Board members, your worst nightmares are only the genesis of where Cottonmouth is going and he is also well aware that eventually somebody is going to try to stop him. He has therefore built a formidable security net around himself and his very mobile operation."

Dave tapped another key and hybrid satellite pictures appeared on the large screen showing the many estates the General owned. He ended with a screen sized picture the Columbia Villa which he indicated was indicative of the Cottonmouth's lairs and would be the primary target if they were to assail this monster. As the pictures of the grounds zoomed in, Dave described the protective security surveillance devices of this Villa in more detail.

"Seen here are some of the live computer driven weaponries," Dave stabbed the red laser bead at several points on a photo, "and their locations as well as the placement of the highly trained personnel in and around the Cottonmouth's Columbia estate. So it becomes quite obvious that with the state of the art defenses and personnel, these fortresses and especially the Columbia Villa, can only be breached without severe collateral damage by an elite team such as Kodiak. At the same time we must be allowed preemptive lethal force in our rules of engagement. I cannot emphasize too strongly that if any team has to go on the defensive, they will have already lost the mission and most probably their lives. Lastly, if your decision is favourable I would request at least three but preferably six more highly trained soldiers. The extra firepower will further ensure the positive conclusion of the mission to shut down Cottonmouth."

Dave glanced around the room and was encouraged to see the Board now in rapt attention.

"Finally, I hope that you can render a decision that will be favorable to both my requests. Thank you for your time."

"Some questions Lt. Colonel?" the Director asked.

Dave nodded.

"You stated 'Cottonmouth' spirited away Saddam's WMD. Due to the UN investigation as well as other searches I was of the opinion there were no WMD. Do you have other intelligence?"

"Sir, the United States intelligence community is well aware of the existence of the material. They know it was there because they are the ones who sent it there. Although they cannot admit that without losing a lot of face and possibly even some allies, they indeed know it was there."

Sage nodded affirming he understood and another person spoke up.

"Wouldn't it just be easier, safer, and more cost effective to drop some high altitude bombs and eradicate the entire estate?"

"No Sir. First, the Cottonmouth keeps many innocent people in his employ to use as a human shield. Second, we need to accumulate any Intel which will tell us of his resources and thus allow us to deal with them. Even if Cottonmouth is neutralized, there is still a huge possibility that his organization will just appoint a new leader and carry on. Neutralizing Cottonmouth is of supreme importance but bringing his organization to an end is equally a top priority."

The Director scribbled some notes and resumed.

"What makes you so sure they have the resolve to continue to a cataclysm?"

"Sir, as you are aware I just returned from Israel where I was the target and almost one of many victims of a human bomb. I was about to get on a bus, when a man pushed in ahead of me and got on. Once on and back a couple of seats he turned and stared at me. I had made the first step and then remembering I had one more errand to make. I stepped back down. As I did I happened to catch the eyes of the man who had pushed in ahead of me." Dave slowly glanced at each person for effect.

"He was a human bomber and had been watching me to see where I would go and when I approached the bus he hurried past me to make sure he was on the same bus as me. As the bus pulled away from me I could see the defeat he was feeling for losing me, in his eyes, but those eyes quickly steeled with a determination and seconds later the bus came apart with at least thirty people being killed. Determination? You bet they have, and at any cost."

There was silence for the next sixty seconds while the entire group digested the information.

"How long would you take to bring a highly trained recruit up to speed with the rest of your team?" Sage asked.

"Generally, given the soldier is already trained in multiple skills it would take a maximum two to three months, but if we intensify that we could complete it in four to six weeks and still have a fluent workable combatant. A JTF-2 recruit might fit in within a few weeks."

The Director gave a questioning glance at Colonel Benton. She hunched her shoulders and nodded toward Dave.

"The Lt. Colonel is our resident expert," she said.

"Okay, thank you for the informative presentation Lt. Colonel We will discuss your request and give you our decision later today. You and Colonel Benton are dismissed.

Joanne and Dave left the boardroom and headed for the parking lot. As they conversed on the way to their cars, Dave gazed towards the white caped pinnacles of the mountains to the north east and pointed at them.

"Those mountains are so majestic and yet have a ruggedness to try the physical strength of any man. I've been to the top of a couple of them and I can tell you it's damn hard work, but yet hard work is not enough. A person has to be highly trained, have the right equipment, and the physical stamina to get up there. Make no mistake about it, those mountains are unforgiving and similar to this Cottonmouth obstacle. We've got the training and the best equipment in the world but we have to be able to use it to the best of our ability to get the job done. I wonder if I said enough of what needed to be said in there?"

Joanne chuckled. "You certainly did. If you had said any more, Sage would have had you spirited away as some high level secret or maybe even relegated you to a funny farm."

Dave looked at her trying to pretend he took it to heart, "They really do that kind of thing? Wow." Joanne chuckled again in spite of herself.

"Okay, I'll call you the minute I get any word," she said as she got into her car.

Dave returned to the Global Tech offices. He had a water cooler meeting with Gail before he went to his office, where he fidgeted, paced, and drank coffee. He had a bad feeling about what the board's decision would be and it had little to do with the number of new recruits or at what level of urgency the mission might rate. These were of utmost importance but he was worried about the loss of George and who would replace him.

He had this real bad premonition that somehow things would get twisted around and because she had scored so well on the last exercise, Lt. Levine would be George's replacement, and that in his eyes was unacceptable. The minutes ticked by like hours and the hours were like eternity.

The phone finally rang and it was Joanne summoning him to her office. Dave figured he would have a chance to talk to Gail on the way in but when he got to the reception area Gail wasn't there. Dave entered Colonel Benton's office and two glowing female faces greeted him.

"Ah, Come in Lt. Colonel and have a seat."

Dave knew from the formal salutation that his worries were the beginning of his second worst nightmare. Dave sat down waiting for the proverbial shoe to fall.

"Lt. Colonel, the Board has made its decision. Your request for an Operation into Columbia to capture and arrest General Smith with an elevation in rules of engagement was approved." Joanne looked up from the computer screen and smiled. "However, given the time required to bring new personnel up to speed the Board felt that, although you will be authorized to recruit all six, because of timing you must go with what you have on this mission. You and your team have authorization to extradite Beauregard Smith from Columbia to either the U.S. or Canada. I want him in Canada. You've also been authorized to use as much force as you deem necessary at the time. In other words, you're going to jump in and take him, one way or the other. This operation, from here on out, will have the codename of Cottonmouth until he is apprehended or dead." She passed him the manila file with CODENAME: COTTONMOUTH in big letters and Top Secret stamped across it. "Any questions?"

Dave quickly glanced through the folder.

"Looks like I got exactly what I wanted," Dave said.

Colonel Benton's face lightened.

"That is with the exception of Lt. Levine. She will fill the slot made vacant by Lt. Seagram."

Dave began to rise from the chair to argue.

Lt. Levine will replace Lt. Mussleman as backup shooter," she raised her voice as if to quell any opposition, "and Mussleman will become primary shooter. You will proceed to Columbia on August 20th. That's day after tomorrow, where you will do a night HAHO insertion. You will make a commando raid of Cottonmouth's estate and take him, alive if possible. Any other Intel will be a bonus. You will do demolition of the villa for total destruction. Are there any questions?"

Dave glanced over at Gail, then back at Joanne and decided it was a crazy world.

"Colonel, I'm really not comfortable with Lt. Levine going in on this operation," Dave said.

"Lt. Colonel," Joanne said with a sharp voice, "these orders are not negotiable and unless you have knowledge of a serious deficiency in the Lt.'s capabilities I expect you to carry out your orders."

Dave really didn't like the idea of sending her into harm's way. On the other hand she, in all honesty had performed better than either George or Marty on exercises.

"Yes Ma'am. I will develop our operational plan and submit it to you for your approval later today."

Dave returned to his office and began planning the intricacies of the mission. The part he didn't like was for Gail to be involved, but worse, she and Lt. Mussleman would be first in. The two shooters would need to jump in a safe distance from Smith's compound twenty four hours ahead of the rest of the team and would secure a hidden position in the compound with only their stealth and cunning as backup. They alone would safeguard the team's arrival the next night.

Dave mused about this little lady guarding his arrival on enemy turf and then wondered if in the annals of warfare, this kind of thing had ever happened. The hours flew by and Dave had just put the final additions to his plans when the phone buzzed. It was Joanne summoning him to her office again. Minutes later Dave was standing beside Gail in front of Joanne's desk listening to something almost unbelievable.

"I know this is a terrible time to make you two aware of this but better forewarned. We have received information that an assassin has been contracted for you and possibly you as well, Gail. It was awarded by General Smith. Got to admit you really got this guy dancing."

Dave stood listening to the report his CO was relating to him. He knew there was only two ways to go. They could tuck tail and run, which meant trying to hide both Gail and him and eventually that would deteriorate into shame. The other was to strengthen his resolve, get Cottonmouth before he got them. If he stopped Cottonmouth's assassin, all he would accomplish is to cut off the tail, so to speak and the General would just grow it back by hiring another. No, he thought, what he had to do is go in and get the General himself. In addition, it wasn't as if it was just his life or that of Gail's. This sociopath would kill thousands or maybe even millions if he wasn't stopped.

"Our best course of action is to proceed with Operation Cottonmouth," Dave said, "and his assassins as the need arise. Colonel, until then I would like you to appoint the Lt. here as my aid; a kind of protective custody." He laid his hand on Gail's shoulder.

The Colonel glanced at Lt. Levine and then back to Dave.

"Alright, Lt. Levine, you'll have your new orders by noon and in the meantime you are on special assignment as Aid to Lt. Colonel Hart. You are to be his shadow and take orders directly from him. However, during the mission you will be the team's backup shooter," Joanne said smiling and giving him a wink. "Nice try though Dave."

Dave entered the CO's office later that day and gave her a briefing of the operation starting with the plan to send the shooters in as a type of Pathfinder. They were to do a HALO ten kilometers south of the villa, work their way into the compound and unseen, set up separate shooting platforms. They would also set up the Satellite beacon so the rest of the team could pin point their target the following night. Dave described the new carbon fiber bat wings the main group would use when they did their HAHO the next night.

"These carbon fiber wings having a wing span of six feet, made from a carbon fiber composite, and weighing in at less than a kilogram will allow us to do our jump over one hundred and fifty kilometers from the target area. These wings are virtually radar proof so the stealth should be perfect. Once on target we will do a search, arrest or destroy mission, mop up, and call in our ride home."

Dave gave Colonel Benton a salute and left her office. Gail joined him and they decided they would stop by her apartment so she could grab a few things and then go to the barracks in Abbotsford.

They were enjoying each other's banter as they traveled down Kingsway, when Dave noticed a car doing some excessive lane changes behind them. He mentioned it to Gail and then began some easy evasive tactics to see if the car was following them or just another hotshot driver. Sure enough after a couple of corners, the Crown Vic was still on their tail. Dave made a few turns, drove down some alleys and copped a u-turn until he wound up headed straight for the Ford.

Both cars came to a halt nose to nose and both Dave and Gail jumped out behind their doors with their weapons pointed directly at the driver's side windshield. The sun's glare on the glass made it impossible to properly identify the person inside the vehicle but not so much glare that they couldn't see any moves.

"Alright, come on out of there nice and slow. Get out and keep your hands where we can see them," Dave shouted.

The tension was thick as the Ford's door slowly opened. Both Dave and Gail had their weapons trained on the driver's front window just above the dash and were ready to dispatch him to the infernal highways below. First a pair of shiny black boots stepped down on the pavement and then the hands rose above the door glass with a weapon still in one. The man gently laid the weapon on the roof of the car and slowly rose to full height. Finally the man was in full view.

Chapter 10

Dave and Gail lowered their weapons.

"Marty, what the hell are you doing following us?" Dave asked.

"Colonel Benton gave us orders to become a security wall. I guess she's worried about you two, LC."

"You mean to tell me she's got the whole team out here on protective security? Oh, what the hell, I was going to have everyone report to the barracks anyway. Meet us at the barracks and I'll call Captain Rodriguez to direct the rest of the team out there. I want a briefing and an equipment check and we may as well practice some maneuvers."

      *   *   *

      *

Eight hours later Lt. Musselman and Levine were on their way to Columbia where they would do a night HALO jump into the jungle somewhere south of Smith's estate. They would be Alpha Team and would secure a good but hidden sniper observation position on the estate grounds near the villa. They would stay concealed there throughout the day waiting for cover of darkness when they would also set up EHF (extra high frequency) beacons for the guidance systems. This would assist in guiding the rest of Kodiak team to a precision landing on the villa's rooftop. The rest of Kodiak would be Baker and Charlie Teams and would follow twenty-four hours later. They would land directly on the flat roof of the Villa, which was easier than it sounded with the electronic beacon guiding them to a nine thousand square foot landing area.

The next evening, as the big Hercules with the rest of Kodiak team approached the drop zone, Dave received a transmission from Lt. Musselman. "Alpha team on location." The ground below was mostly black with areas of illumination off to the northeast and northwest indicating the major cities of Bogotá and Cali. The team had been breathing one hundred percent oxygen for the last two hours when Dave gave orders to prepare their jump equipment and especially their 'Bat Wings'.

As the C-130 reached the drop zone the hatch opened and Kodiak team spilled from the plane, falling into the darkness like a bunch of hornets leaving the hive. They performed the HAHO, which in this case was forty thousand feet, glided with their special carbon fiber wings at nearly three hundred kilometers per hour to eight thousand feet, jettisoned the wings and opened their glide parachute for the rest of the distance to the roof of the villa. This allowed them to exit the plane more than seventy kilometers away and enter the Villa's airspace undetected. As Dave glided toward the lower elevation the frost cleared from his goggles and he could just make out the men ahead of him in the darkness. They were completing the procedures perfectly.

Dave detached his wings, pulled the rip cord and opened his chute steering towards some lights from the Villa a little over five miles from his position. Each man used his GPS and other navigation devices to maneuver the glide chutes toward the LZ until they had a visual and then quietly landed on the roof of the Villa.

Dave was the last man to land and immediately began giving orders.

"Alpha, are you in position and ready?" Dave asked.

"Just give us the word LC and we'll give these guys a light show they'll never forget," Marty responded.

"Roger that Alpha one. Is your backup ready?"

"I'm ready," Gail replied.

"Then listen up, Alpha, when I give the word, I want at least two thermo baric grenades fired into each of the three barracks." Dave was banking on these new state of the art grenades to use up the oxygen in the building to increase the explosion so that any combatants in there wouldn't come out alive. "If any combatant survives and isn't ready to surrender you will continue to use lethal force. Do I make myself clear?"

"Yes Sir!" was their unified response.

"Baker and Charlie, we're going over the side and swing into both upper floors just as we planned."

The two small groups moved to the edge of the roof and secured their ropes. Everyone quickly fastened their lanyard to immovable objects and lined up along the roof with their weapons slung to the front, ready for use. Within seconds they were all ready.

"Okay let's go."

Dave's team ran down the wall almost like they were on level ground, but then halted just above the upper level verandas. They hung there facing the ground until Julio's group got into position just above the ground floor and then on Dave's signal they all swung into the piazzas. Dave began to get an uneasy feeling as he found one bedroom after another empty and other areas void of the General or any of his minions. By the time Dave and his group had search the entire upper level and found no-one, Julio was reporting in with the same info. Dave began to contemplate a possible ambush.

"Baker, be prepared for an attack," He said quietly into his Com-Tac, "defend your perimeter. We're coming down to join you."

Once they formed up, Dave left Julio with a couple of men to stand guard near the Ballroom and led the rest to the only area that hadn't been searched, the Villa's basement. The entire Villa was deathly quiet. Dave's group moved with near total stealth as they made their way down the staircase. Harvey received an instant glare from Dave when he stepped on a stair and it squeaked.

Dave held the team motionless until he was certain the noise had gone unnoticed and then motioned for the group to continue cautiously toward the basement. They reached the lower floor and found most of the hired domestics in a common room used by the employees as a dining hall. He ordered them to stay put and in a half broken Spanish with the help of some innovative sign language made them aware they weren't in danger and asked if anyone else was in this area. He wondered if the General could be hiding with his bodyguards in one of the rooms. One of the maids pointed to a room down the hall.

"Hay dos hombres por el vestíbulo," she said nervously.

 Dave didn't know a lot of Spanish but he caught dos, Hombres, and vestibulo, meaning two, men, and room. He left a man to guard and the four remaining team members moved cautiously down the hall. When they got to the door the maid had pointed to, a member cautiously tried to open it from the side. It was locked. Dave motioned for everyone to stand back and be ready to storm the room. He let blast with his silenced XM8 on the door lock. The wood splintered all around the lock allowing it to fall to the floor as the door flew open from the impact. Four automatic assault rifles were leveled on two men dressed in British button down suits. The two were shaking with fear.

"Who the hell are you two and what are you doing here?" Dave asked.

"We're General B. Smith's associates. Top military aids actually. Among other things we are responsible for communications and logistics," said the braver one on the right with a strong British accent.

"We're also responsible for much of the accounting and general business administration. I'm

Andres Little and this is Jonathan Jenner," the left one added.

"Well fellows, I wouldn't go broadcasting that you're responsible for anything around here; just in case there's someone within ear-shot who's not a big fan of the General's." He gave them the meanest look he could muster. "Like me for instance. Consider yourselves under arrest. Turn around and place your hands behind your back."

They complied and Dave's men lashed their hands with neoprene handcuffs.

"Where is your General Smith anyway?" Dave asked.

"We are not privy to that information. He seldom informs us of his whereabouts," Andres replied. "But I do know he's not here. He left late last evening."

Dave moved them to the kitchen with the domestics and made them all aware if anyone came out before called they would be shot on sight. He told Jonathan to tell them to have coffee and stay where they were. When questioned as to where the main computer that operated the guidance equipment and guns Andres told them it was next door from the room where they had been. Dave swiftly moved to that room and disabled the entire system with several well placed sprays of gunfire.

As the electronics arced and crackled Dave and his group left the basement and rejoined Julio on the ground floor. He knew there was something wrong and decided they had better get to a position they could defend and that was the jungle.

"Captain, take your men out the north side of the building and be prepared for engagement."

Julio nodded and led his three men out the north door into the night to blend into the jungle while Dave moved to the south to do the same. Julio's group had almost made cover at the tree line when automatic fire raked the ground near them. They opened up on the darkness where they had seen the enemy weapon's muzzle flash. Dave heard the sound of the firefight just as others opened up on his group as well.

"Alpha, do the barracks, now," Dave yelled into his Com-Tac while switching his XM-8 scope to night finder. "There you are you suckers." He laid down a heavy pattern emptying his thirty-shell clip. With his weapon still up where he could use the scope he slammed in another clip and continued to creep toward the area the fire had come from. When he reached the area, he found five of the estate guards had ended their career. At about the same time the thermo baric grenades from Marty and Gail began in quick succession to level the three long barracks buildings and light up the entire compound. Dave could see about twenty of the enemy being blown out the doors of the Barracks. He checked over his shoulder and saw one of his men, Warrant Officer Williams, pulling himself slowly toward the cover of the edge of the jungle. Dave ran out, grabbed him by the shirt collar with one hand and ran forward dragging him until they were under the cover of foliage.

"Thanks LC. They blew the hell out of my knee and I thought I was a goner out there."

Corporal Kowomoto spotted the incident from his vantage point, crept up, and began taking care of William's wound.

"Alpha, do you have any visual?" Dave said into his Com-Tac.

"I've got three just off the compound to the east. Looks like they're trying to regroup," Marty reported

"I'm watching four to the west," Gail said.

"Take them out," Dave commanded, and a volley of automatic weapons fire from the two XM-29s filled the area with an almost solid staccato.

"Baker, how are you doing over there?" All that returned was silence.

"Baker, Julio do you copy?" After another brief silence, Master Warrant Officer Kelly Jones, one of the men with Julio, came on.

"LC, the Captain's been hit, bad, and I took one in the arm. I think he's dead LC. I really think he's dead."

"Stay cool son. I'll be there right away." He glanced at his own wounded man.

"Are you okay? Can you hold the fort here if need be?"

"Yeah, I'm good as long as I don't have to move."

"Okay doc, you stick with William and help defend this flank.

Dave ducked around some wide leafed flora and staying under cover as much as possible, made his way over to Julio. He knelt beside his friend and slipped his hand under his head to see if he could do any preliminary first-aid. What he felt made his stomach want to empty itself. His fingers slid inside a gelatin which was Julio's brain tissue.

Dave didn't need to check any further to see if there was anything he could do for his best friend, as the dead man's eyes blankly stared toward the night sky. The bullet had entered above the left eye and fragmentized, taking away nearly half the back of his head. The night's darkness hid the tears in the Lt.

Colonel's eyes as he gave orders for the team to sweep the area and neutralize any combatants they found. When the sweep was completed, the enemy body count was forty-four plus three enemy guards under arrest.

Dave certainly wasn't feeling victorious. He'd lost a wife and now a close friend and loyal officer. How many more would have to die before this serpent was stopped?

He ordered his men to remove anything that even hinted at Intel and had the prisoners brought to the compound. The domestics from the basement were questioned but they knew very little. Dave spoke directly to them.

"Alright, I want all of you, except Andres, Jonathan, and those three to head for the nearest farm or town. If we see any of you around here in thirty minutes, my men will have orders to shoot to kill. Now get going." Andres translated the message and pointed toward the entrance driveway.

The people hurried down the driveway nervously watching the computerized weaponry.

As the darkness turned to grey of early morning Dave brought the team together. They had already set up a camp about fifty meters from the Villa where the prisoners were being held under armed guard.

"Corporal Shaw and Kowomotto, front and center." The two immediately ran to where Dave was.

"Yes sir!" They both exclaimed at almost the same time.

"I want you to get the explosives from Kelly and upon his instruction set the villa for complete demolition. I don't want one stone left standing on another." He waited a few seconds for impact as the two soldiers stood at attention in front of him. "Alright, get at it."

"Yes Sir!"

When all was ready, Dave called in the extraction chopper and then pulled his Com-Tac around.

"Leader to Alpha you two can stand down now and make your way to our camp just south west of the Villa.

Dave had just turned toward the Villa when Lt. Levine stepped into the clearing of the camp.

"I thought I told you to stay in position until I ordered you to stand down?" Dave yelled.

"I-I did sir."

"Then how the hell did you get here so fast Lt.?" Dave asked in a sarcastic growl.

"My shooting platform was only five meters from your camp." She pointed in the direction she had just come from.

Dave looked from Gail to the direction she had come from and back to Gail.

"You mean to tell me you were that close in all the time without being found out?"

"Yes Sir, Lt. Colonel Sir. Best scout, best team, best army and best CO in the world Sir."

"Okay Lt., grab some chow, we got a chopper coming in for extraction. Stay clear of the buildings though."

It was a tight squeeze to get the Cyclone on the helipad between the villa and the remnants of the barracks, but the pilots managed to land. Julio was loaded first. The larger weapons were stowed in the baggage compartment and finally the team escorted Jonathan, Arthur and the three guards aboard.

"Welcome aboard Colonel Hart. I'm Captain Fred Marsh and my co-pilot here is Lt. Simon Shavers. Please accept our condolences for the loss of your man. We're to shuttle you to the HMCS Regina which is off the west coast and they will return you to Victoria," the pilot said. Dave sized up the new helicopter and motioned toward it.

"Hey, I thought you weren't getting these birds until next year?"

"Test flight. How are we doing so far?" Lt. Marsh said with a wide grin.

"Certainly rates a pass as far as I'm concerned," Dave said.

Once airborne Dave ordered the aviator to swing around and get images with the digital camera under the fuselage. When the pilot had switched on the camera Dave flicked a switch on the little remote, a tiny red light flashed twice and the consecutive blasts leveled the entire villa. The camera captured the entire destruction of the buildings as at first it turned to a large dust cloud and then as the dust settled, light grey rubble appeared where the beautiful villa had once stood. Dave watched it for a minute and thought, *Okay Cottonmouth we're in it to the end now* and then patted the pilot on the shoulder.

"Take us home Captain." The Sikorski's nose dropped down again, turned and headed for the ship.

*   *   *

The afternoon was still quite warm by British Columbia's standards as Dave stood on forecastle deck of the frigate Regina and enjoyed the stiff warm sea breeze of the forward motion of the ship. As he gazed around he noted the vigorous flapping of the Canadian flag at half mast. Never had this tradition of the flag at half mast hit home to him more than now. Canada and the world had lost one of its great sons and thus the empty spot at the top of the pole.

He searched the coast peering slightly to his left trying to get the first sight of the harbor as the ship gently rounded Rocky Point on the southern tip of Vancouver Island. The grey warship was about two miles off shore cutting water at fifteen knots and soon Esquimalt, its home base, would end its journey.

The captain had given him a full history lesson about the Regina telling him how it was a second-generation frigate of the original Regina, a Corvette from World War II. The Halifax frigates, of which the new HMCS Regina was a member, were slightly smaller than the Iroquois class destroyers but when push came to shove these frigates had more than enough sting to win the day. The rational was that in any modern sea battle, teamwork by these ships would get the job done. Over coffee, the captain had told the story of his ship. When the skipper had finished Dave had a very healthy respect for the little warship that could. Normally Dave would jump at the chance to immerse himself in these tales but now they were only a diversion from his loss.

Esquimalt had just come into view and Dave was using it as yet another diversion when he noticed Gail standing by his side. She looked up at him for a long while.

"Should I scream man overboard or are you still with us?"

Dave frowned and looked away not wanting her to see his misty eyes.

"No-one should ever have to tell a young wife her husband has been shot and killed in the line of duty. And how the hell do you tell a little boy his daddy won't ever come home again?"

Gail couldn't reply as tears welled up in her own eyes.

Some whoops and whistles were sounding and then a message came over the speaker system ordering Kodiak team to report to the stern and the helipad.

Dave, Gail and the team arrived at the chopper and watched solemnly as Julio's coffin was being reloaded. The rotor blades where beginning to rotate. Dave saw the ship's Captain heading toward him.

"What's going on?" Dave asked.

"You're to report to your Abbotsford barracks for further orders. A Colonel Benton indicated her office had all aspects arranged and will meet you there."

"Thank you Captain, for everything," he said. He saluted the Captain, the flag, and then followed his team members into the helicopter.

The chopper landed close to the Kodiak's barracks and as promised Colonel Benton had a hearse waiting. The team carried the coffin with a Canadian flag draped over it to the grey Cadillac and held a salute until it was off the tarmac and out of sight. Joanne asked Dave if he and the team were up to a debriefing.

"Colonel., I'm not up to anything right now, debriefing or otherwise, and I think I speak for the whole team, but anything that gets us closer to neutralizing the Cottonmouth is our top priority," Dave said.

"Then have them in the meeting room in fifteen minutes and we'll get it over with. Then I want a private session with you to give me your version as to what the hell went wrong."

Joanne marched away before Dave could ask her what she meant by that. Was she accusing him of something? Gail sided over towards Dave.

"What's wrong with the Colonel?" Gail asked. "She really seems miffed."

Dave watched the Colonel enter the building and slam the door.

"Miffed? That's certainly an understatement. She doesn't like losing good soldiers, and neither do I." Not thinking, he walked away from Gail without another word.

After debriefing the team, Colonel Benton led Dave into a makeshift office and closed the door.

"Can you explain to me how a crack covert team like yours gets ambushed by lesser troops?" Joanne demanded in an accusing tone.

"May I remind you Colonel that we are dealing with the Cottonmouth and true to his name he is very capable, and so is his mercenary army." Dave spoke becoming a little upset with the seeming insinuations.

"So you're telling me this General has his troops out in the jungle all the time just in case of a night attack or did they just happen out for a stroll when you dropped in?"

" Colonel, I don't know whether the General left with knowledge of our mission or if it was just coincidence. As far as his troops go, I don't know if they were on some kind of ambush detail or if that was their regular picket duty. More than half of them were still in the barracks as you heard the team tell you. Colonel, what do you want me to say?" Dave asked with his voice raising and his face beginning to warm.

"Let me spell it out for you Lieutenant Colonel I am not questioning your patriotism or your honor but I am wondering, again, if you are not too close psychologically. I wonder to myself, does he have the objectivity he needs for these missions or is he blinded by an inner rage? Would you tell me that, Lt. Colonel? Should we turn you over to Dr. Spock?"

"You bet there's an inner rage and its worse now than ever but it's not handicapping me at all. Colonel we went in there perfect. Every move was executed perfectly. Had we not made exactly the right moves, none of us would have got out alive."

Colonel Benton looked hard at Dave.

"I'm putting a hold on operation Cottonmouth until we can find out how this fatality went down. The funeral is day after tomorrow, you're to give the eulogy, and I want you at the office tomorrow."

*   *   *

The ranch style house was only fifty meters from the base of a sheer rock cliff that rose almost twenty-five meters straight up. The front yard had a lawn and two large walnut trees, one at each corner. A shallow ditch ran along in front of the lawn and the road ran just beyond that. The driveway ran from the road past the house to the garage in the back yard.

Dave drove in the drive and stopped behind Julio and Karen's car. He glanced at the garage and remembered the many evenings Julio and he had spent sipping suds while fixing some engine or bike or just playing a game of chess. He knocked on the back door of the house and it swung open, but when Karen saw who it was, her face went hard.

"And just what do you want? Isn't it bad enough you took my man? Get away from here!" she screamed. "Get away from here and don't ever come back!"

"Karen, I'm really sorry. He was my best friend and---,"

She cut him off in mid sentence. "Get out of here! Best friends don't get their friends killed," she screamed. Then she burst out crying and ran to Dave and threw her arms around him. "Dave I'm sorry. I know you didn't get him killed but why did he have to die?" She was sobbing now.

Karen invited him in and they sat at the kitchen table and drank coffee. Dave talked and cried with her and by the time he had to leave, she had stopped sobbing.

"Karen if there's anything you need, just call," he said as he left.

The drive back across the Frazer River to Cultus Lake allowed Dave time to sort out the events as they had unfolded. As he followed the insurgency through to its completion, some red flags began to emerge.

The next morning Joanne asked Dave if he'd developed any possible causes for the blunder in Columbia.

"Yes, as a matter of fact, I don't know why it didn't become more obvious sooner, but I'm fairly sure we still have one or more moles and he or she will have to be weeded out before we can proceed."

Joanne smiled.

"I came to the same conclusion as well except I'm not so sure we can leave the Cottonmouth alone while we do a thorough internal investigation and cleaning."

Dave gave her a questioning look.

"You don't expect me to lead a squad against him again with the chance of him getting our plans just ahead of our mission?"

"Of course not, but leave it with me for a bit to see what I can come up with. I guess, unless you have something to add," she said, leaving an opening for him to jump in. "Right, then you're dismissed."

Dave left the office and was surprised to see Gail at her desk.

"I thought you were working for me now?" he said with a smile.

"Oh, ah, I just dropped in to gather my personal things. It was so rushed with the change of orders, I didn't have time to pick them up."

Dave offered her a ride home but she said she had an appointment and would use the transit.

*   *   *

Dave moved toward the podium and was overwhelmed by the crowd of a thousand plus people who had packed the church. He had to control his emotions very carefully; otherwise, he reasoned, his grief would spill out and it would become totally uncontrolled. At the podium, he glanced at Karen whose eyes were red and blank, then at Julio's parents who were both weeping. He thought to himself, "I hope I can do you proud old buddy." He almost broke down right then and there. He cleared his throat and as the crowd quieted, he began.

"To say Julio Rodriguez was my friend would be a gross understatement. He was my very best friend. Even in the Bible, Jesus said there is no truer friend than that he lay down his life for his friend. I would have certainly laid down my life for him and he did give his life for us. His wasn't a wasted life, for he gave it defending the freedoms and values he, and we, all cherish.

Julio was more than just a friend however. He was one of the finest officers I have ever had the honor to serve with. He carried out his duties with one hundred percent commitment and wouldn't accept anything less from himself or the soldiers under his command. Many times he covered our backs while putting his own life in danger. He was ever there for every member of the squad.

Finally, he was more than a good friend and a brilliant officer. He was a beloved husband and father. Many were the times when called to see if he would join the team for an evening of fun, Julio would opt out, so as to be with his wife and child. He was a wonderful man, a good friend, a fine officer and a great husband and father. We will all surely miss him."

Dave could say no more and as he stepped down from the podium, glancing at the people, he could not find a dry eye in the building. As the hearse backed into position at the cemetery, the long line of vehicles found places to park and the mourners walked to the ceremony. Karen made her way over to Dave and Gail. She stood all in black, as the tears ran down her cheeks, gazing into Dave's solemn face and then taking an extra step forward, hugged him.

"I'm sorry for what I said yesterday. I hope you'll forgive me for that and that we can always be friends." she said partly sobbing.

"Karen, if you miss him as much as I do and I know you do, then I'm sure you're ready to fight the whole world."

Karen stared into Dave's eyes.

"Will you promise me one thing Dave?" she said.

"Anything."

"Promise me you'll get the people who killed my Julio."

"You got my word on it."

Karen nodded and left to join the procession to the grave side. Dave felt his heart torn to pieces and then looked at Gail whose eyes were also glazed with tears.

"We'll get him for Karen, won't we Dave?" she stated more than asked.

"I suppose that means you're staying with the team?

"Colonel. Benton feels its best all around until you can train in more new people. I like being out there too because it makes me feel I'm doing my part. Come on Dave, its what I was trained for." He nodded.

All branches of the Service were represented as well as the RCMP, which indicated his ascription to them all. Three F-18's did a fly over and one peeled away representing a lost comrade. Shortly following that a squad of seven army officers fired in unison three times for the twenty-one gun salute. The navy did their parade and a group of six RCMP dressed in their scarlet tunics and Stetsons stood at attention evenly spaced around the casket. They were facing out as their emblem the buffalo does when in a defensive position, as Julio was slowly committed to the grave. After everyone had left Dave stood peering at the open grave and silently recommitted his promise to Karen.

Chapter 11

The cool water invigorated Dave as he leisurely backstroked five hundred meters from the north shore of the lake in the late August heat wave. He rolled over and did some dips and other frolicking maneuvers before popping his head above the surface. He had just turned back toward shore when he spotted a car that resembled Joanne's pull into the parking lot just beyond the beach. When she got out he recognized his CO and wondered what she was doing out here. He was quite sure whatever she was here for had to be important so he picked up the pace and within minutes was hauling himself up on the dock. Joanne had walked to the end of the dock and was waiting for him there.

"Is this what the taxpayers of this country pay you for?" she asked whimsically.

"A guy's got to stay in shape. What brings you out here?" He toweled himself off. "I'm sure it wasn't just to investigate misappropriation of tax dollars."

"I thought we might have a talk about Cottonmouth."

"Sure, why not. He's one of my favorite subjects." Dave said with conviction.

"We've unraveled some of the material you brought back from Columbia and it appears your theories on nine eleven are less speculative than we may have thought. We have several important people in Washington and the Pentagon implicated in the conspiracy with Beauregard Smith at the controls. There's also proof the CIA tucked him into a Florida desk carrying out Black Ops and from there he squirreled away companies and money to carry on after the Company realized he was too hot to handle and cut him loose. But no one is about to stand up and say he was one of ours." She looked at Dave who was enjoying this.

"We found, from his records, they actually did engineering studies on computer mock ups, as to what would happen by setting small nuclear charges right into the main footprints and other charges in the main uprights of the two towers as well as the third building. His engineers actually designed the charges to make it appear like the fires from jet fuel brought them down. Smith had some top engineers work the scenarios of how to bring those buildings down and when they were finished; well no-one has seen them since. It seems some of the very people he had used to plan parts of the event were in the towers when they went down." Joanne glanced at Dave whose facial expressions were saying, *just like I told you.*

"What I can't figure is what all the players hoped to gain. I mean Smith is whacked out over power apparently but the rest, what do they get out of it that's worth killing three thousand people?"

Dave was serious now.

"I suspect each had his own personal devil to deal with. Greed, power or even some twisted idea of patriotism and there was probably a lot of intimidation, blackmail, and bribery involved. Those are the kind of things that allow people like Smith to get their dirty work done. Don't forget what Eisenhower said about the arms manufacturers, that they should ever guard against letting them get their tentacles into government. I fear we're far past the point of no return for that problem.

Joanne smirked as Dave was prepared to carry on.

"I guess there's no dispute on your feeling about this subject, however I did want to discuss how we might proceed to bring this thing to a satisfactory conclusion. I have some ideas that don't exactly follow standard operating procedures and for that reason I felt we should discuss these plans to see if they could work."

Dave smiled and began to escort her off the pier.

"Okay Joanne, sounds like it's right down my ally. My place would probably be the best place for that kind of meeting. I can guarantee there are no bugs there."

Joanne stopped and turned to Dave.

"I'm generally tucked away in my office so I want you help me a bit with your field expertise. Do you know of a way we can plan this without some mole or bug getting all the information?" They shuffled toward Dave's cabin talking as they went. Once inside the house Dave offered Joanne a chair at the kitchen table and proceeded to the sink.

"First it really isn't so much expertise as you put it; it's just common sense. I'll brew us a pot of coffee and we can set some parameters." At his table he suggested they not discuss anything to do with the mission at the office and always have their meetings where there was plenty of noise interference such as traffic or load music. He also said he would come up with code names for meeting places so they and only they would know where their meetings would be.

Joanne eyed him incredulously.

"Wow, do you think maybe you're over dramatizing this just a hair? I never took you for being paranoid."

Dave's facial features became stone.

"If he could infiltrate our organization, which he has, and intercept a covert mission like the one he just did, I think it only prudent that we go completely covert. Only you and I can know about the future plans until we're ready to spring on him. My life and the lives of my people depend upon it."

"Alright then, that's the way it will be. Oh, one last thing I wanted to tell you is about the list of new people you requested. I was able to transfer six of them into your command and they've begun training as per your specifications. You know Dave sometimes I feel like I'm a Corporal and you're the C.O."

"It'll never happen. You're much too good at being the boss and I just do what I do."

They continued the conversation while finishing the rest of the coffee and then Joanne had to leave. She gave Dave a smile as she got into her car and hit the down button for the driver's side window. Dave leaned down toward the window.

"There's one more thing Joanne. I've been having a visitor the last few nights. By the professionalism the person displayed I'm thinking it's the General's hit man."

"Then I'll put some people on a detail out here to watch you or we can move you again."

"Negative. I'll take care of it myself this time. Just keep it quiet until I call and then send in the troops."

Joanne nodded, hit the up button for the window, and drove away.

*   *   *

The night was hot and the humidity made it feel worse. The August full moon wasn't exactly what Phillip would have put on her wish list but she would just have to blend as transparently as she could with the shadows. After all that was her claim to fame and besides didn't she have her ace in the hole set aside for insurance? The professional killer had taken black tactical apparel which she had bleached in dark grey vertical waves and added a hood of like colors. If she didn't move she blended so well with the birch trees and other plants surroundings it was almost impossible to see her. She watched the Lt. Colonel's house grow dark and she knew it would soon be time to move in. She crept to a back window where she had been surprised earlier to discover that it was not only wide open, but had no anti-theft bars or sensors. Normally this would have sent warning bells ringing, but due to the heat Phillip allowed her quarry was trying to stay cool.

Making absolutely no sound, she slipped over the window sill and entered the house, sliding onto the floor much as a snake would do. Quietly, on her hands and knees, she crawled across the room and had just silently cracked the door open a little further, when the light came on. She twisted around and her eyes quickly ran up the six foot four frame of her quarry. Dave leaned against the wall with his Glock 9mm aimed at her.

"Well, well, what have we here? I suppose you are aware that break and enter is illegal," Dave said.

Phillip stood up now to her full five foot six and pulled off the hood of the cat burglar apparel. Dave now had a shocked expression. Phillip had seen the same expression many times just before she had killed her victim.

Dave had an aching thought in the back of his mind. *This has been way to easy*, he thought. *A pro doesn't cave this easy.*

"So can I ask what you're doing sneaking through my home?"

"Certainly, I was here to whack you," she said and then moved so fast Dave barely had time to move.

She swung her foot up and around catching Dave's gun hand knocking the weapon across the room and then in a continuous circle moving like a bolt of lightning caught him the second time with the other foot on the side of the head. She twisted and turned hitting him repeatedly with lighter blows, but with enough force to disorient him. Dave was only able to partially deflect the blows and he knew if he didn't find an opening soon this little lady would kill him.

With the same thought running through his mind he saw her move toward the killing maneuver where she would deliver a one - two blow knuckle slam to the temple and then the carotid artery in the neck. One or the other or both would guarantee his demise. Dave moved his head a second before her first fist reached its target and as he moved sideways he also moved ahead locking her arm in his and twisting it up and over. With her forward movement and his opposite action her arm broke with a loud cracking sound. Phillip gave a loud shriek from the pain. Dave continued on behind her with a swift motion to wrap his arm around her neck and kick her legs out from under her. She went down hard and lay on the floor. Dave twisted around and sat down; his second sidearm was now in his hand pointed at her.

"So now that we've had our little tussle I suppose I need to call the police. Before I do, just for the record, who hired you?"

She was trying hard to eat the pain as she held her arm, which hung at a strange angle. Dave checked her for a weapon but found none.

"Hey, just for the record," she nodded to her arm, "Go screw yourself."

Dave's face tightened.

"I'm going to ask you nicely one more time and if I don't get my answer it'll be the M.E. instead of the MPs."

"You won't do that." She forced a smile. "That is, if you want to see your girl friend again."

Dave was taken by surprise but he tried not to let it show.

"I don't even have a girlfriend."

"Oh? How about five foot eight, blue eyes, blonde hair, Lt., Canadian military, as of now missing? And if anything happens to me, she'll stay missing." She produced a winner's grin.

Dave didn't believe either of them were supposed to get out alive so he decided to run his own bluff. He somewhat feigned exasperation and cocked the hammer of the weapon.

"I'm getting sick and tired of this crap with you scumbags going around killing my friends, so unless you cough up some information like who hired you and where the Lt. is, you will be dead when the MPs get here."

Phillip glanced at Dave and he made a gesture as if to say 'your last chance.'

"Okay, okay, a guy using the name 'The General' hired me. That's the only name I know him by. He's already paid three million for your early departure."

"And?"

"And your 'Lt.' is in an old abandoned ferry across the river from Fort Langley near the McMillan Island Albion ferry dock. She's downstairs in a state room."

Dave replaced the hammer slowly.

"That's better, now let's get that arm taken care of and then we can go find this ferry."

"Wait a minute! What about the MPs?"

Dave motioned with his weapon for her to move out to the kitchen.

"I'll have to do; I'm their boss," he said.

He was rummaging through a large first-aid kit looking for a triangular bandage when he caught a movement from the corner of his eye. Dave drew his gun and swung toward Phillip just in time to see her lifting a small derringer toward him. He fired off six shots and left a row of red dots from her heart to her forehead. Her eyes portrayed surprise and as her knees buckled, blood pulsed out of the wounds in the chest and the neck while around the center of her forehead a nine millimeter red dot also grew larger. She collapsed face first into the floor.

Dave wondered where she had been able to hide that weapon. He gave a sigh of disgust and thought why couldn't she have just cut her losses and stayed alive. His next thought was for Gail. Was she alive? He reasoned she might be. Then it hit him, Phillip was using her as a final trap. She had no intentions of going to the ferry. She had figured she would be arrested and Dave would go there. And, that meant the old ship was probably booby-trapped.

Dave called Joanne and informed her of the shooting and his suspicion of the booby-trapped ship. He asked her to get a hold of Marty, tell him what was happening and bring the new high tech sensing equipment. They would put it to good use finding the location of the explosives. He told her he would also need the fire department, the RCMP and their tug boat and the closest bomb disposal unit, and to have them meet him near Fort Langley at the north branch of the Fraser River on McMillan Island at the ferry dock. Dave headed for Fort Langley.

Edging the limit for the Cadillac, Dave managed to get to the ferry dock in forty minutes. Two fire trucks were already there and the firefighters were wandering around, giving the impression that they were about to pack it up and return to the hall. Dave pulled into a small lot just as the bomb disposal unit from Langley arrived. Dave hurried over to the dock and checked the upriver shore. It was four in the morning and still quite dark so it took some time for his eyes to adjust. He gazed up river but there was nothing but water, sandy banks, and trees slightly back from the shoreline. He searched downstream and after his eyes adjusted a bit more he could see a faint outline of an old ferry.

The small ship had run the McMillan-Albion crossing until maintenance outstripped its usefulness and a new ship was brought into service. When she was retired they run her a ground and had her winched up onto the sand bank where everything of value was removed. Dave estimated the old ship to be about five hundred meters from the roadway.

Marty's car came screaming into the parking lot and Dave ran over to fill him in and ensure he brought the high tech equipment. After talking to Marty, Dave called the police, fire crew and the Bomb disposal personnel to an impromptu meeting.

"Okay people, listen up. My Name is Lt. Colonel David Hart and this is Lt. Martin Musselman. We are attached to the military and we have an old derelict ferry grounded on shore about five hundred meters down river. We've been led to understand it has been professionally rigged with explosives and booby trapped. We believe a Lt. Gail Levine from my unit is confined in the ferry below deck in a stateroom. My colleague and I will work with the bomb disposal people and our equipment to find, if possible, the trip mechanisms and a solution for entry. Once we have neutralized them, we will do what is necessary to remove the young lady and then the bomb disposal people will remove the explosives. Are there any questions? Alright, let's get the area secured and, people, no one enters that ship without my approval and by all means keep your wits about you."

The bomb squad, Marty, and Dave worked until midmorning plotting wires on a blueprint of the ferry. These were ferreted from x-rays and infrared photos the bomb squad had taken from a distance. Dave was growing frustrated.

"All these wires, pressure switches, motion sensors, temperature sensing devises, electrical interference switches, and they all have multiple slaves. Here it is ten o'clock and we haven't even been able to board the ship yet."

Dave was in the forty foot, fifth wheel trailer that was designed as a mobile emergency command center. Along one wall was a bank of telephones with satellite computers which could tie into almost any emergency network in the world. Many of the stations were vacant today for lack of necessity but at one station Marty had plotted the many packs of dynamite using their special equipment. All told he suggested there was more than enough C-4 to morph the ship into tooth-picks.

"Hey Colonel over here," yelled a member of the bomb squad.

Dave stepped over to his station and watched the screen as the man moved an x-ray camera with the computer mouse that in turn produced a skeletal picture of the old ship.

"This equipment of yours helped us find the switch used to turn on the device," the squad member said.

"That's something anyway; how many slaves on that one?" Dave asked.

"Appears to be six, Sir. One more thing, all this wiring feeds into a mainframe that has been wired to run the show. Before you ask, it has several fail-safes and it looks like about three hard drives working in tandem. The way this is designed it looks like even if we could get one or two drives shut down the third would still send the required voltage to the igniters and set off the caps, which I guess is immaterial because even if all of them shut down the slaves would simply close the circuit to the igniters anyways."

Dave was studying the schematics of the wires, sensors and C-4 and where they had been penciled in to the approximate location on the blueprint. He turned to Marty.

"This has me baffled; getting into the motherboard and shorting it out won't work on this one. It would only burn out the boards and the circuits would automatically close and set off the whole damn---"

The bomb squad captain cut him off.

"What if we just cut a large shaft straight down through the deck and on through the ceiling of the cabin the lady's in? We could use a crane to suspend the workers and then once the hole is cut, we use the same crane to lower rescue personnel down and bring her up. We wouldn't have to set foot on the decks."

Dave snapped a glance at Marty with an incredulous smile, and began looking over the blueprints.

"It sounds so simple, but you know I think that's the key to our problem." He turned around to face the other computer stations.

"Listen up people, I want you to double check the locations of all the motion, heat, and pressure sensors with particular attention to any inside the cabin and especially ensure that the lady's not sitting on one. If our bomber was only thinking of someone setting her masterpiece off by entering the ship by way of the hallways we just might be able to use this shaft idea. Let's check this out as thoroughly and as quickly as possible."

Dave scanned the schematics again and sat down at one of the communication stations. He requested two large cranes and also ordered four welders with cutting and welding equipment from the Base. Dave checked with Marty and found the perimeter was cordoned off with guards about every fifty meters. As Dave re-entered the trailer one of the radiology technicians informed him that all the x-rays and infrared pictures showed that although there was plenty of C-4 in the room with Gail, all the sensors were in the corridors leading to the stateroom, and the area above the stateroom was absolutely clear.

Dave checked the schematics and found there weren't any electrical wires from the deck straight down to Gail so he decided on a three meters square vertical shaft opening straight down into the cabin exactly over Gail. When the opening had been cleared down to the ceiling, he would be lowered in, cut out the last square and bring her out.

The cranes and the welders didn't arrive until three and when the cranes arrived, they realized they would need large Caterpillar tractors to help drag the large heavy equipment into location on the soft sand. By the time two D-8H Cats arrived, it was after supper and beginning to get dark. The fire department had ordered lighting to flood the area so that the work of positioning the equipment could continue until it was in place just after midnight. The welding trucks were pulled into position between the cranes and the ship and the dangerous part of the rescue was about to begin.

Two welders from CFB Chilliwack strapped into harnesses to be hoisted over the deck. The first job was to weld large eyes or hooks onto the area of steel deck they would cut out. The cable block from the second crane would be fastened to these eyes; thus when the two meter square of two inch thick steel was cut through, the second crane would carefully move it away. After the steel was removed, the wood underneath had to be cut by firefighters with extrication equipment and removed in similar fashion.

The people worked carefully but feverishly throughout the night and as the cool dark night transposed into a second grey dawn, they were ready to remove the ceiling square in the stateroom. Dave donned the harness and the crane moved him over the hole and began inching him down into the belly of the ship. Once suspended in position and with the panel to be removed secured, Dave carefully used a small angle grinder to cut the remaining square of ceiling tile.

As soon as it was loose, he took a deep breath and signaled the second crane to lift it out. Peering down he saw Gail, tied and gagged and a little dusty from the work above her, but very much alive. This was it. If there were any sensors in the room that they had missed he would soon be tuning up his own harp. He signaled to be let down until he hovered just above Gail. He carefully checked to ensure (as much as possible) that she was not booby-trapped, then took the gag off and cut the restraints off her hands and feet. As he still hovered above her he helped get her into a harness, fastened it to the cable, and gave the cord a double jerk as a signal for the crane to lift them both out.

Gail had tears of relief and was still clinging to Dave as the crane operator swung them away from the ship where the tired rescue personnel clapped and cheered. Colonel Benton who had been watching the entire operation since early morning joined in to congratulate Gail.

Gail was transferred to the Langley Memorial by ambulance where she was diagnosed with a slight concussion, some scratches and bruises, but otherwise given a clean bill of health, and released. Both Dave and Joanne were waiting for her as she slowly made her way down the hall. Joanne was the first to speak.

"I want you to escort her to some relaxing, quiet, faraway place and care for her for a week. Remember she was transferred to you as an Aid. You both need a quiet week before we jump into the Cottonmouth thing again. All I ask is that you let me know where you are. You know, like we planned." She winked at him and left.

"What was that all about?" Gail asked as they moved toward Dave's car.

Dave had to think fast.

"Oh, that? The Colonel's trying to be funny. I'll explain it to you someday. So you heard the boss, we have to take a week somewhere quiet, to un-ruffle our feathers and give you time to heal."

"I don't know of any nice quiet place. They all have people swarming everywhere."

Dave opened the door to the car and helped Gail in then moved around and slid in behind the wheel.

"I think I know just the place," he said with a grin. "It's a small island between the main land and the north tip of Vancouver Island. There's a cabin on it and I know I can rent it for a week. What do you say?" Dave was now heading for Surrey.

"Sounds exactly what the Colonel ordered."

"It is and it just happens to belong to the Bentons as well. That's what Joanne was winking about, but because it's John and Joanne's cabin don't expect luxury. I think they must've built it in the back to the earth movement days. It's totally Spartan but it has two bedrooms, a living room, and kitchen."

Dave had arranged everything with Joanne while waiting for Gail at the hospital so when the couple arrived on the island the next day using the Benton's pleasure craft, Joanne had had the small cottage stocked with all the necessary provisions. They settled in and before lunch they struck out on a hike. The plan was to circumnavigate the island by way of the beaches and get to know the place. They started down the beach but the two hundred and fifty meters of sandy beach in front of the cottage on the east side of the island was the only easy access to the water available; the rest of the shoreline rose to sheer vertical cliffs straight above the sea.

Happily they searched out a path and began to climb into the more interior part of the island. Dave watched Gail as she climbed through the rugged rocks to finally reach a grassy plateau. Without realizing it, they had already worked nearly half way around the island and Dave, who had carried the backpack with their picnic lunch, called out to Gail to set up a picnic site a short ways back from the fifty meter cliff. It was a grassy area in a cozy spot under a giant Douglas fir tree. Dave searched the area for ants and was glad the little varmints hadn't chosen this place to set up shop. Gail spread the blanket on the ground while she hummed an old song of the same name.

They both sat down on the blanket and as Dave started pulling sandwiches out of the pack, Gail set a mug in front of him, took one herself, and poured a creamy colored liquid from the thermos into each of them. Dave eyed the beverage and motioned toward it.

"What's that anyway? You wouldn't be trying to drug me, would you?"

"Try it. I really think you'll like it."

"It looks like Buckley cough syrup."

Gail made a face.

"T r y I t!"

Dave pretended he was nervous but following orders as if under duress. After a small sip his eyebrows went up.

"Hey this is good. It tastes like Pina Colada."

Gail chuckled.

"Good guess. That's what it is. Well it's Virgin Pina Colada. There's no alcohol in it."

They sat together on the blanket and gazed in awe at the ocean and the rugged coastal mountains of mainland British Columbia. After the snack was done Dave swung around and laid his head in Gail's lap as the sun warmed the air and a mild sea breeze gently moved the upper most branches of the tree. He caught her gaze and held it until he was sure she could hear his heart pounding. After long minutes he raised his head ever so slightly and Gail moved hers down and their lips met. As they embraced they eventually moved to where they were lying side by side and broke off. Gail sat up first, not as an end, but rather to get air. Dave followed her lead and panned the ocean view again.

"You know what this reminds me of?" Dave asked.

"No, what?" she asked quizzically.

"When I was about ten my uncle and his friend took me on a fishing trip, on Harrison Lake; it looked a lot like this. His friend had a fourteen foot run-a-about with an out board and we headed up the lake to test it out. We were doing more sightseeing than testing and never even got our hooks wet. After stopping in many inlets to explore as we proceeded further and further up the long lake, it should have come as no surprise when the motor quit. We had run out of gas.

We were a considerable distance from where we had started, but my uncle motioned south suggesting it was only around a rocky point we could see across a small inlet. He said we could hike back to the dock in half a day and come back for his friend and the boat. He figured we would get back there before suppertime. After hiking all day on the rugged rocky shoreline, my cheap city deck shoes had fallen apart and we wound up on a cliff just like this, with the sun going down. As we looked out over the water, we spotted a ferry; I'd guess it was more than five kilometers out.

My uncle suggested if we were to put my white tee-shirt on a pole and wave it, someone on the ferry might see the white flag and send help. We proceeded to carry out his plan, but as we waved the long pole over the edge of the cliff a gust of wind caught the fabric, undid it from the pole and my tee-shirt went sailing out over the water, landing at least a kilometer out on the lake, leaving me without a shirt, shoes and getting chilled. No one knows if anyone saw the flag, but no one sent help."

"What did you do?"

"I got very cold and was thankful for my aunt who called the police and reported us missing. The RCMP spotted us from their search plane later that evening and sent a search and rescue tug from New Westminster to get us. It took that tug well over an hour (at fifteen knots crossing the water in a straight line) to get us back to the dock, so hiking around the rugged shoreline probably would have taken a week."

Gail snickered.

"Bet that was the last time you ever went fishing with him."

Dave looked up at Gail with his eyebrows lifted in shocked surprise.

"Are you kidding? That was one of the most exciting days of my young life. A few weeks later we were up country trying to find colour in a creek bed. Never found any, but we didn't get lost either."

He looked into her eyes and as that same old wave of emotion washed over him he pressed his lips to hers and kissed her long and deep. Gail seemed to melt into his arms as they continued in a tender embrace.

*   *   *

On the third day, Joanne stopped in. She was actually wearing beachwear and Dave had to stare for a bit as he had never seen his CO in anything but uniform or fashionable business suits. After asking Gail if she might borrow Dave to have a word alone with him, Joanne asked Dave if he had seen the view from the highest peak on the island and they left for the lookout. Gail was happy to grab some time for tanning on the beach. After they were out of earshot of Gail, the Colonel became very somber.

"We have more Intel on our favorite General. It seems he's doing a lot of moving around. He's been to his place in Argentina and then went to Korea. Our last Intel had him in Middle East. We know he's preparing for something but we're not sure what. Have you come up with a solution of how to stop him from setting up a repeat of the last fiasco?" Joanne asked.

Dave stopped and turned to her.

"As a matter of fact I have," he said and then began walking again.

"If we are going to nail this guy we are going to need some real time Intel on the ground. Intel as to exactly where he is and what kind of security we're up against. We can use our Israeli friends but only to a point. Seems when they get into something it evolves into a disaster. I can check with my contact and get inside info but that won't be enough.

We need our people on the ground watching the action and reporting directly to us. I would say we need three teams of two JTF-2 recons to be inserted at the different locations where we might expect Cottonmouth to show up. At present those three areas would be Syria, the Myanmar island villa and Argentina. These teams would send information and I would adjust my plans accordingly. Then at a point of which we alone would decide, my team would storm whichever of his headquarters he is at. The JTF recon team in the specific area would join us in the raid."

Joanne looked out over the ocean.

"You've really been giving this some thought haven't you?"

"I've never stopped thinking about it. It's either that or memories of Mexico."

"Will you require any extra recruits?

"If we can get those six new recruits up to speed in time that will be enough. I'll also need transport to location but if it's the Myanmar Island, an air insertion is a no-go. In my research I noticed some of the sat photos showed a high concentration of skywards security on the island. So if it's to be the island it would have to be a sea landing which may not give us a great advantage. Cottonmouth is expecting an aerial insertion so there would be an element of surprise to give us some edge though." Dave stopped, implying that's all he had.

"Okay Lt. Colonel, I'll see what I can do. Now, how are you and Gail getting along?" she asked as they started back for the cottage.

"Oh, it's been nothing but fighting and bickering since the day we arrived."

Joanne shot a glare at Dave and then realized he was teasing and smiled.

Dave saw Joanne off and was comfortably sprawled in a reclining beach chair watching Gail frolic in the water, when suddenly her head disappeared beneath the surface. When she came up she appeared to be in a panic.

"H-Help," she managed before she went under for the second time.

Dave sprinted into the water making a spray with his feet and legs. As he reached the area where he'd seen her go under, he frantically searched for a sign of where she was. Suddenly she burst up from directly under him throwing him off balance. As they both broke the surface they were gasping with laughter while the adrenaline high subsided.

"Sure is taking more and more to get you to come to me," she said with laughter.

Dave's laughter turned to a grin and then he put both hand up in the air and pretended to growl as he imitated a wolf man staggering toward her. Gail squealed with the pretention of being frightened while she tried to get away, but Dave thrashed through the water and got hold of her. They happily wrestled and splashed around in the water until both had used up their excess energy. They relaxed, tanned, made love, and all too soon their time in the sun was over and they had to leave their island paradise.

*   *   *

Dave called Marty and Gail to his makeshift office at the training base. Both officers stood at attention until Dave had given them their ease.

"I recommended you both for promotion and I'm happy to say it has been approved." He shook hands with Marty and then turning to Gail he shook her hand. "Congratulation Captains. You've both done an admirable job with those new recruits but now I'm giving you the task of polishing them to perfection within the next few days." Dave passed them their new patches. Captain Musselman caught Dave with a side glance.

"Is that how long we have before we move against Smith, Sir?" Marty asked.

"I strongly suggest, sir, you refrain from questioning on any reference to any mission. I simply want those men trained the best they can be in the time specified. Am I making myself fairly clear Captain?"

"Yes Sir!" both Captains shouted in unison.

"Alright then you're both dismissed."

Chapter 12

Beauregard peered through the heavily tinted windows of the cream colored Mercedes Van as it and three others sped from Damascus towards a rendezvous in the Bekka Valley. The landscape seemed to become slightly greener as they travelled north- west in the mountainous terrain, although it remained almost as hostile. As the vehicles turned onto yet another smaller road, even less travelled, the General was becoming impatient to see his underground lair. This was where his state of the art weaponry was being assembled and would be the pivotal point of his world domination plan. He focused on the matter of the meddlesome Canuck, which irritated him to the point of raising his blood pressure thirty points. Soon, he thought, at least one headache will be taken care of. Still it excited him conjuring up gruesome methods the female assassin might complete her task.

As the vehicles rolled to a stop in a single line, General Smith scanned the sheer rock cliff directly in front of the vehicles. Although he knew better, the vehicles facing the wall of stone gave the perception that the drivers had made a wrong turn and now were in a single line with nowhere to go but crash into the solid rock of the mountain. Suddenly two large areas which were camouflaged to exactly match the rock cliff began to move to each side creating an opening large enough for two tractor- trailer units to pass easily. The vehicles moved slowly and uniformly into a large cavernous parking area and the big doors slid closed returning the perfect camouflage of the mountain cliff. As the entourage exited their vehicles several men from the facility hurried over to greet the honored guest and owner. With an outstretched hand one of the men directed the way to the laboratories and workshops.

As Beauregard toured through the labyrinth of large tunnels and caves with the other men, he pictured the Kings of Babylon, Assyria or Persia using these very caverns to hide their armies until the time was right and then ride out, pouring down on their unsuspecting enemies, killing and plundering them. Of course, the caverns looked different now.

He scanned the large belly of a subterranean room from the catwalk that was built out from the rock wall twenty feet above the working area. From his vantage point, he inspected the high tech centrifuges to his left with all sorts of machinery and computer driven devices. Then, straight ahead, was a large lab with glass tubes from hundreds of small containers swirling all around and bubbling up into larger flasks. This was the area that would create the chemical ingredients of the mini blue lightning fission bomb which only weighed ten pounds, but in theory would level five square kilometers of any city.

To his right and just into another almost detached cave further towards the center of the mountain, was a modern sheet metal fabrication shop. These were not just tin bashers as the trade calls them, but highly skilled technicians, artists in their own right, who were very carefully constructing precision aluminum briefcases. Their work was meticulous with the dimensions measured in microns.

The General moved down to the shop floor and to the metal shop. He talked to the sheet metal workers and heard that the bomb that would be inserted into these cases would fit perfectly at twenty-one degrees centigrade. Ten degrees higher would cause the indentation to expand to be too large allowing, the possibility of movement of the bomb and pre-detonation. Ten degrees cooler would allow the case material to contract and the bomb would not fit into its sleeve. The completed aluminum case was insulated on the inside and wrapped with insulated leather covering on the outer shell. It would be identical to the briefcases many of the diplomats of different countries carried and, with the device inside, only marginally heavier.

Smith looked over the first finished case and set it beside a regular attaché case. The aluminum case manufactured here was slightly larger but not so much as to be noticeable. The General felt victory in his grasp and to him it seemed a small axiom that tens of thousands, probably even millions would die.

He finished the tour and continued even deeper into the catacomb of caves to the boardroom, where his deputies and associates were awaiting his arrival. All the others were seated and General Smith nodded to them as he took his chair at the head of the table. An envelope addressed to him sat before him on the table. He tore it open and began to read.

General Smith,

It is my unhappy duty to inform you of the demise of my client who met her death before she could fulfill her contractual duty to you. Please take heart that she was shot while in conveyance of that duty by a Lt. Colonel David Hart. It is also in the contractual agreement that in the event of the premature death of my client working in the completion of that contract that you are to forfeit an extra two million dollars.   As her legal executor, I request immediately monies owed to her estate in the sum of three million dollars. Thank you in advance for your attention to this matter.

George Culvert, Attorney at Law.

With each sentence, Beauregard's breathing became more rapid and labored. Finally Smith screamed obscenities and crashed water jugs, glasses, papers and lap-tops to the floor. In the next breath, he grabbed the man next to him and proceeded to choke the life out of him. Three men from around the table drew their sidearm and would have shot him but one of his own bodyguards grabbed a bottle of Champagne and re-enacted the launching of a large ship by christening him across his head. General Smith stared in shock at his own guard, let the man go, and fell to the floor with the victim collapsing on top of him.

Quickly the General was moved into an anteroom where a medic applied six stitches to the head wound, dressed it and gave the General an injection of antibiotics and something for the enormous headache he would surely have. A short time later, reeking of Champagne, he regained consciousness and glared at the guard who had hit him with the bottle. The hatred emanating from his eyes spoke to the guard in a way that words could not. The guard didn't know when or how but he knew he would soon be dead.

Beauregard returned to the meeting room and immediately became aware that he now had two armed guards with machine pistols, one on either side of his chair, to ensure there would be no further attempted homicides. The General looked around and then reasoning that he had lost his temper which would diminish his persuasion in negotiations, gave an Oscar winning performance of a truly penitent man.

"Gentleman, I truly apologize for that unfortunate outburst. In way of explanation, let me relate to you the cause of my fury."

He was not at all sure he could get through this without his temper getting away from him again.

"The letter I was reading was from my lawyer who has informed me that one of my true and trusted comrades has been killed by the infidel. I am feeling such grief. I am sorry and hope you can forgive me for my outburst."

He did not find it easy to apologize, but all the conspirators seemed to accept his duress and the rest of the meeting went well with almost everyone in attendance pledging their total support to the General's Middle East plan of conquest. Some felt he was going too far too fast and some wanted to forge ahead even faster but in the end they simply said glory be to Allah, pledged their support, and allowed the General to choose the pace and extent of the attack. That is except for the attaché from Syria whom he had choked. He would never agree with the General again and thus he would join the champagne bottle swinger to meet their Allah a little sooner than they had anticipated.

After the meeting, General Smith was lavished with praise for his exceptional plan to rid the world of the infidels, both big Satan and little Satan, America and Israel. The tour, meeting, and celebration were a success and the General could leave with the knowledge his plan was forging ahead as planned.

The other delegates said their goodbyes and then he was ushered to the vehicles to be driven back to Damascus where a private jet whisked him away into the desert sky and once again he would disappear into the crowds of some city, and be lost to the world.

Except, he thought, for that crazy Canuck that seemed to be part Bloodhound, part Mongoose, and part Captain America, and he wasn't even American. *Where were guys like that when we needed them?* He mused. *There were some back in the horse and buggy days.* He grinned to himself. *That is, before crooks*

like me took over. No matter, even this Canuck
cowboy can't catch me in time to stop these fireworks.

   *   *   *   *

   Dave was rehashing the information that had been gathered from their raids. Something just wasn't adding up. He couldn't put his finger on it but if Smith had so much to do with 9/11 as the evidence indicated and the CIA, NSA, and God knows who else knew of him, then how come they didn't have agents on him. He was still working on it when he received a message from Colonel Benton.

   The message, 'Meet me at G-2 for coffee. Sixteen hundred hours,' came up on his computer screen.

   Dave knew from a pre-arranged list that that meant the coffee shop on Carrel Street in Gastown. He glanced at his watch, deleted the memo, shut down his computer and headed for the rendezvous. He found Joanne in the small cafe and with a coffee and Danish, sat down at the small round table and waited while Joanne picked her words carefully.

   "We have Intel that Cottonmouth is headed for Dubai. He'll be flying there within the next few hours, but it looks like he might not stay there too long either. The same source says his yacht, The

Encounter, is at port there and has been preparing to set sail."

"Dubai?"

"That's the word we got. Apparently the JTF-2 men in Damascus witnessed his departure on an executive jet to several different cities but the end of the flight will be UAI. They also reported he had a dressing on the back of his head. He must have been in a fight or had an accident."

Dave gazed around the small coffee shop.

"The question is where is he headed? Is it his island fortress or somewhere else?"

Joanne found his eyes and held the stare.

"If he is headed for his 'Island Fortress' are you ready to go?"

"Just give us the word, we've been training hard for the last week and even the new members are honed to a razor's edge. Captain Levine and Musselman have done an exceptional job."

Joanne reached over and put her hand on Dave's forearm.

"I suspected she might fit into the team and there really is no safe place for her, at least not until Cottonmouth is stopped. Furthermore, I sure in hell wouldn't want to be the one who told her she's off the line, would you?" she asked.

"You know, I hate it when you're so damn right." Dave took a sip of the brew, a bite of his Danish and frowned. "But yeah, she probably is safer with the team than if she's sitting it out alone; and the team seems to be safer with her there." He gave a slight snicker. "God knows she's the best '*man*' I got."

"Good. I'm relieved to hear that from you. It means she's as good as her paperwork says she is," she said. "Okay, I might as well let the other shoe fall. For what it's worth, I happen to believe the Cottonmouth is heading for his island so I've decided to deploy Kodiak immediately. I've already sent out requisitions and found the HMSC Victoria in the South Pacific. She will arrive in Perth, Australia day after tomorrow.

It will have a turnaround time of seventy-two hours so you'll have plenty of time to get down there. Luckily, they were doing maneuvers in the south Pacific and were due for a dockside. I requisitioned it for you and your team to be transported to the Indian Ocean so the navy reassigned the ship and will keep it on standby until you get there. Also, it just so happens that the Victoria has been testing a new highly secretive weapon which just might be useful for your mission.

So when you and your team report aboard the Victoria, Kodiak will need to train on this new piece of equipment. They call it a Submerged Rapid Transport Vehicle or SRTV for short. Apparently this device travels at up to one hundred and eighty to two hundred kilometers per hour while submerged and with two of them they could get your whole team into shore in one trip and double quick. You'll train while on route to the deployment area."

Dave frowned.

"So when do we leave?"

"I have already cut your orders and you have air priority out of Comox for early tomorrow morning. The sooner you're on your way the less chance of a security breach and if Cottonmouth does head where I suspect he's going, we'll have the jump on him."

At that Dave told Joanne his questions about why the American Intelligent community didn't seem to be on Cottonmouth. He told her it had been a concern of his for some time. They discussed it for some time and after passing ideas back and forth they came to the consensus that the Southern Spooks especially the CIA would get a black eye if they got involved seeking him out and something went wrong, so distance between him and them was the plan. That way if Smith did something they could say they had no knowledge of what he was up to.

*   *   *   *

Dave traveled to the Abbotsford base, made all the last minute preparations for their deployment and gave the team half an hour to be ready to move out. The larger Kodiak team was lined up on the tarmac when their Aurora taxied up for loading. All their special equipment was loaded into the cargo hold and the members boarded. Dave slipped into the cockpit handed the pilot his flight plan orders in hard copy and then gave them verbally as he crouched between the pilot and Copilot.

"Captain, I'm Lt. Colonel Hart."

"Captain Johnson here and my co-pilot there is Lt. Crems." Dave shook their hands.

"I want you to fly at a heading of zero one zero degrees for forty five minutes at an altitude of eighteen thousand feet at two hundred and fifty knots. At the end of that line, bring us around to two zero five degrees and fly on that heading for approximately forty minutes at the same speed and altitude. Is that understood, Captain?"

The Captain gave Dave a side glance as he spooled up the engines.

"Sir, if you don't mind me asking why the hell fly all the way to Prince George just to turn and head for Comox?"

"As a matter of fact, I do mind you asking. This mission is on a need to know basis, Captain. Just fly the flight plan. I guess it shows you're awake though," Dave said smiling.

Dave moved back into the passenger area and then on to the back of the plane that was configured into an office. He closed the door and sat down at a desk with a computer monitor on it. Marty and Gail were seated across from him with identical monitors.

"So LC, are you going to let us in on the mission?" Marty asked.

"We fly to Comox via Prince George, just in case anyone is paying attention. Hopefully it might throw them off. We lay over at Comox base and leave for Australia at zero five hundred." At this all ears were tuned in. "We will board the HMCS Victoria in Perth, Australia and head to our deployment area some twenty kilometers off an island in the Indian Ocean. You and I will have some special training on route to the deployment area."

"You said the Victoria? That's a submarine," Marty queried.

"Give the man a cigar. So what?" Dave asked.

"Oh, nothing. It's just that submarines and I don't get along too well," Marty said with his head down.

"Yeah, I read your file, but take heart, you should be okay. The Captain has asked that we stay in our quarters as much as possible, other than our training, until we deploy and the ship will be traveling under the surface for stealth and speed as much as possible, so it will be fairly smooth. You'll be able to challenge the team to a chess tournament and while away the hours."

"You make it sound almost bearable," Marty said as he grimaced.

"The sub should get us into position in about seven days, eight at the most."

"Eight days cooped up in a submarine with all those men?" Gail asked with a smirk.

"You for one will have a fairly comfortable room. You'll bunk with another woman. After all it's the new navy." Dave pulled the lever on his seat and reclined. "Wake me up when we get to Comox."

Marty looked incredulous.

"I swear this guy sleeps everywhere we go. I'll bet he sleeps away the whole seven days on the sub."

"Count on it, as much as I can anyway," Dave said without opening his eyes.

*   *

*

The CP-140 Aurora lifted off from Canadian Forces Base for its seven-hour flight to Hawaii. There, Kodiak team were sequestered at Hickman Air Force Base and had an early lunch in a mess hall. The team re-boarded and the Aurora was airborne by twelve hundred hours. This flight would tax the Aurora in distance and the 13 hour flying time would exact a toll on the team as well. It would also be difficult to get used to the idea that they would seem to lose a day and arrive around twenty-one hundred hours the next day. None of the members were used to spending so much time doing nothing and so it was that two hours into the flight a chess tournament was underway as well as the inevitable poker game.

Dave completed all the preliminaries on his computer and Operation Cottonmouth came up on the screen. He scanned the real time digital satellite imagery of the island showing it was about ten kilometers long and with an hourglass effect about one kilometer wide half way down at the narrowest spot. It actually took on a similar shape to a peanut in the shell. Most of the island was covered with typical jungle flora, but other than snakes and birds, had few other creatures. A twenty meter ridge ran along much of the west side with sheer rock cliffs in places and others with large boulders and an eighty percent grade.

As Dave looked at recon pictures, he thought of another battle on an Island closer to Japan. Back then, in the closing stages of World War Two, the Marines stormed the beach on Iwo-Jima and were slaughtered by the Japanese guns that were waiting for them. They took a month to take that island and thousands of brave young men just like Julio had died. Here Kodiak was charging a slightly smaller island with a small elite force, probably outnumbered ten to one, but Dave hoped he would have the element of surprise.

Another difference from this mission and the famous one was his team would come in on the side of the island where there was no beach or at least very little. Although this had its own hazards, he hoped it would give him the element of surprise he needed and not have to contend with the General's high tech security. Dave searched along the shoreline trying to get the best advantage and again searching the Sat photos, he saw the large boulders and rocky out-crops and realized a heavy surf could be lethal. He also hoped the two JTF-2 recons had kept their heads down and would be able to join his forces. It was evident Kodiak would need all the help they could get.

Another unknown was how the team would work with the two new underwater personnel carriers. Only Marty and he would be trained as backup operators, but the others would have to ride in them and they had never done a lot of underwater work. The SRTVs had room for nine persons, traveled at over one hundred ninety kilometers an hour and the batteries at that speed lasted a half an hour, which meant the sub could deploy the team about ninety kilometers from the fortress with a very limited risk of being spotted. Dave went over the operational plans so many times he no longer needed the computer. An announcement over the speakers brought him out of his concentration.

"Welcome to tomorrow lady and gentlemen. We are now crossing the International Date Line and so today is your yesterday and tomorrow is already today. This also signals the approximate half way point of our journey. We will be landing in Sydney at twenty-three thirty hours, about five and one half hours from now, today which is already yesterday so we'll be there tomorrow which is today, --- I think."

Dave smiled at the attempted comedy of the pilot and thought what it must be like crossing the equator by ship. He had heard stories from some of the sailors how first timers had to pay subservience to those old hands and especially the one dressed as Neptune. Just then Marty poked his head in the door.

"LC, you got a minute?"

"Sure Captain, come in. What can I do for you?"

Marty quickly moved through the doorway and closed the door cautiously.

"Sir, can I speak freely."

"Of course, what's on your mind?

Marty moved to a chair, sat down, and told Dave that he also had a problem with the SRTVs. After a long talk Dave convinced him it was no worse than flying a multi engine plane which Marty was licensed for. Finally Marty returned to the poker game.

Dave had reclined his seat and the nightmare of the Vallarta fiasco was well underway, when the shots from Sal's automatic woke him only to realize it was another knock at his door. He awoke and realized this time it was Gail. He motioned her to come in and have a chair. They talked for a long time and Gail brought the conversation around to their personal situation. Dave felt sad but knew he had to be stern.

"Captain you should be aware that until this mission is complete we have no personal situation. If you have one, get rid of it and that's an order." Dave felt bad and immediately felt he was sorry about his referral to their relationship as that personal thing, but believed that she was a professional and believed she would understand.

"You're right of course sir and I agree totally." She had morphed from the relaxed lady in fatigues to the battle hardened combat soldier.

"Now Captain, why don't you rustle us up some coffee and maybe bring a couple of those week old doughnuts from the galley as well. I think we should have us a meeting."

"Yes sir," she said as she left with a smile.

Dave paced the floor, returned to his chair, sat down, got up, paced the floor and sat down again. Gail returned after a few minutes with the goodies and pulled up a chair across the desk from him. They talked about the mission of which Dave was still somewhat closed mouth. Their conversation wound down and Gail decided to check out the poker game.

Dave reclined his chair again and slipped back to sleep and relived his personal horror and awoke to the pilot announcing over the speaker they would be landing in Sydney in twenty minutes and everyone should find their seats and fasten their seat belts.

Chapter 13

The executive jet landed at Dubai International just as the sun was slipping over the horizon. The General's staff had made the usual arrangements for the hotel's Rolls Royce Phantom to meet his plane. A quick glance out the window told him the chauffeured vehicle had anticipated the jet's stop and was now slowly moving to a position close to departure ramp of the aircraft. The General smiled and sauntered to the front of the cabin and then scowled at the co-pilot for not having the door open by the time he got there. He exited the jet but stopped on the top of the stairs to gaze out over the area. *This is where I want to be*, he thought, and then continued on down to the limo.

The chauffeur stood at attention holding the rear door of the limo and closed it the after he had entered. The General immediately closed the divider for privacy and picked up the phone.

"John, you and the others get rooms at the Holiday Inn but send my two guards over to my hotel. And John you watch the tab. I'm not paying for a lot of parties and extras. He hung up and turned on the radio to hear the stock quotes which in his mind were never good enough. When they were finished he pushed the button opening the divider.

Once the chauffeur had slowly edged off the tarmac and onto the roadway he glanced in the mirror.

"Will Sal A Din be visiting us again during your visit Mr. Smith?"

"Not that it's any of your business but Sal won't be visiting anyone, anywhere, anymore. An infidel killed him in Kirkuk. Now just do what you're paid to and get me to the hotel." He closed the window again and picked up the phone and punched in his assistant's number.

"John did you make sure my reservations are made for a late dinner in the Al Mahara?"

"Yes Sir, but I had to pay an extra surcharge to get you in."

"And just how much was that?"

"Ah, a thousand dollars, I had to come in above three others who were also late getting reservations."

"Someday son, I'm gonna have to personally take my H&K and blow a hole in your head to let all that stale air out. And did you find that man Cain?"

"Cain Sir? Oh, you mean Mohammad, the assassin. Yes, he sends his warmest regards; he said he would be honoured to dine with you, and he'd be there promptly at seven."

Smith hung up the phone and then dialed another number. There was a brief wait while certain security switches closed and when a female receptionist answered, he asked for Admiral Joyce. After exchanging niceties, General Smith got to the reason he called.

"Joyce, I need a small problem eliminated. I want a CSIS agent surgically removed from my back. This guy is costing us and if we don't get rid of him he very well could screw up the whole Op."

"Beau, that's going to be a tough one. Remember we're not involved and Washington has turned up the heat out here."

"Damn it George, what kind of chemical are you guys playing with out there? I said I want this guy dead and I want his Colonel dead and I want his girlfriend dead. In time I'd like to turn that damn north into a third world country. Is that plain enough for you?"

"Can't be done old buddy. Too much illumination for an elimination so to speak. Is *that* plain enough for you? Now if there was nothing else,

I'll say goodbye. I've got a stack of recruit applications to approve."

The General almost smashed the receiver through the telephone's console as he slammed the receiver down.

He could feel the heat in his face and remembering the doctor's caution to watch his hypertension, he tried to put David Hart out of his mind by watching the city as the driver whisked him towards the hotel.

*   *

*

Smith always liked the five minute virtual submarine ride to the Al Mahara and was soon seated at his favorite table mesmerized by the fish swimming in the giant tanks. He glanced around the dining area and noted that the whole restaurant was in front of the curved glass aquariums. The giant tanks were set up so well it gave the feeling that the whole restaurant was beneath the sea and it always gave Smith's twisted mind pleasure to think the very relatives of the food on his plate were swimming by watching him eat.

At one minute to seven a man with bronze colored skin was ushered to Mr. Smith's table. Smith noticed the man grabbed quick glances at each of the tables around the room as if he might be watched and Smith realized this man might well be, for he was Mohammad al Abbas, reputed to be the best assassin in the Kingdom.

"Thank you for coming, Mohammad. I thought we might conclude a small business arrangement over our meal."

"As you wish, General Smith."

They conversed about the world situation and their rather extreme political rationales until the tantalizing meal of wonderful sea foods was presented at their table. The General had ordered the most expensive wine in the hotel if not the entire Emirates to impress his guest but now thought he might have done just as well with a bottle of Jack Daniels.

"Mohammad, I believe I might have a very special project that requires your reputable skill. I have already tried a person in the States who failed."

The General was fishing to see if this man was as well connected as had been claimed.

"Yes General, I have heard she was shot by the very man she was sent to kill."

"You are very well informed. I only learned of her demise yesterday."

"I, actually, was made aware of the incident today," Mohammad bragged.

"The question is can you complete the task?" The General rinsed his fingers in the bowl and wiped them with the linen serviette while chewing a morsel of lobster.

"I'm afraid my associates and I are booked up for at least the next year, but if you would wish I could take the particulars and enter your request on the list. It would seem everyone wants someone eliminated and they are all willing to pay outrageous sums of money to have it carried out."

The General smirked as he glanced up at him, dipped the crustacean's white meat in the melted butter and took another bite.

"Yeah, life's a bitch." He said with a condescending smirk.

The cold dark eyes of Mohammad glared at him and told the General that he was not dining with a friend.

"I'm afraid Phillip was well known as the best in the business and if what I hear is true about her demise, I would warn you to get as far from this Mr. Hart as you can."

The General could feel his ears getting warm and knew this was no place to kill this impudent pup.

"Then my friend, I suppose that concludes our business for this visit. Possibly I might call on you in the future, if I'm in need of your talents." There was a pause and when Mohammad didn't interject anything, "I suppose you must hurry to return to your group of cutthroats now with so many commercial ventures in hand to carry out?" the General said in a sarcastic tone.

The big man didn't miss the sneer on Mohammad's lips as he slapped down his fork, stood, threw his serviette on his unfinished plate of food and left the restaurant. *No matter*, the General thought, *he would have probably just got himself killed anyway and cost me another chunk of change.* Reaching to his holstered H&K and flipping the safety on, he continued his meal.

*   *   *   *

The General peered at the gulf ocean gleaming in the morning sun as he furiously pedaled his stationary bike. He wasn't getting much further on the bike than he was on his cell. He had been talking for five minutes and getting an argument from John, one of his body guards, with every order. He finally told him to have the ship ready, period.

General Smith continued to pedal the exercise bike as he reminisced how he had come by the 'Lady'. He had been feasting at a memorial supper for one thing or another when a marine architect named John Ralston Wiles had begun an unwanted conversation with him. Beauregard had only just been promoted to a Brigadier General and told the man he wasn't in the market for a yacht and especially a large one, but the man continued until the General had asked the price. Only two hundred million was the reply.

"Well I sure as hell couldn't even afford the brass doorknobs of a ship like that." He had said.

"That, my friend is the icing on the cake. You don't have to afford it. You just have to order it, and the US taxpayer is responsible for payment. The ship is built to your specifications and when the whole deal is sealed, you renege on it by saying you don't want it or some other lame excuse. It really doesn't matter what. The ship is paid for by the US Government, but they don't really know anything about it, or would want it, so it is put up for auction to sell at market value which turns out to be you because you're the only one beside my lawyers and myself privy to the whole transaction. And your price is one Andrew Jackson. You get a two hundred million dollar ship for twenty dollars."

"And you suggest you can put this whole operation into effect?"

"My associates and I have worked all the fine points and although it may not be morally right it's absolutely leak proof legal. Our dockyard is in

Sweden and we can deliver the craft within six months."

"So what do you get out of it?"

"Why we get commission above costs from the sale of the craft of course."

Beauregard eyed the man trying to find the angle.

"Tell me why don't you just do the same thing and sell it for the whole price?"

"That's the thing; we need someone who is connected to the government with the authority to make such a large order but with the imagination to become involved in such a scheme. That makes a person like that an integral part of the project. I believe you're that person."

Beauregard stared at the man for a few moments trying to decide how to take the comment about the imagination and then decided that this fellow must know a lot about him. After all, the truth was the truth.

The two men discussed the contract over several weeks and Smith did research with a background check on Mr. Wiles and his associates. When the General was comfortable that he wasn't being setup by anyone, he ordered a two hundred and thirty-five foot craft with four decks and powered by four V-twelve diesel engines. It was sleek and streamlined and had all the luxuries available, including a small heliport at the stern. Smith named her *The Encounter* but usually referred to her as simply *The Lady*.

*　　　*　　　*　　　*

The sun was directly overhead when the General pushed the intercom in his lavish lounge on the second deck and ordered the Captain of his yacht to cast off as soon as possible. Almost immediately, the skipper had given the order to cast off all lines and prepare to be underway. The General gazed out the large picture windows as the ship began to move away from the dock and passed all the other fishing vessels, yachts and larger commercial ships. He hardly noticed the occasional deckhand running to and fro preparing for open water by stowing the large lanyards used to secure the ship while at dockside. The General poured himself a generous glass of Bourbon and pushed the intercom.

"Tell the Captain to take *The Lady* to sea, John, and tell them two body guards to come in here."

"Yes Sir."

Within seconds, the two bodyguards knocked on the door and Smith summoned them to come in.

The two men entered casually, trying very hard not to give the impression they were nervous about what the General might do because they were fully aware no one ever knew what the General might do.

"You called for us Sir?"

"I sure as hell did and you took your own sweet time getting here too. What would I have done if there had been some little shit trying to kill me or something? Ah, come on in, I guess your response time wasn't too bad. Sit down. You want a drink?"

"A soda would be nice if you have it."

"Good for me too, Sir" said the second body guard

The General poured and passed them large glasses of iced soda.

"I think since you two know the ropes each of you should team up with the two new guys until they get the idea of how things work around here." He raised his eyebrows as a question and both men nodded.

"Good. Now has there been any word on Andres? John is good, but not up to Andres' caliber."

"None sir, not since the raid. The good news is we did hear our platoon took out one of the higher ranking officers and injured several of the attacking team."

The General whirled around.

"You think that's good news?" He began raising his voice. "I spent over fifty million on that place with its security, and a handful of grunts come in and wipe the entire platoon plus all the high tech equipment in a few hours, to say nothing of the several million for the Villa itself, and you think because these dopey mercenaries kill one man and wound a couple of the others, that it's good news."

The General held up his first finger and thumb close together and feeling his facial blood vessels almost ready to burst, continued.

"We're only that far from finalizing our mission. That far, but if this Hart character gets in my face again we could lose it all. Do you understand? We could lose it all." The General was totally agitated and the blood vessels stood out on his neck and forehead.

"What can we do to help, General?"

The question seemed to break the tension as he glanced at them and then broke down into a chuckle.

"Do to help? Not a goddamn thing boys. Not a goddamn thing. Tom, you all just make sure this Hart fellow doesn't get to me. That's your entire job." He looked more relaxed. "Okay, you boys get out of here, get those ladies I hired in Dubai and escort them in here."

The General scanned the beautiful ocean and wonderful weather outside through the window and thought for a second maybe he should enjoy some salt air. The thought vaporised as the two ladies entered the room and he chose to play his special version of sex games with the couple from Dubai.

When the two evening shift guards entered the room to check on their boss they were not prepared for what they found. One of the guards called Tom. By the time he arrived the General was having an altercation with the new guard.

"Give me your weapon," the General yelled at Tom.

Tom hesitated.

"Give, me, your, weapon," the General repeated forcefully.

Tom slowly passed his Beretta to the General, who took it aimed it at the new guard's head. The new man stared at him in disbelief but didn't have time to start to sweat. The General unloaded the entire eighteen round clip into his skull, turning it into a pink and scarlet jellied mush.

"Try to tell me what to do will you."

He glared at the dead guard and then swung around to Tom.

"Don't ever tell me what to do or you'll wind up like him." He threw Tom's gun onto the lifeless guard.

Tom and the other new guard stood stupefied, feeling as if they might be sick as the General scowled at the three dead bodies and turned to leave the room.

"Clean this up and throw the three of them over the side. Those two sluts weren't much good for anything but shark bait anyway."

Tom hunched his shoulders and motioned for his partner to help him get the bodies on some plastic and drag the three of them to the stern area where they could slip them into the sea.

The next morning the General acted as if the situation had never occurred. As he sat in a plush recliner in second deck lounge he called John again.

"Tell the Captain to head this floating bordello through the strait and let's get to Bombay."

"You mean Mumbai, Sir."

"I mean what I said. You just tell him to get us there, and make it full speed ahead. Understand?"

Almost immediately a slight vibration could be felt as two of the four large diesel engines torqued up to max RPM's as the huge ship began reaching for its maximum forty knots. Beauregard leaned back, sinking into the plush recliner, poured himself his second Bourbon of the day and started the DVD with his favorite movie, *The Godfather*.

*　　　　　*　　　　*　　　　*

Kodiak's plane landed at the Royal Australian Air Force's Richmond Aerodrome. The single runway didn't leave much doubt for the pilot as to which one to use. They would go in against the wind on a north westerly glide path. The C-17's were lined up on the tarmac and a couple of made over 747'S were near one of the large hangers. The Aurora made its way over to a separate hanger where Joanne had arranged a blacked out bus to ferry the team to a barracks so they could freshen up, eat, and then later be airlifted to the Victoria.

After showers, Dave ordered up a huge amount of food that ranged from Buffalo Burgers to Cantonese Kangaroo Tenderloin and from Rock Oysters to Marlin fillets. After the long hours and uninviting menu on the plane, the team enjoyed the unique and varied cuisine. At 0:400 Dave rousted them to attention and directed them to an Australian Military helicopter in which they were transported to the HMAS Kuttabul Naval base. The ultra modern helicopter ride was more to keep the lid on the mission than for speed. The newly acquired MRH-90 set down after only fifteen minutes of airtime and the team disembarked about a hundred yards from the submarine.

Dave noticed the two shrouded containers fore and aft on the submarine decks and felt the hairs on the back of his neck bristle. He mused to himself, *A hundred and eighty-five kilometers an hour now that's going to be moving.* Dave directed the movement of the team unloading their equipment off the chopper and onto the sub. The last man with the last of the equipment was no sooner on board, than the sound of the diesel engines starting could be heard and all lines were cast off. They were beginning a week of sea duty.

The Kodiak Team were escorted to their billet and requested, because of the size of the ship, to remain in their sleeping quarters except when training, at meals or at exercise times. Once the ship was in open water, the ship's Captain requested Dave and Marty join him in the Captain's Wardroom. The two Kodiak members sat down at the meeting table across from several officers and the Captain. The Captain was the first to speak.

"Welcome to the Victoria. I'm Captain Villeneuve and to my left here is my XO Commander Douglas 'Chip' Shillington." Pointing to each one with his open hand he went down the line and introduced the other officers present, ending with Lt. Porter. These men are the only personnel on board beside your people who know the mission. Our ship will only surface during training exercises for you and your team. This little lady will take seven days to reach our destination, where you will be deployed some twenty kilometers off-shore of a small island we have dubbed *Island Fortress,* situated in the Andaman Sea."

From there, we will use the two SRTVs that are housed on our decks fore and aft to transport you to the Island. My XO and Lt. Dorchield will operate the SRTV but as a safety consideration, the two of you will have to learn how to operate the equipment as well. As a final backup, Lt.'s Paroit and Porter have qualified on the craft in the remote possibility either or both of the primary navigators are unable to go. Commander Shillington here has worked out a training schedule to educate and familiarize you with the underwater vehicles. Are there any questions?" The Captain glanced at the two Kodiak members.

"First, Captain, I'd like my team as a group to join in on at least one of the exercises with the small crafts before the deployment. Second, after we are deployed I'd like you to take the Victoria in an ark around the island and stand by about thirty kilometers off the eastern side. "

The Captain nodded to his XO.

"Chip, what have you got laid out for their training?"

"Okay, you'll get ten hours of classroom for you two, possibly your team might want to read the manuals, but I don't think they need the in-depth version. Next, incorporated into the training I have four exercises with the vehicles of which the last one could be full team participation."

Dave nodded.

"Sounds like we got our work cut out for us," Marty said hesitantly.

"It's actually more fun than work. Where else can you get to play with two forty-six million dollar high tech aqua toys?" the commander asked with a grin.

Dave glanced over to Marty who was frowning.

"Should be a fun week," he said more for Marty's sake than anything else.

As the Victoria swiftly and silently slid through the Indian Ocean, Dave and the crew worked hard to learn what they could about the new submersibles. Finally, Commander Shillington took Dave and Marty on deck and had some crew members launch one of the little subs. When they had unlatched the canopy that had covered the mini sub the commander waved Dave and Marty to move closer to him so they could hear.

"Alright then, these are the Submerged Rapid Transport Vehicles, the SRTVs. They cost forty-six million each, but from a stealth viewpoint are worth every penny. This one is called the Langley. It can travel at depths from zero to two hundred meters and a speed of one hundred knots. That's about one hundred and eighty five kilometers per hour. The down side is it can only travel at that speed for twenty minutes and then the batteries are drained. It takes twelve hours with this vehicle sitting for the small reactor to replenish the batteries to full power. Any questions?"

Each of the three men had donned special breathing apparatus and although they probably wouldn't need the breathing equipment on this exercise, it was a safety factor. In turn, they crossed over to the mini sub and slipped down the hatch. The commander was the last to enter and gave the command for the sailors to cast off all lines. The sailors unhooked all the cables and returned to the deck of the Victoria, pulling the lines and the gang plank up and away from the Langley.

Dave looked around the small craft and realized, although it would be tight, the two small ships would indeed carry the entire Kodiak team.

The Commander sat down at the controls, which didn't look all that different from that of a small aircraft. In front of him the clear, thick glass of the upper nose cone was similar to the windscreen on an airplane or car.

"Alright then, let's put this little bullet through its paces," he said with a pinch of excitement in his voice. He punched a code into the onboard computer key pad in front of him and a slight whirring sound began. With one hand on the steering wheel and the other on the throttle lever he moved the throttle just slightly and steered the craft away from the Victoria. He turned a dial to begin compressing the air from the ballasts which would automatically open another valve and flood them to submerge. Dave and Marty watched with the enthusiasm of a teenager taking their first driving lessons.

As soon as the depth gauge showed fifty feet Commander Shillington began moving the throttle down. The whir began to increase and soon sounded like a large waterfalls. The Commander explained the excess noise was from the super-cavitations of the pumps not the electric motors and the only obstacle they need worry about would be whales and other large aquatic life. He assured them that the computerized sonar would automatically divert the small sub away from the larger creatures and it worked exceedingly well. He put the craft through dives and rolls, twisting and banking into one-eighty degree turns.

Shillington slowed down and let Marty do a stint at the wheel. To Dave's amazement, Marty really enjoyed operating this expensive toy and took it up to the maximum one hundred eighty knots. Dave also took the controls but all too soon 'Chip' signaled that he had to take over the controls and get them back to the Victoria. Back behind the controls and guided by an underwater GPS system, he made a banking turn and headed back to the ship. When they surfaced, they were about a hundred meters from the mother sub. They had been out for fifteen minutes and had traveled more than thirty kilometers.

The sailors re-hooked the Langley to the deck crane and as Dave, Marty and Chip made their way down to their state rooms, the sailors hoisted it back on board, secured, and covered it. Once the deckhands reported the SRTV was secured the Captain ordered a dive and the submarine slipped below the surface, making twenty knots toward its destination. After the second and third day the team fell into a pattern of meals, physical exercise and sleep. They also pulled their turn of a trial run in the SRTVs, which went off without a hitch. Dave watched the team with pride and realized he was leading the best commandoes in the world.

He was also, however, waiting for the all important call from Colonel Benton that would either shutdown the operation or signal a go to completion. On the fifth day out Dave was summoned to the radio room and rushed there only to have to wait while the young officer decoded the message. Dave paced up and down the corridor, concerned about what the message might say. After what seemed like eternity the communications officer slipped out of the room and handed Dave a paper with the brief message. Dave read it several times.

Lt. Colonel David Hart. Cottonmouth is proceeding directly toward Island Fortress. At present rate of speed he should arrive tomorrow A.M. Have monitored via satellite at least three bodies over the side on the second day of voyage. Also tensions have heated up between Israel and Lebanon. We will not be able proceed into Lebanon. Your orders, however, remain as planned. I will forward final orders as of thirteen hundred tomorrow. Please advise of status of operation and if possible, reply thoughts on Middle East problem. Colonel Joanne Benton.

Dave knocked on the Com. Room door and the officer opened it.

"Would it be possible to send a reply?"

"Yes Sir. The Captain has already authorized the traffic."

Dave quickly scribbled his reply.

Colonel Joanne Benton, Please be advised we are on schedule and training on the SRTV's is complete. We are able to be ashore in seventy two hours, full readiness. Waiting to receive green light to proceed. Don't be concerned with M. E. The tension there justified. IDF to overcome objective. Should be a blast. Lt. Colonel Hart.

Dave handed it to the communications specialist.

"Please code this and send it Attention: Colonel Benton, CSIS Vancouver."

"Aye, aye, Sir!"

The status hadn't changed and that had helped Dave relax somewhat but there was still a chance General Smith would bolt and run before they got there. Dave could almost picture him getting the jitters and casting off in the yacht before they could get to him.

Dave returned to his state-room and re-evaluated the attack plan and for the first time began considering a diversion to divide the island security if that should become necessary. He wondered why he hadn't thought of it before. The more he studied the map, the more he liked the idea of setting a small force (maybe two or three men) on the east side of the island. His reasoning was if his force was found out, the diversionary force could be used to throw the enemy off enough to give his main team a chance to gain the upper hand.

If in fact they managed to frame the attack without being intercepted, the diversionary team would join forces with the main force. The more he studied the new idea the more he liked it. He decided he would use the JTF-2 men for the diversion. He would call the two men when the time was right and have them position near the beaches of the east side of the island at locations north and south of the Clubhouse (which is what he was calling the Cottonmouth's Villa), set some explosives and await the attack. If a diversion became necessary they could set off the charges. This would hopefully confuse the enemy and draw some of the security fire. After ensuring he hadn't left any glaring holes in the operation, Dave altered the attack plan orders and then sent for Captain Musselman. He told him of the new plan to use JTF-2 men as diversions and detailed the rest of the changes.

Marty studied the map and with a grin glanced up at Dave.

"LC, I think we'll get him this time."

Dave raised his eyebrows.

"My God, I sure do hope so."

Chapter 14

The Captain announced that the Island
Fortress was in sight as the sleek yacht cut through
sizable swells. The spray was splattering the lounge
windows but the General could still make out the
rocky shore line with its white surf and the swaying
palms trees of the northwestern tip of the island.
With the ship closing the distance, some of the
western cliffs and the jungle flora further south also
were discernable. The far southern portion of the
peanut shaped island was still too hard to make out,
but General Beauregard was more interested in the
east side anyway because that's where he believed
the trouble would lie if there was any. He had had
the villa built two hundred meters into the jungle on
the east side, making it almost invisible from the sea
and that's where his harbor was. That's where the
beaches were and so in the General's muddied
military mind that's where an assault would first be
made.

Smith ordered the Captain to circle the island
twice, staying about two kilometers off the coast

before going dockside. He had the crew scan the coast-line for anything out of the ordinary and while the ship cruised two kilometers off shore, the General called his security chief.

"Major Akemi, how are things on my paradise island?"

"General, how nice to hear your voice." He almost choked on the words. "Everything here is as it should be. We have our patrols leaving and returning at staggered intervals as you requested and have seen or heard nothing. None of the various sensors have indicated any movement on the island and the drones have not found anything out of the ordinary."

"Alright Akemi, I'll be docking within the next couple of hours. Notify the staff to prepare the Villa and meals."

It took an hour and ten minutes to circle the island twice and when the General decided it was safe, he gave the order for the Captain to put to dock. The General had his entire entourage disembark and enter the villa before he left the ship. His thoughts were always in the area of self preservation and he concluded if anyone was going to ambush the party he would have a good chance to escape. The General prided himself with a sixth sense when it came to his own survival.

He considered this island fortress as his Camp David for the present and for that reason he had security checks so strict that not even guests whom he had invited ever made it to the Villa without having passed through a battery of sensors and x-rays.

The General gazed through the panoramic window that offered a view that took in a wide expanse of aqua blue ocean with only a couple of palms on either side to act as a frame. He sipped his bourbon and took deep drags of a very expensive cigar. Soon the real Camp David would be his as he ruled the world from the American Capital and this little gem in the ocean would be one of his get-a-ways when the pressures of wealth far beyond Solomon's would get too great.

The General sunk into the kangaroo leather recliner as though he were settling into a cloud and proceeded to lift the phone and dial a number.

"Tri-ex Industries, how may I help you?" a female voice chirped.

"Tracy, get me George. And, start putting sir on my salutation or you'll be cleaning oil barrels in the high arctic."

"That would be George Andrews. Just one moment, sir. Whom may I say is calling?"

"Quit tooling with me lady. The monitor shows damn well *whom* this is."

It took a few moments before George, a compatriot of Smith's came on the line.

"General, phoning on an unsecured line from overseas could be dangerous at this point."

The General wondered for whom.

"Look, George, by the time they get this encryption decoded and figure out what the hell I'm talking about the mules should be dispatched. I just called to let you know I'm going ahead with insertion in a few days. We finalized the plans three days ago. You may want to be out of Washington for a while."

"General do you think it's wise to be so specific on the phone?"

"It won't matter in three days once the mules are dispatched, it'll take a miracle for any intelligence organization to find and stop even one, let alone thirty."

"General, I don't know whether you're drunk or just crazy, but I'm going to hang up. Good bye."

General Smith looked at the receiver that was now buzzing. Finally, he put it down in the cradle wondering if maybe he was feeling the effects of the sippin' whiskey more than he realized. The sun still shone high above the western horizon even though the shadows on this side of the island were lengthening. The General yawned and then stretched. The thought of sleep became too enticing and he slogged off to his bedroom.

Meanwhile at Fort Benning, NSA personnel had intercepted the General's communication, documented it, and tried to interpret the meaning of the conversation. Special Agent Angela Brooks checked a list and found a Colonel Benton's request for intercept and forward of any information coming out of Myanmar. Brooks called her superior, Sergeant Major Jones to confirm clearance because of the subject matter. He thanked her but because of the unusual wording he told her he would talk to the Canadian authorities himself. He asked his aid to get Colonel Benton on the phone and that he would take it in his office.

The Sergeant Major swaggered into his office and closed the door and as he sat behind his desk to wait for the phone to ring he became engrossed in the peculiar wording of the transcript.

The phone rang twice before he picked it up. He outlined the information he had received and then asked if Colonel Benton could shed any light as to what this General Smith was talking about. Colonel Benton told him they were watching this individual, thanked him for the heads-up, but lied that she knew nothing more about what the conversation implied. She told him as of yet it was simply file fodder and after exchanging courtesies they disconnected.

Colonel Benton normally would have liked to inform the American Sergeant Major all but at this point, with leaks even in Global or CSIS and due to the situation she felt it imperative to keep a tight lid on the pot until Kodiak Team hit the shore.

The Victoria had just surfaced in heavy seas when the XO brought the message to Dave. Joanne had relayed everything the NSA Officer had given her and added she felt it prudent for the Team to proceed ASAP. She gave him operational authority to begin the assault on Smith's Island and wished him luck.

Dave found the captain in his state room.

"Sounds like we've just run out of time, Captain. Think you can get us close enough tonight?"

The Captain led Dave over to a table with the charts, took a protractor, measured the distance, checked the time and entered the data into the computer. Instantly the data came up on the screen.

"We're still about two hundred kilometers from your drop point but it looks like if I put this girl through her paces we could conceivably be some fifty kilometers out in about seven hours. You'd still have some three hours of darkness left, and there would be no moon due to the storm that will be over the area. On the other hand that storm is going to make launching the SRTV's and hitting the beach difficult and dangerous for your team."

Dave digested the Captains words and thought for a few minutes but no matter how dangerous it would be he didn't feel they could allow this opportunity to slip by.

"Captain we'll just have to risk it. Cottonmouth is planning to carry out some kind of mission and the mere thought of allowing him to proceed is too awful to contemplate. Who knows how many innocents could be killed. No, we have to go now no matter what," Dave said with urgency in his voice. "Oh God now it's beginning to sound like a suicide mission." He turned to the Captain again. "Can you make it happen?"

They moved to the operations area and the Captain nodded to his XO.

"Take the lady down to snorkel depth and all ahead full. Let's make the lady swim, gentlemen."

As he turned back to Dave, the orders were being relayed to the Chief Petty officer, who in turn relayed them to the various sailors controlling the ship. A slight vibration could be perceived as the propellers began pushing the water faster than the ship.

Dave called the team together in the mess deck and informed them of the latest word from Global. He told them that the deployment time had been moved up almost eighteen hours and they would be hitting the shore in a storm with a shortened time to get inland before daylight. He suggested they try to get some sleep and told them he would roust them at zero one thirty hours to prepare to leave the sub.

Dave was too keyed up to sleep when he got to his berth and imagined it was the adrenalin free flowing through his brain. He wondered if his crew were suffering from the same insomnia and decided it was probably a pretty good bet.

Dave lay in his cot with his hands behind his head and his mind strayed to the awful picture of Puerto Vallarta. His mind quickly replayed the horrible scene in the basement and the memory brought tears to his eyes and his breath became short and rapid. He had to purposely remind himself that this was not just about Bev or now Julio. He was here to rid the world of a very dangerous menace and not just to avenge the brutal and untimely death of his only true love. He went on to consider the overview of the assault plan but was vexed by wanting to get to it.

After checking his watch for the twentieth time in the last hour, he got up and headed for the small mess deck for coffee. His reasoning was if he couldn't sleep he may as well be wide awake. As he entered the narrow corridor leading to the mess hall, he could hear conversation coming from the small cafeteria. Dave was not totally surprised when he was greeted by the entire team who were already half way through their first cup. As he entered the room all conversations stopped as they glanced over at him. There was silence for a few breaths while they awaited an expected rebuke from their CO.

"I guess if we're going to be up anyway we might as well do another briefing." Smiles broke out and some nodded as they all took a swig of coffee.

Dave spread out a map of the island on the table, got a coffee, and turned to stand at the head of the table.

"Marty, you'll take your team to a point just north of the middle of the island at this indentation, here." He pointed to it on the map. "You won't be making contact with the northern JTF-2 Scout as previously planned because I'm going to deploy them on the east side of the island to be used as a diversion if necessary. You will make a wide arc toward the northeast and swing down to the compound which we will call the *Clubhouse*. You will act as your own sharp shooter and deploy on elevated ground with good visuals, somewhere around here, to afford covering fire if it should be required.

I will take my team, and make an arc southeast and then north up to the Clubhouse. I will also position a sharp shooter, Captain Levine, on some elevated ground to the southwest of the compound where she will also give us covering fire as required. I want demolition set for all the buildings here, here and here. They will be remote, not timed and fired when I give the order. As you're all aware, Captain Musselman is second in command. Be careful. This island is very well secured.

Tel-sat will be frying their air communications and JTF2 will take out the land lines so our man won't be calling in reinforcements from other parts of the island. Are there any questions or can anyone pick out any flaws in this plan?" Dave waited and when there was no feedback he continued. "Alright then, unless the JTF-2 report any drastic changes we go with this. We'll have one more, hopefully short briefing on deck before we head for the beach which will be in---" He checked his watch. "Two hours and thirty minutes. I suggest you use the time to check your gear and prepare."

* * * *

The speaker system bellowed a loud low and then high whistle and then an announcement.

"Now hear this, all Kodiak Team on deck. Launch group, be prepared to launch SRTV's."

Dave looked at his watch. It was zero two thirty. The Captain had managed good time.

Dave had just arrived on deck and was standing on the forecastle when a call came on his cell. It was the JTF-2 scout on the island who gave Dave a final update on the island defenses and warned Dave of the squadron of Unmanned Air Vehicles. He indicated they were equipped with infra red camera and that they were armed.

Dave gave the soldier the change in his orders and then signed off.

Chapter 15

The rain and driven sea spray stung Dave's face as he held his head down and watched a wave swash across the deck of the heaving submarine. Dave noticed the eleven members of Kodiak team huddled close to the downwind side of the conning tower trying to keep as dry as possible as well as fighting for balance on the rocking ship. The only illumination was the powerful spot-lights directed on the decks fore and aft, allowing the sailors visibility to launch the submersibles. Dave knew it was just about time to board the SRTVs so he waved his arms for them to gather in close.

"Okay, listen up. Our condition is green." He glanced around at the three to four meter swells combined with the wind and rain. "Even if it's about as off coloured green as I'd want to stray. This guy has armed UAV's doing surveillance so getting to the Clubhouse is going to be tricky at best although the weather might be to our advantage on that point. As far as we know we haven't been detected and of course I want to keep it that way. The name of this operation is Codename Cottonmouth and it's called that for a reason. Make no mistake, this General Smith has all the attributes of the Cottonmouth snake and he is the head of this organization so we hit him hard and fast with total surprise. Our Intel suggests Smith has at least a fifty-man contingent around him so our objective is strategic. We take no prisoners who are combative and we destroy any and all enemy structures. The head gets severed today, people. Captain Mussleman, I'll see you on the east side of the island." He glanced over and noticed the sailors had finished launching both SRTVs. "Alright let's move out." He directed Alpha team aft while he led his Baker squad to the forward sub...

Baker team tried to follow, as the two navigators with little difficulty moved down the ramps to the submersibles, but the Kodiak members, however, stumbled from the chain railing on one side of the ramp to the other side and a couple almost flipped over the railing into the sea before finally managing to get down the hatch of the crafts. Dave gave a worried glance at the sea which was now developing four to five meter swells. He considered the landing and wondered how many of his men would get thrown into the rocks and be maimed or killed before they even had a chance to engage the enemy. Dave was the last man in and as he took the ten steps down into the tiny sub, Captain Shillington closed the hatch; side stepped past his passengers, and took his seat at the controls. Both vehicles silently slipped below the surface and the propulsion systems thrust them toward the island.

Twenty minutes later both squads were on the ocean floor in very deep water about three hundred meters from the shore of their appointed landing sites. Dave listened to the warning from Chip Shillington to the squad that they were about twenty-five meters below the surface and that they should swim to the surface in stages. He then gave orders for everyone to turn on their breathing apparatus as he flooded the vehicle. As Baker team's sub filled with water in preparation for the team to swim to the surface, the storm above had strengthened to a full gale and even at the depth they were at, Dave could feel the breakers move the small craft as they came down into the water. Dave followed his team and slowly began fighting the turbulence half way to the surface.

Dave was concerned that Alpha team, under the command of Captain Musselman, who would have to fight the same killer storm, could also have casualties. For the first time he began to contemplate scrubbing the mission in hopes of waiting for better weather. His resolve hardened just before he reached the surface, as his mind raced over the fact Smith was in the final stages of something globally devastating and deadly.

Once the entire Baker squad surfaced, they began the arduous task of swimming to shore. The wind driven rain and the high surf made it almost impossible for Dave to get his bearings straight even with the aid of his GPS. He continually checked it and corrected their direction trying to hit the ten meter piece of sand he had chosen from the satellite photos. He kept the group close together and continually gave orders so they would keep their mind on him and not on the pounding surf. As an especially large wave lifted them, Dave suddenly saw the island and the small slice of sand no more twenty-five meters in the direction they were headed.

"Okay people," he barked, "swim like hell to beat the next breaker or it will punch you into the seabed. Now let's go!"

They swam as if their live depended upon it, as in fact it did. Gail was the first to stand up wobbly on the course sand and then the others got to the ankle deep water just as another curl crashed into the gravel twenty meters out and brought four feet of water to the shore where it almost washed them back out again. Dave grabbed Gail as she washed past him and held her until the current disappeared.

The group made their way onto the ten meter gravelly beach where the soldiers formed around Dave at the water's edge. After twenty minutes in the turbulent water, Dave was bent over with his hands on his knees catching his breath. He glanced around at the meter and a half towards the rock cliff and motioned in that direction.

"That's the next obstacle team. Get up that cliff as quickly and quietly as possible and then we can get rid of these wet suits." Dave led the way up the sharp incline of slippery rain washed rocks and boulders with each member of their squad cautiously picking their way behind him. The job was made more difficult and dangerous by the totally black night and howling wind driven rain. Dave was almost sure some hidden demon had been sent in the howling wind, determined to rip them off the face of the cliff and deposit them back in the sea. Several members slipped and more than a few times the soldier would have fallen to their death except a comrade grabbed them and held steady until they once again got a grip on the rock face.

Atop a twenty meter cliff on a reasonably level piece of terrain, they all stripped from their wet suits and breathing gear stowing the equipment cautiously out of sight for possible later use. Dave checked his GPS and was thankful for the submersible's navigation officer. Shillington had landed them right on target and even with the raging seas they had been able to land exactly where he planned. He thought maybe something would start going right for them yet. Dave pulled out his Sat cell and dialed the special number for Oscar. There was an agreement to co-ordinate their attacks and it was crucial that the caves in the Bekka Valley be neutralized before Smith's people could mount a mission.

"Oscar this is Badger. We have landed and have condition green. You can begin your assault. I'm informed the mutts in the caves haven't moved yet."

"That's affirmative Badger. My people are ready to move within the hour and our commandoes are already in the air making ready to jump. They will surgically eliminate the caves. Good luck on your end."

Each Kodiak member double-checked their weapons while Dave Called the JTF-2 scouts. Dave gave them the co-ordinates where he wanted them to deploy and the scouts moved toward their position. Dave called Captain Musselman on the Com-Tac as well, but his efforts to raise Marty got no response. Had the whole team been hurled into the rocks, or maybe captured by a security patrol?

As the Baker squad rested, Dave rechecked his map and GPS. He assured himself proper orientation and then gave the order for them to move out. The team cut straight east into the jungle and then sliced southward where they quickly came across a path.

Although hiking would have been easy on the path no one had any misgivings about using it. Dave motioned for three members to move to the left of it while two others and himself moved along the right. They skirted the south side of a small mountain. It was really only a large hill of maybe fifteen hundred meters, but here it was a mountain. Dave looked the area over and with the harsh rain that was falling he thought to himself, *rain to grow the flowers for paradise.* They trekked through a valley to the north side of another smaller mountain further south. The heavy rain continued and although it wasn't the best hiking weather Dave told the men it was a pretty good bet the UAV's wouldn't be up in this wind and rain so it was all for the best.

He continued to check his map and GPS as their trek formed an arc from the south around to the north just as was outlined in his briefing. It was still difficult hiking through the dense jungle in the heavy warm rain, but after just over two hours of sloshing, a member on point raised his left fist and everyone froze. He held up his fist while pointing ahead to the right indicating that the clubhouse was just a ways ahead. Dave ordered Gail to proceed ahead to the left where there was a significant rise and find a concealed shooting position. He led the rest to the right and north-east.

Marty and his Alpha squad were having a considerably more difficult time. When they reached the surface the high seas made it extremely difficult to account for everyone. The Captain had just got the group together and was about to head toward the island when one of the men let out a yell.

"What happened over there?" Marty called.

"I think I just got hit by a shark Sir. I think my wet suit is ripped but I don't think I'm cut. At least there doesn't seem to be any pain and I can still feel my feet and legs."

"Everyone take defensive measures and for God's sake don't panic," Marty ordered.

The men joined in a loose circle and became as still as possible for almost ten minutes. Finally, thankful that there were no more incidences, Marty gave the order.

"Okay people, I think we can assume it was a hit and run, so let's not wait around for another one. Let's get to shore as quickly as possible."

They headed for shore but the strong wind and current had pulled them north and by the GPS Marty gauged they landed more than a kilometer north of their objective. The waves and the rocky shore line were no less formidable here as they had been for Baker squad but somehow Alpha made it ashore with no other casualties other than the shark attack.

Once ashore, Marty checked the man's ripped wet suit and saw that the man did in fact have a laceration, which the medic dressed. Marty was sure it was a shark hit and run and had the medic give the man an injection against infection.

The Captain chose to head inland to intersect the trail rather than try to trek south along the open cliff and rock strewn shore. He believed they could angle over to the path and save time. Instead, he found a swamp that wasn't shown on the map and guessed Cottonmouth's people had probably created it by flooding some lowland. Marty thought it could have booby traps set in it. He contemplated the situation they were in for a moment. This swamp was between them and the designated route and given the time, he recognized that moving back to the beach to start over wasn't an option. He decided to cross the swamp.

"Listen up. We're going to have to cross here and get on our course. Everybody, heads up for anything from crocs, to security devices, to hostiles."

Alpha inched their way through waist deep water. Marty reckoned once they were out of the swamp and got to where they would slowly turn south, it would use up another hour. They would still be some distance from the Villa and he was going to be close to an hour late. He tried to call Baker squad with the information they would be late, but found there was no response. It was only then that Marty realized the two-way that transponded the signals from the headsets had been carried in a pack by the same member who had been brushed by the shark. The shark had sliced the strap and fled with the pack with the sat cell and transponder in it. It had probably saved some lives because the shark had taken it for food. Afterward, when it recognized the equipment as foreign material, not food, the hunter moved on for other quarry.

But their communications were dead at least until they got to within the close proximity of a few hundred meters, so the Com-Tac headsets would transmit directly with Baker team's headset.

Captain Musselman carefully led his men across the swamp and at times, when he and his men were in water up to their waist, wondered if he had made the right choice. He moved back and forth ensuring all his men were kept together in the dark rainy night. The Captain was relieved as the water level dropped first to the thighs and then to the knees. As they crawled up a small embankment out of the swamp everyone was feeling more at ease. In the excitement of leaving the algae covered water the squad began to converse a little among themselves. Captain Musselman crept closer to the group making motions with his hands and offering a frown.

"You guys had better get a lot quieter before you wake up the whole damn jungle."

He continued to quietly whisper and give hand signals to the squad as he led them into the jungle. They picked up a little time as they stealthily made their way toward the clubhouse. Suddenly their point, Harvey, put up his fist and the squad froze in their tracks and then silently slipped into hiding. A patrol of four guards doing an early morning perimeter inspection were meandering down the path. Marty tried to get his people out of sight in time but one of the guards thought he heard something and wandered off the path to check it out.

Marty stayed hidden until the guard had passed him. Incredulously, the guard took two steps past him and then began an ecological hydration of the jungle plant life. Marty wondered if maybe he would allow this man to live, but his orders had been eliminate all combative personnel. Knowing his men would wait for his signal Marty waited as the man became preoccupied. Just before the guard completed his improvement project, Marty stood up behind him. The motion caused a slight whisper of sound which the guard heard. Marty's Kukri made its lethal entry into the guard's back at about the second or third vertebrae severing the spinal cord. The Guard's mouth opened as if to yell but nothing would come out because the lung muscles wouldn't work. Then his eyes went to his AK-74, but his hands and arms wouldn't work either and the weapon fell to the jungle floor. His eyes showed terror as his legs buckled under him and the only sound he made was the cushioned fall to the jungle's moss floor. Marty used his kukri once more, incising the man's neck from ear to ear. His eyes went large, his mouth moved slightly, but none of the commands from the brain seemed to go anywhere. The jungle floor where he lay absorbed the scent of raw blood and after a few more seconds he simply had a blank stare. He was dead.

At the same instant, three other Alpha members who had silently slipped up behind the remaining guards used their kukris in unison and instantly the three other guards met a similar fate as their comrade. Marty ordered the squad to move the bodies into the jungle and cover them with mulch. After the quick burial, for security purposes he again led the squad toward the Clubhouse at double time, knowing the guards would have set report times and when missed it would in itself set off an alarm.

*   *   *   *

Dave studied the lay of the land as he decided where he was going to deploy his people. From the jungle where they were concealed, it was two hundred meters of almost flat ground with only a slight decline down to the clubhouse. To the left of the clubhouse about a hundred meters there were several smaller buildings that were the guard's barracks. To the right only seventy-five meters he could see maintenance, utility and possibly storage buildings. From the Clubhouse, Dave guessed it was about seven hundred meters down to the high water mark that then dropped another two meters down to the beach. The dock and harbour area was on the south or right hand side of the beach. As he studied the area he marveled at the artistic way the conflict of the jungle and the man made landscaping had been integrated to complement each other. The entire landscape was expertly grassed and had hedges of trees, large shrubs, and low stone fences.

Dave decided to position his team individually in scattered positions using these hedges and stone fences for cover. The positions created an arc just in from the edge of the jungle so they would have a solid field of cross-fire. As he delegated his people to their assigned positions he tried several more times to raise Marty on his sat cell and Com-Tac hoping against hope he might still be able to organize this attack with more firepower. He hoped Marty was just late but he was beginning to fear the worst.

Baker squad was ordered to hold their positions in hopes Alpha Squad would soon show up. Finally, as the grey of dawn overcame the dark of night with images made visible only by flood lights beginning to transform into daylight objects and the storm slowly also moving away, Dave made a difficult decision. He would have to move in and stage an attack with the people he had. It wasn't the way it was planned but he couldn't postpone the show any longer. If Alpha squad had been overcome, the longer he waited the worse the enemies' strength would be and with daylight any operation was going to be more risky.

Dave instructed Troy and a helper to plant charges near the barracks and utilities buildings. They had orders to ensure, as much as was possible, non-combatants were removed from harm's way. He waited while his resident expert completed the tasks. When they gave him the thumbs up, Dave slipped out of the jungle to a position behind a small utility shed where he could direct the action and offer the most cover fire.

He was going to have to initiate this assault even though he had the bad feeling he had insufficient forces. He tried once more to raise Captain Musselman and Alpha Team. There was no answer and Dave began to wonder if this was going to be a repeat of the Columbia raid.

"God, I hope not," he thought to himself.

Chapter 16

Dave stood with his back flattened to the wall of the small utility building. He did a visual around the right hand corner of the shed and then quickly glanced to his left as he whispered into his Com-Tac.

"Listen up people, I don't know what happened to Alpha squad but we can't wait any longer. Captain, mark your kill zones and be ready to find your targets. Lt. Williams get the rest of those devices in the required locations and be ready to detonate on my orders. Everyone get ready to move when the C-4 starts to pop."

Dave tried to raise Marty just one more time with no better luck and was just about to give the order to commence when he felt the cold steel of a nine millimeter move just under his helmet and press near his temple.

"I'd guess Lt. Colonel David Hart? I don't know how the hell you got this close but I'm sure the boss man is really gonna enjoy this. How many you got with you?" When Dave didn't answer immediately the man smashed the barrel of his of Beretta across Dave's chin. "I asked you a question asshole."

Dave's continued silence brought a second more volatile blow with the weapon that knocked his helmet off and almost rendered him unconscious. With the weapon pointed at the base of Dave's skull the guard handcuffed him and then shoved him stumbling along a path in the direction of the Villa. A trickle of blood found its way down to his right brow, then down the side of his face before it joined up with the gash on his jaw and ran down his neck. The man shoved Dave into the Villa and then into the study where the General was enjoying his morning Bourbon.

"Well well, what have we here?" The General raised his eyebrows at the guard.

"I found him out behind one of the utility buildings. I sent Josh and Sean to find any others."

"So Mr. David Hart, I presume you're the individual who thinks he can upend events, which will soon change the way the world is governed. Really Mr. Hart, do you suppose a queasy little Canuck like yourself could accomplish what the CIA, NSA, and the FBI couldn't? I'm led to understand you believe I had a lot to do with nine - eleven?

Dave continued to stand silent and steely eyed.

"That's very perceptive of you," the General finally said after he had given Dave plenty of time to acknowledge. "Well it's true, sort-of. You see many Americans just don't like to get into wars what with its awful killing, plunder and wretched waste of resources. Surely you can see if we left it to the average citizen, some two bit dictator from a derelict country would be ruling the world."

"So a two bit dictator like yourself and a few of your really intelligent people, thinking you're some kind of Master race, kill three thousand of your own people because only you're smart enough to determine how, when, and where the people should go to war?" Dave said in an enraged disgusted voice.

The General raised his head from the drink in his hand and gazed at him with a demeaning smile.

"Oh you poor misinformed man. Those decisions are not made from a patriotic view or even a militaristic one. Someone has to grab for the golden ring. You understand as President of The Group of Twelve I must mold the world and make plans to sustain our way of life. And if we don't cull a few million every now and then, why, we'd be over populated. You know the maintenance of life, liberty, and especially the pursuit of untold wealth, or in other words happiness. We make these accords at the highest level and then I or one of my associates ensures they are brought to birth."

"Are you inferring the President of the United States ordered 9/11?"

"Not at all. He certainly couldn't become embroiled in such things. He's not one of the twelve, but on the other hand I'm not even sure we made him aware of it beforehand. No, I'd have to say it was more on a spiritual level. Enough to know however, I am the man used to orchestrate the entire performance."

"You call murdering over three thousand innocent people a performance? How about my wife? Was that a performance too, you murdering psychopathic son-of-a-bitch? You're a pathetic piece of dirt, Smith and you're going down."

Smith slowly moved in and with his entire two hundred and sixty five pounds smashed Dave with a hard left into the mid-section and then followed it with a crushing right hook to the jaw. Dave doubled over, vomited and nearly passed out from the heavy blows. He certainly would have been on the floor had it not been for the guards holding him up.

"So go ahead Mr. Hart arrest me." The General laughed hysterically as he moved to the bar to pour himself another victory drink. "You know Hart, I do admire you. Your dogged determination isn't at all the norm these days, but then you did have your wife to avenge. Candidly, you weren't supposed to live through that attack that Sal carried out. I suppose the three bullets probably was a dead giveaway." Smith broke out in another fit of laughter.

"They took five slugs out of me, not three you scum bag. I would have thought such a high spiritual form as you would be better informed." The General shot a glare at Dave and stopped smiling.

One of his soldiers came in and whispered in his ear and a sneer was added to the hatred on his face.

"Bring them in here," he ordered.

"Mr. Hart, we've just captured your two confederates as it were." He turned with a wave of his arm.

"Hurry up and bring those two in here."

Dave looked around and was shocked at the appearance of Gail and one of his new recruits, both handcuffed. He caught the Cottonmouth's eye and held it with contempt.

"And what do you plan on doing with us? You know we won't divulge anything." Dave demanded, trying to gain any negotiating chips he might.

"Well let me demonstrate." Smith took a nickel plated revolver off of his desk and in one motion aimed it at the young officer's head and put two nine millimeter holes in his forehead which blasted red, pink and grey brain tissue in a spray on the wall behind him. The man collapsed to the floor dead.

"Does that give you any clues? We will interrogate you first to see which of our operations have been compromised and then if you co-operate we may choose not to kill you. If you don't tell us what we want to know after torture, we will kill you. Of course, I will probably find some sport with the young lady,--" he looked her up and down. "--before I eliminate her. Take him down to the cell block and then get out to the yard and make sure there aren't any other rats around. The two guards began leading the two away but the general interrupted them.

"I said take him, not her. I'll watch her for now," he said with a sadistic smile.

The guards roughly threw Gail at the sofa and the two of them, one on each arm, almost dragged Dave out the door.

*   *   *   *

There was a pink glow in the east when Marty and Alpha team finally arrived at the compound.

"Baker squad this is Alpha, Badger are you here?"

"Alpha, this is Baker. We haven't heard from LC for nearly twenty-five minutes. The last transmission from him was we were to move in when he gave the order. Looks like you're in command now Captain. What do we do?"

Captain Musselman pondered on the situation for a few seconds while looking over the geography and then rattled off orders to prepare to detonate the demolition charges in and around structures on the compound. The sun was up when Marty ordered the assault to begin.

*   *   *   *

The two guards wrestled Dave through the mansion to a white wooden door off the kitchen. They had not seen Dave fashioning a bobby pin, which he always kept clipped to his back pocket, into a small key for the cuffs. He had practiced the procedure in training until he could do it with his hands behind his back which was exactly the way they were secured now. He had grown a little rusty but soon he had the desired 'S' curve he wanted.

One guard moved ahead to unlock and open the door to the cellar and Dave took advantage of the split in forces. Just as the guard opened the basement door and turned back to help escort him down the stairs, Dave kicked his foot as high in the air as he could, connecting exactly in the guards crotch. At the same time he lashed out with the handcuffs and caught the second guard across the face. As the first guard doubled over Dave put a foot on his shoulder and propelled him through the open door backwards, crashing down into the cement floor and wall on the lower landing head first. Dave made an anti clockwise turn and again lashed the second guard across the face with the handcuffs which now resembled bloody hamburger more than a human face. With his right hand he grabbed the Berretta that was holstered under the second guards arm. The guard tried to charge, but Dave side stepped and as the guard went hurtling by, Dave tripped him and then gave him the added propulsion required to fly off the top stair. He touched nothing until he hit the wall just above his compatriot, his head and shoulders smashing against where the cinder block wall and cement floor joined. The breaking of the cervical disks of his neck were audible and when Dave glanced down at the two of them, they were both staring up at the ceiling, but seen nothing. Dave threw the door closed and removed the cuffs from his left wrist.

"I guess that closes the door on your life of crime," he said in a self attempt at humour.

Now he wondered how he would rescue Gail without getting her killed. He was cautiously working his way back to the study when a series of explosions shook the Villa. To Dave that was a partial relief because it indicated Alpha team had not been captured and were beginning their assault. He dashed down the hallway to the study, but when he got there it was empty.

Smith had bolted and as Dave frantically searched for a clue as to which way he had left, he continued out the front door. He was just in time to see the dust from a vehicle the General had used to flee the half kilometer to the docks and his Yacht. Dave crouched behind a disabled Land Rover as a building close by went up in an explosive inferno. He was just about to make a dash for the building where he had been captured when he spotted a guard aiming at someone. Dave took a double handed stance and fired twice. The guard folded to the ground somewhat like an accordion. As he charged toward the area where his Com-Tac lay, another building burst into fragments and somebody from the tree line laid down suppression fire. Dave rushed zigzagging down the path as at least a couple of Smith's guards blasted away at him with the slugs spraying grass and dirt up behind him. Dave made it behind the building and found his helmet with the communication gear still intact. As he donned the apparatus he called Captain Musselman.

"Alpha leader, do you read?" Dave called.

"Loud and clear Badger. Where were you?" Marty responded.

"Never mind that. What's the situation here?"

"Everything is clockwork. We're taking out the buildings surgically to our advantage. More or less just mopping up now."

Marty had no sooner spoken than a UAV swooped down laying a line of fire only centimeters from Dave.

"Captain, you'd better dispatch a couple of people to take out that air strip; and fast. Mop-up here and send a man down to meet me at the dock, on the double."

"Yes sir."

Dave saw a Peugeot but in line with the luck of the day, he took two steps toward it and the car exploded into a fiery inferno, lifted off the ground, flipped over and landed on its roof. Sometimes these guys can be just too damned efficient he thought. Instead of wasting any further time he charged down the hill at the fastest gait he could muster. He got to the dock as the General's yacht was rounding the breakwater about a kilometer away and heading for open water.

Dave knew that the yacht in open water could make about thirty to forty knots. As he scanned the docks, his eyes fell on a thirty foot Condor type speed boat. He ran over to it and jumped in but when he got to the control console he saw that Smith had the wires for the ignition quickly ripped out. As Dave searched the docks for another boat that might catch the yacht, one of the new Kodiak team members came tearing onto the dock.

"Specialist Potter Sir," he said somewhat out of breath.

"He's trashed the ignition on this one but I can't see any other boat that would come close to catching that ship," Dave yelled out to him.

The young soldier ran up to the side of the boat, looked at the wires hanging down, smiled and jumped in.

"Piece of cake LC. Ever watch the movie, Gone in Sixty Seconds? I always wondered why they took so long."

"You telling me you can fire this thing up in less?" Dave asked incredulously

The young man pulled out a small pocketknife and stripped some wires.

"I can if they didn't do anything else to stop it."

"I don't think they had time to do a whole lot." Dave just finished speaking when the engine coughed and fired up. He raised his eyebrows.

"Well I'll be damned. Get the bow line," he yelled.

The two men untied the dock lines and Dave steered the speedboat into the harbor. Once away from the dock Dave pulled back on the throttle about a quarter of the way and the launch lifted and skimmed the smooth water. He wasn't sure how it would take to the open water of the Andaman Sea, but as they turned past the break water he pulled it back to half and was cutting the tops of the half meter chop at about forty knots.

As they became more familiar with the small craft he pulled the throttle all the way back and sent the condor almost flying across the tops of the waves now edging sixty knots. They continued at that speed for a short time but, as they moved further out the swells got higher and he had to cut back to keep the craft from becoming totally airborne.

He turned the controls over to the young soldier and scanned the ocean with a pair of binoculars he'd found on one of the seats. It took several minutes but finally Dave honed in on the large ship and once he knew where it was he could pick it out with his eyes. The General had turned south and now the race was on. It would take the Condor about fifteen minutes to catch the yacht and Dave started laying a plan as to how he would board the craft when they had caught up. The sun was bright and there was a slight breeze so the Condor's speed was hindered only by the swells. Potter seemed to be an able seaman and was maintaining his speed although occasionally the long boat jumped from crest to crest.

"Okay Specialist Potter," Dave yelled to be heard above the engine and wind noise, "When we catch up to her I want you to cut speed equal to the yacht. I'll be on the starboard side there and you will sidle up to her on her port. I'll want you to get me as close to the swim platform as possible. If necessary you will cover me with your side arm because I'm going to need your XM8. Once I'm on board you veer away and standby off the port side about five hundred meters until I need you. Is that clear?"

"Yes sir."

Potter brought the Condor to the back of the yacht and sidled up alongside the port stern as well as any seasoned sailor. Dave was almost ready to transfer when one of the General's guards popped up and fired at him. Potter reactively swung the boat away from the yacht in a natural defensive motion which threw Dave off the edge. As he began to fall, he was able to give an extra push and jump just enough to get a grip of the railing on the edge of the swim platform. The drag of the water at forty knots on his feet was almost more than Dave could handle, but he managed to drag himself up and onto the platform. In the fall he had lost the XM8 and had only the Beretta he had taken from the guard. As he slipped up behind the Transom, one of the guards popped up again and quickly ducked when Potter put two shots over his head, almost hitting him. Dave tried to open the door on the transom but the handle and latch were locked on the inside.

If he was going to get in the ship, he was going to have to go over the transom and that meant he would be in an open kill zone for a few seconds, which was of course more than enough time for the guard to kill him. He motioned to Potter to lay down some suppressive fire and the young specialist caught the idea right away. He put the sidearm on full automatic and when Dave was ready he fired a burst towards the area where he'd last seen the guard. Potter didn't intend to, but his volley coincided with the guard coming up to check or shoot at Dave. Two of Potters bullets hit the guard and he dropped his weapon and fell. Dave was over the back of the ship in an instant and waved Potter off. He grabbed the guard's pistol while cuffing him to a large beam and then slipped along the side of the main aft deck. Dave stuffed the Beretta in his belt and since there didn't seem to be any more action on the main deck, he moved up to the second deck. Moving in a crouched position, he had just entered the lounge when a shot from a door at the far end of the large room made him dive behind a wet bar for cover.

"Smith it's all over," he yelled. I've given orders for our submarine to torpedo this ship if it doesn't stop. It's all over."

Dave was bluffing. He had given no such order. He sure as hell wished he had, but at this point praying had a lot more bite than wishing.

The General shot again, this time splintering hardwood and smashing several bottles of his liquor directly above Dave's head.

"Then I don't suppose I have a lot to lose, now do I?"

Dave began very slowly and cautiously to move around the corner and as he crept into the large open area of the lounge, the General suddenly burst through the door on the opposite side firing several times. Luckily for Dave, Smith's shooting was off that day but one of the bullets managed to hit the weapon in Dave's hand and it was torn from his grip. One of the General's guards slipped in behind Dave and before he realized it he was between the two, the General stood only a couple of meters away with the H&K pointed at his head. He picked up the phone and gave orders to stop all engines.

"I don't suppose you would like to give me any information about how much of my organization is compromised?" the General asked calmly.

Dave looked up at the man and held his face like flint.

"No I didn't suspect you would. Well I guess this is goodbye then." He raised his weapon and Dave could see his trigger finger squeezing, but then his eyes grew large as he looked out the window beside him. Potter roared straight towards the encounter on the starboard side firing just like a cavalry charge and at the last minute veered away almost colliding with the Yacht. The General heard a noise and turned toward the door of the lounge where Gail was now standing with an automatic weapon pointed at him. The General dropped his pistol and looked back at Dave who by now had drawn the Berretta.

The General stared at Gail in awe.

"But how on earth did you get out of there? You were handcuffed to a beam?"

"Sorry, I'm not giving lessons on escape and capture today," Gail said

A smile came over the General's face and he quickly began pulling a concealed weapon from his side pocket which was out of Gail's view. Dave saw him and yelled as the General moved the weapon up to fire on Gail. Six shots were fired. The first one was the General's. It hit Gail's left shoulder with such force that it spun her to the left and knocked her to the floor. The next two were Dave's which caught the General in the right arm and the leg which caused him to buckle slightly and distract him. The next shot was from the guards H&K and it hit the wall at head level where Gail had been standing moments before, splintering mahogany wall board. Number five was Dave's again and this one found its mark. The General had glanced over at Dave and begun to swing his weapon to kill the Canuck but Dave's shot centered just above the eyebrows. The General never even closed his eyes but instantly crumpled to the floor. Dave heard a rustle behind him and simultaneously rolled, twisted, and fired catching the guard, point blank in the face.

Dave quickly checked to ensure Smith and the guard wouldn't be coming back for another round and then ran to Gail. He slid up to her on his knees. The impact of the bullet had rendered her temporarily unconscious. He checked for a pulse and breathing. There were both. He checked the shoulder, which was saturated with blood that was now dripping into a puddle on the floor. He grabbed a field dressing from his leg pocket, ripped her sleeve open, and pressed the dressing firmly, but gently on her shoulder while he tied it on.

He called the Victoria for medical assistance and within the hour the sub arrived. The yacht was secured to the sub and within minutes the yacht had half a half dozen seamen from the Victoria all carrying automatic weapons. They rounded up what was left of the yacht's crew and sequestered them in one of the staterooms. Dave took a 360. Such a beautiful place and yet such a violent dark spirited man, he thought. Kind of has a touch of poetic justice he mused and then he wondered how many more were in this twisted group. Dave was beside Gail as she regained consciousness.

"How are you doing, beautiful?"

She glanced toward her shoulder.

"It hurts like hell."

"Doc, can't you give her something," he said with a tinge of panic in his voice.

The medic pulled out a prepackaged syringe and prepared to inject the morphine.

"Don't sweat it, LC, she'll live."

Dave was about to grab the corpsman by the neck when he felt a tug on his shirt. He glanced down and Gail was smiling up at him. She gave a slight frown when the doc injected the morphine and again when he gave her a shot of antibiotics.

"I'll be fine LV," she said and drifted off to a dreamless sleep from the morphine.

Dave gave the medic a smile.

"Sorry Doc, take good care of her."

The Medic glanced at him with a smirk.

"Maybe next time you put a field dressing on make sure it's not soaked in salt water."

Dave thought for a moment and then sheepishly chuckled as he felt his face flush.

Dave searched around the yacht for the General's cabin and soon found it. He rummaged through the desk and file cabinets but found nothing. Then he booted the computer and after fifteen minute of not being able to get to the files he wanted, he decided to get help. He transferred to the Victoria and called Vancouver. He got a couple of computer specialists and set up communication on his sat phone. He then returned to the yacht and with their help proceeded to break into the files. He found a list of the General's associates back in the States and Canada, and having found the evidence he was after, e-mailed it to Global. When all the Intel had been downloaded to his CO's capable hands, he shut down the computer and headed back to Gail.

Chapter 17

Dave and the medic from the Victoria moved Gail into one of the staterooms and gently placed her on a large four poster bed in a comfortable position. As she lay on the luxurious bed she appeared so small and helpless; Dave felt a twinge of guilt that somehow he should have taken the Cottonmouth out before he had a chance to do this. After all, he thought that bullet was only a short distance from killing her and the second one from the guard hadn't really been that far away either.

Dave gave a quick glance around the room and had the instant feeling he was imposing in some person's private boudoir until he realized just where he was. His gaze took in the grandeur and the opulence even in the guest's room. As the medic took care of Gail, Dave slipped out into the corridor, and called Colonel Benton.

"Have you arrested the Cottonmouth?" she asked.

"We had some dicey moments but as for Beauregard Smith, he's dead. We have quashed all resistance by lethal force, that is except for a few of the guards and the island's Chief of Security who chose to commit suicide. This part of his organization has been annihilated and won't be causing any more problems. I suspect you've already seen the list of his associates back there?"

"That affirmative and we've already acted on them. We, in partnership with the NAS and FBI, are rounding up the remnant of the organization's leaders back here. Your list should help us find the ones who have deeper cover and we can use it for evidence as well. So far our arrests have been quite impressive too. Two Congressmen, a Presidential aide, another General, two Admirals, and a number of agents from the Intelligence field, both Canada and U.S.. By the time your team gets back home it should be all mopped up." Dave then changed the subject.

"Joanne, the reason I called is I need to get Gail to a hospital and I thought if you could arrange it, we could take her to Point Blair on the Andaman's and from there get her a medivac to Singapore."

"Good God, what happened to her?"

"She was shot, but she'll be okay. I just want to make sure she doesn't get infection, although the medic has assured me he gave her antibiotics."

There was silence for a bit and then Joanne answered.

"Point Blair is not an option, but getting her to Singapore could work. I'll get an air evac set up. Are you on the island now?"

"We're on the General's yacht, the Encounter, about twenty five kilometers east of the island." Dave looked at the GPS and map on the control console.

"We're at Latitude 9.3189 and Longitude 91.098."

"Hmm, seems to me I remember reading in a report that ship was a huge thing, something like eighty meters and it cruises at thirty to forty knots. And you say Gail is okay?"

"She was conscious until the doc gave her the morphine, but she's got this terrible hole through her shoulder. We don't know if there are any broken bones, although the Doc doesn't think so. Look can we skip the twenty questions for now? I just want to get her to a hospital."

"Keep your shirt on Lt. Colonel I'm going to authorize you to commandeer the ship and use it as an ambulance. Make sure you're good to go and then set course for Singapore. By the time we could get air priorities in place and it could get to you, you'd probably be there and using the yacht would be diplomatically better. You might request the Victoria's Captain allow the Corpsman to be relieved to your command to accompany Gail if that's necessary. You be the judge of that." Dave looked at the phone in amazement and half laughed.

"You mean take the yacht and just go?" he asked incredulously.

"We are formally seizing the yacht and all possessions on it and as of now you are the Collection Officer. So to avoid messy intergovernmental red tape with unfriendly countries, I would suggest you get under way as quickly as is possible."

"So should I bring the team with us as well instead of sending them back to Australia in the sub?"

"I don't see a better or safer way to do it. You might need them if you run into pirates or the like and when you get to Singapore you can send the boys back home by commercial flight. Then maybe you and Gail could---." She let the sentence trail to imply something naughty.

"You devil," Dave said as he chuckled.

"At any rate, get that soldier to Singapore Lt. Colonel and get me a full report on the mission as soon as possible."

"Yes, Ma'am."

Dave slid the small phone closed and went back into the stateroom where the Corpsman had just finished cleaning the wounded areas and replaced the dressing. Gail had surfaced, but was still in somewhat of a euphoric state

"Thanks Doc," Dave said and swung his attention to Gail as the Corpsman left the room. "Well, I've been issued new orders."

"What! I get shot and you just leave me behind? Just like that?"

"Take it easy; nobody said anything about leaving you behind," Dave said defensively. "I've been issued new order to take you to Singapore University Hospital and this," he waved his arm to indicate the yacht, "is your ambulance."

Gail settled down, looking dazed and took in the room for the first time.

"Wouldn't it be nice just to travel in something like this and just relax?" She gazed at all the expensive furniture and surroundings.

Gail sat up and then took Dave's hand. She was still somewhat under the influence of the morphine and spoke softly.

"Then you won't leave me behind?" Dave squeezed her hand gently.

"I'm not in the habit of leaving my wounded people in the field, Captain." He said with a grin.

When she finally lay back on the pillow, she grimaced.

"It may take several months of convalescence on a south sea island, though, before I'll be ready to head back."

He glanced at her with a smirk.

Dave stayed with Gail a while longer and then went up to the wheel house where he conferred with the Victoria's Captain. Dave arranged to have Victoria's doctor give Kodiak's medic the necessary information to care for Gail until they reached Singapore. They were just about to cast off from the submarine, when Lt. Williams came charging in the door. He told Dave that there was C4 attached to various places on the hull and it had twenty minutes on the clock.

Dave passed the order to abandon ship and with the subs medic helped Gail across the gang plank to the Victoria. Everyone who could move, plus Gail were on the sub and it moved away from the Encounter. They were half a kilometer away when the hull of the yacht lifted slightly in the water and then a fireball erupted out all the windows and openings. Much of the top side of the yacht blew into small fiery pieces leaving the hull fully engulfed in flame temporarily sitting on the surface of the water. Dave watched what was left of the once beautiful ship slip beneath the waves as the diesel continued to burn on the surface.

Commander Villeneuve strolled over to Dave on the forecastle. He questioned him on what he would do now and Dave suggested he might have to catch a ride back to Australia. The Commander just smiled and told him they weren't headed for Australia but rather for the Philippines after which the Victoria would regroup with the American fleet and continue exercises in the south Pacific.

Dave called Joanne and related what had happened and told her about the Victoria. She told Dave to have the Victoria put the civilians ashore with provisions and take Gail and the rest of Kodiak Team to Singapore.

Within the hour The Victoria was underway.

    *   *   *   *

The doctors X-rayed Gail's shoulder and found that the projectile had shattered the upper outside corner of the clavicle. They did an emergency surgery to clean it up the shattered bone and held her in the hospital for observation. They allowed her to leave after only two days but admonished her to take it easy and not to lift anything with that arm for at least six weeks.

With Gail in tow, the entire team was booked onto a commercial flight back to Vancouver and arrived in a heavy drizzle. Dave gave them a twenty-one day leave and once the CF bus had left he found the rental vehicle Joanne had provided. Dave and his aid, Captain Levine with her shoulder in plaster and her arm in a sling, headed for the Global Offices.

Dave figured the young Lt. at the reception desk would probably stop him if they tried to just walk into the CO's office so he went to the desk and inquired if the Colonel was in. The young man glanced up at him.

"Oh, go right in Lt. Colonel, Colonel Benton is expecting you."

As they entered the room Dave was surprised to see his old CO General John Benton seated on one of the sofas. John stood when Dave and Gail entered and seeing Gail stiffen, told them to take their ease.

"General, it's good to see you again." Dave said as they shook hands. The General then spoke to Gail suggesting it was too bad Canada didn't have the Purple Heart medal but that the wound would be a reminder of the bravery she had shown. Colonel Benton was smiles ear to ear as she glanced at Dave.

"John wanted to be here when we gave you the news."

Dave searched their faces for some clue as to what '*the news*' would be.

"Which is?" Dave added when Joanne wasn't immediately forth coming with the information.

Joanne now picked up a manila envelope and moved toward Dave.

"As I told you I submitted you for promotion to full Colonel and although you're ten years shy of normal time requirements, given your special circumstances it was unanimously granted. Congratulations Colonel David M. Hart." She presented him with his new four stripe patches saying nothing for a few moments and then carried on. "Also John and I have for some time been contemplating retirement and we came to the same conclusion; that you would be the perfect replacement for me at Global. I recommended you as the new CO of Global Tech and with an endorsement from John, that also has been approved."

John stepped forward and shook Dave's hand.

"Congratulations son, you've earned it."

"I'll do my best to continue the high standards you both have led Global in," Dave said feeling very honoured. He then turned to Gail, who had been silent too long and showed her the patches.

"And what does the Captain think of all this?" Joanne said with a grin.

"I think you made the best choice in the world," she said, wanting to give him a great big hug, but realizing it would be out of place in the General's presence.

Colonel Benton gave Dave his new orders and the start date of the second day of the New Year. When the short ceremony was over Dave and Gail left the office together. Dave escorted Gail to his car and once inside turned to her.

"Do you think a newly promoted Colonel could take you to dinner? he asked with a grin. Gail tried to appear coy and replied, "Well Sir, I'm not sure of the protocol, but I might agree anyway if you were to escort me to the same restaurant where we went on our first date."

Bibliography:

1. *fivestaralliance.com ---- Burj Al Arab Hotel, Dubai*
2. *mtronline.net/mt/mtstories.aspx ---- Northup Grumin developes 100 knot underwater personnel carrier*
3. *gpoaccess.gpv/911/ ---- 911 commission final report*
4. *011research.wtc.net/wtc/evidence/photos/collapses.html#south ---- 911 Twin Tower collapses*
5. *911review.com/errors/ ---- 911 Conspiracy Theories*
6. *911truth.org ---- 911 Conspiracy Theories*
7. *Whatreallyhappened.com ---- David L Graham ---American Airlines 11, Conspiracy Theories*
8. *BBC News ---- Hijack Suspects alive in middle east, Conspiracy Theories*
9. *boeing.com ---- Technical specifications*
10. *answers.com ----Canadian ranks and insignia*
11. *konformist.com/2005/911-flight-school.htm ---- Conspiracy Theory*
12. *911-strike.com ---- Jerry Russel ---- Conspiracy Theories*

13. *dailymail.co.uk ---- (Bat wings) ---- Matthew Hickley ---- strap on wings*

14. *welfarestate.com/911/#16 ---- Conspiracy Theories*

15. *csis-scrs.gc.ca ---- Canadian Security Intelligence Service*

16. *airforce.forces.gc.ca/site/equip/index_e.asp ---- Canadian Air Force aircraft*

17. *navy.forces.gc.ca/ overview of Canadian navy*

18. *sikorski.comn ---- CH-148 Cyclone Helicopter*

19. *world.guns.ru/smg/smg13-e.htm --- Automatic and assault weapons*

20. *fraserhealth.ca Royal Columbian Hospital, New Westminster*

21. *dc.indymedia.org/newswire/display/73011/index.php ---- Blue lightning*

22. *batnet.com/~mfwright/miljump.htm ---- Michael Wright ---- Military Skydiving*